PATHFINDERS

Aidan J. Reid

ISBN – 13 978-1523245727
ISBN – 10 1523245727

Copyright © Aidan J Reid 2016

All rights reserved.
No part of this publication may be reproduced, stored in a retrieval system or transmitted, in any form or by any means, without the prior written permission of the author, nor be otherwise circulated in and form of binding or cover other that in which it is published and without a similar condition being imposed on the purchaser.

–

Cover Illustration and Design: Design for Writers

ABOUT THE AUTHOR

Aidan J. Reid was born in the small village of Cloughmills in Northern Ireland in 1982. He moved to Dublin in 2001 to study a degree in Accounting and Finance.

Despite the glitz and glamour of the accounting profession, he became tired of the daily grind and as a form of escapism began writing the book that was to become PATHFINDERS.

Ever since his first, and only lucid dream experience at the age of twenty-one, he has been desperate to return.

This is his first novel, and his way of bridging that gap.

-

www.aidanjreid.com

For Da

What if you slept
And what if
In your sleep
You dreamed
And what if
In your dream
You went to heaven
And there plucked a strange and beautiful flower
And what if
When you awoke
You had that flower in your hand
Ah, what then?

Samuel Taylor Coleridge

- - -

They've promised that dreams can come true but forgot to mention that nightmares are dreams too

Ester Escalante

ONE

Grooming himself in front of the bathroom mirror until it reflected a satisfied expression, Norman stepped into a cleanly pressed suit, and made his way downstairs.

It was early Monday morning in the house and his mother had her back turned as he entered.

Noreen Adams was in her element scurrying about with boundless energy that showed no sign of tapering off as she approached her sixtieth year. Hinged at the waist to accommodate an old injury, she looked like Mrs Pacman. Placing a bowl of cereal down in front of her son, alongside the plate of sliced and buttered toast soldiers, she hurried back to the fridge. In silent observation she reminded Norman of those old entertainers who would spin plates on long beams, darting back and forth to each plate to add spin when it began to stagger. He wondered if there could possibly be a more expensive hobby to learn.

"What time will you be back this evening?" she asked, returning to fill his glass high with freshly squeezed orange juice.

"Around five thirty," he said and rubbed the sleep from his eyes.

"What would you like for dinner tonight? I could make your favourite again?"

His favourite was burger and chips and had been since he realised that food went in that hole. As a child he had picked up the strange desire to stuff crushed salty chips up his nose, a detail that his mother still delighted in telling family friends at gatherings, much to his embarrassment.

"Sounds nice," he replied, before assembling the soldiers in rank file and chomped off their heads.

He rose and walked to the counter with his juice and knocked it back in one go, setting the glass on the surface. Ripping a paper towel, Norman made a bed for the injured soldiers and pocketed them inside his suit pocket.

They exchanged byes and each went their separate way; Norman to work and his mother to a cold bed to continue the hopeless task of finding a comfortable spot that didn't hurt her spine.

Arriving at the offices of Richmond and Regan Ltd. at 8.25a.m., he swapped greetings with the only other person in the room at that early hour, before sitting down in silence at his station to await the arrival of the rest of the employees or his workload for the day, whichever came first.

"I need you to have these completed and filed before the end of the day."

The boss slapped a thick band of invoices onto his desk. A wiry little man with a scowl permanently etched on his head, Walter Richmond looked like a child in a man's suit, such was his tiny frame with the clothes hanging off his body like a scarecrow. The only thing that belied his youthful appearance was his balding hair. His expanding forehead was winning the war against his hairline, pushing enemy lines back beyond the comfort zone. For the follicle challenged, it seemed every single strand counted and would have to be aligned with the other troops to make a strong, thick battalion.

Richmond walked away and stood below a ventilator fan in the centre of the room. Pulling the hanging cord, he waited for the cool breeze to blow from above. Norman watched the blades gather pace, until the wind began to lift the thinning hatch of Richmond's hair up and down like a trapdoor.

With a deep sigh, Norman looked down at the mountain of papers on his desk tray and glanced at the empty trays of his neighbours.

Richmond, invigorated by the shower of cool air, took up sentinel in the corner of the room. His desk was positioned to give a clear view of all the staff with their tables facing his direction in a horseshoe formation. Perched upright in his seat, he drew a thin notebook from his drawer and placed it on his desk. By its side lay two fat markers, one that he uncapped and held over the notebook in anticipation.

Fifteen minutes passed until the next worker appeared; a thin rake of a man, who in his eagerness not to be late burst through the door and greeted the frowning Richmond through a series of wheezes. Having first kicked over a wastebasket bin, scattering then gathering a couple of crumpled paper balls, he then crashed down at his station.

"Morning Norman," he managed in two breaths.

"Morning Clancy."

One by one, the remaining staff filtered into the room with Richmond taking notes with each arrival, matching their entrance with glances at the wall-clock. The solid oak desk was higher than the other tables and as Richmond wrote, his thin arms were almost parallel with his rounded shoulders. He wiggled in the seat, straightening his back, the fidgeting distracting Norman who glanced up to see the man's unease.

As the hour approached, the room filled with nine suited men and women, sorrowful expressions matching their drab grey and charcoal suits. All the seats were occupied except one, with the frown of tables missing a front tooth. Leafing through his notes, Richmond stood and addressed the group.

"Christ," he mumbled. "Has anybody seen Victor?"

The group looked up from their stockpile of assorted letters, papers and documents first at the empty chair and then at each other in baffled silence.

With no response forthcoming the speaker sat back down, a sour expression curdling his face. He began riffling back through his notes, casting a periodic glance at his desk phone and then at the wall-clock for a second opinion. With each passing minute his face became more animated. At 9:10 a.m. there was a sudden rattling on wood of a vibrating mobile phone at his desk. Hopping from his seat, swiping his phone off the desk, Richmond paced across the room to the exit, tiny fists pumping back and forth like pistons.

As a group Norman and his colleagues breathed a sigh of relief when he had gone, the poisonous element that had infected the room suddenly removed to charge itself elsewhere.

"You think he'll get the chop?" Clancy asked to his left.

"I don't know," Norman replied. "I hope not."

"You remember that graduate? When was it, six months ago? Sure the ink was still dry on his contract when he was booted out."

"Fair point. One thing is for sure though, I wouldn't like to trade places."

Suddenly Richmond burst through the door. Coiled into a ball of fury he marched straight to Norman's desk which took everyone by surprise, not least Norman who had already made a solid start on the invoices. Looking up from his stack of papers he looked into the bloodshot eyes of his superior.

"Outside. Now!"

TWO

It was becoming more difficult to focus on anything other than the raised network of blood vessels bulging from his temple. Staring up at him with indignation, a furious Walter Richmond stabbed a bony finger into his solar plexus as he berated the young accountant.

To add insult to injury with Victor James calling to say he would be running late, the cork in Richmond's bottle of composure finally popped, shook by a more pressing concern. An oversight in the books meant that Richmond & Regen Ltd.'s most notable client was being investigated for fraud. Norman had been responsible for the account and the resulting error. Being a good employee, he stood still, wilting under the tirade, soaking up the saliva from Richmond's spat words like a sponge. Head hung in penitence, he chipped in with an apologetic word when needed. Nothing more could be offered and when Richmond was in this sort of mood you just had to ride out the storm.

***

The raindrops were getting fatter as he watched them slap against the glass pane. Things were looking bleak. Hanging the phone back on its receiver Victor shook his head at the realisation that his lift wasn't coming and the conditions which he wasn't prepared for. He buried his hands deep into blazer pockets for warmth, anticipating the Arctic temperatures outside. With upturned collar he left the shelter of the phone box and emerged into a monsoon. What would have been a short walk was going to feel a lot longer in this weather. His pace quickened as he glanced at a rain-specked watch. A cold bead of water wound its way from the nape of his neck along the length of his spine, sending a little chill through his body.

He felt the rain begin to collect inside his shoes, as he weaved his way through the lines of traffic, tip-toeing as best he could through fresh puddles. Each footstep squelched beneath him as the cheap shoes breathed bubbles of foam out the sides. He watched as other people around him struggled to maintain their umbrellas against the harsh wind. His attention was drawn to a tiny middle-aged man skipping through the crowds, dressed in a suit that looked badly worn. The man seemed completely unaware that the fabric had torn from his own umbrella, and he was left holding the metal framework in his hand as if using it as a lightning rod. Big bushy grey eyebrows helped to soak up the rain as it bounced off his pink scalp and he gave Victor a big toothless grin as they passed each other, and he continued on his merry way down the street.

As he rounded the corner of Filmont Park, the wind hit Victor with sudden gusto, using his blazer as a sail, whipping him back several paces. Staggered, he caught his breath and surged forward through the gale, tucking his head down to his chest. Squinting his eyes against the pellets of rain that struck his face, he caught sight of the offices a kilometre ahead. Assuming the wind didn't use him as a kite, he would be back behind his desk soon enough, but he quickened his pace, entering into a slow jog.

By the time he reached the little road that tucked into the industrial estate, he was thoroughly drenched. His suit sleeves only smeared the wet rain on his brow, already soaked. The big orange bricked building on his right had three resident companies encamped there. Top floor was a printing and binding company. Middle floor was a sales office, packaging and selling the dream of unlimited, super-fast broadband. He entered the offices of the ground floor, stamping his feet on the carpet when he had passed through the doorway.

The receptionist gave him a smile which Victor took and reflected back, only wider. She handed him paper towels which he used to pat his face and hands with before stepping through the hallway and entering a door on the left.

"Making a mess again?"

Clancy Andrews turned around to see the speaker enter before returning to mop up spilled coffee on his table.

"Half day mate?" he replied.

Each footstep from the new arrival left a water print on the carpeted floor. All eyes were drawn to him as he removed his outerwear and hung it on the rack, allowing the tepid gear to drip itself dry. His shirt was glued to his chest with damp, and he tried patting it down with a dry tissue which had little effect.

"Where's Norman and Richie Rich?" he said to no one in particular, as he claimed his seat.

"They both just left the office. Back shortly I reckon," returned Clancy, whose desk was daubed with soaked paper towels.

"Cool. Funny story Clance," Victor said when he was seated. "Bumped into some looper on the way here."

"Oh yeah?"

"Yeah. Bald as a coot. In his fifties, maybe sixties. Big goofy smile." Clancy smiled. "Do you know him?"

"Know of him," he replied. "Hope you gave that one a wide berth."

"And the rest. What's his deal?"

"What do you mean?"

"He was out there prancing around in the rain like some fruitcake, warped version of Gene Kelly."

"Bad news mate. Nuttier than a squirrel's turd," Clancy answered. "Luisa'll tell you the same."

Clancy interrupted his cleaning and called to a woman a couple of tables down who looked up from a book entry she was making.

"Saul. What's the story there? You've been here a lot longer than me."

The woman smiled and looked at Clancy's desk, which was now more towel than wood. She swung her pencil frame around in the swivel chair to face the men.

"Growing up, me and my friends were always told to avoid him, and run as far away as possible if we saw him, especially if we were on our own."

"Paedo?" Victor asked.

"Worse. He's from the city," she said and Victor offered her a mock laugh. "No, I don't think he's anything like that. The grownups always used to tell us…"

"Newsflash Luisa," Victor interrupted. "You're a grownup."

"No," the woman smiled. "I mean when we were kids!"

"Go on."

Clancy was seated again, chair pulled flush to his desk. Luisa rolled closer on her own chair, out of earshot of the other accountants who until that point had expressed little interest in their narrative.

"Depends who you speak to in town. The story I grew up with was that he bludgeoned his family to death after serving in the Kopachi War. He was the only member of his unit that made it back. Some sort of Post-War Syndrome or whatever you call it."

"Unlikely that he'd get away with that," Clancy said.

"No shit Sherlock," she replied. "Those were the rumours back in the day. Police did a botch job on the investigation."

"What else you heard?" Victor asked.

Victor's body was turned toward the woman but his feet still tucked under his desk, hidden from view. He rubbed the bare feet together and was careful to screen the radiator directly behind him from his two colleagues.

"It's a small town. You'll realise soon enough."

"What does that mean?"

"It means that everyone's got an opinion," Clancy interjected. "What was it that Eastwood said? 'Opinions are like assholes – everyone's got one'?"

"Which is why I'm asking your opinion," Victor said and nodded to Luisa again.

She arched her waxed eyebrows high and considered his question for a moment, until her expression changed, poking her nose out to draw a breath before pinching her nostrils shut. The bemused looks of the others confirmed it wasn't her imagination and they scanned for its source and a guilty looking Victor James reclined back in his chair.

"What?" he asked, feigning surprise, finding it hard to compress his smile.

Seeing the black socks being grilled on the radiator they protested in unison until Victor conceded defeat and with reluctance peeled the socks off. Instead he put them inside the shoes and moved them beside the radiator when they had all returned to their work.

The office door opened and in walked Norman, looking worse for wear. Blushing, he wobbled back into his chair, Richmond trailing close behind.

"Victor, I'll have a word with you later," Richmond said in passing before slotting back behind his own desk, jotting a note in his book.

"Thanks for covering for me," Norman whispered out the side of his mouth to his neighbour.

"Don't worry about it," Victor said. "You alright?"

Norman nodded, offering a weak smile as he sorted through the invoices, looking for some composure and calm under the pile.

"Just another day in paradise."

Late that afternoon as the staff were packing up and preparing to leave the office, Richmond approached Norman again, this time with a little more trepidation.

"Norman, could you stay behind for a few minutes?"

"Sure," he said, "I've made a good start on the accounts."

Richmond looked away in deference, watching the employees one by one. When the room had finally cleared and in the middle of a terse silence, Walter Richmond returned to his solid oak bunker and practically hid behind it.

"Pull up a chair," he said, motioning with a flick of his head to the one nearest.

Taking his lead, Norman brought it close and sat opposite. Richmond was unable to match his eye contact, which made the accountant uncomfortable although he couldn't pinpoint the reason.

"Norman, I've been director of this company for close to ten years now, as I'm sure you're aware. During that time, I've worked with many accountants helping to shape this company into the fine practice it is today. We have built a reputation that has helped us attract more and more business; a reputation that cannot be built overnight and one that ultimately, through your thoughtless actions, you have impaired."

Speechless, Norman continued listening, fearful of where this lecture was headed.

"I've been monitoring your progress lately and worry that you are becoming more distant."

Their eyes met in a fleeting glance, before Richmond diverted them back to the table surface.

"You've been at the company for…"

He thumbed through the notebook flicking its pages, searching for a reference.

"Th… three years," Norman said, his voice catching in his throat.

"It says you've been here three years," Richmond said. "We appreciate what you've done for the company, we really do. But we feel that, going forward, we have to let you go."

Ordered to pack his things, Richmond asked him to leave the premises with immediate effect. He withdrew a notebook and started to scribble into it, ignorant of the man sitting opposite who he had shared three years of a corporate life with. They sat in silence, Richmond a picture of patience waiting for the accountant to stand up and move to his desk and begin the clearance. When Norman did so, it was with slow movements, as if the pace would bring with it some eventual clarity or understanding. Richmond's continued supervision in light of this task seemed justified in his mind, fearful of a final act of defiance or that something would be stolen.

A final rushed handshake minutes later included a short word of gratitude from Richmond. Norman didn't respond and offered little by way of resistance before his former manager ushered him from the building and, before he knew it, he was suddenly alone in the car park holding a box of office junk he didn't need.

Arriving home, his dinner was on the table, covered in a tea towel to ward off the flies.

"That you Norman?"

"Yes ma," he said, and lifted the towel and felt for the pulse of the burger which was dead cold.

"Everything OK pet? You're late tonight."

"All good. How long should I stick it on for?"

"Two minutes should do it."

He waited for the food to be nuked and took it to upstairs to his bedroom, where he salted it with his own tears. Finished, he let the empty plate sit on the table and undressed in silence without turning on any of the lights.

Dusk had fallen on the room, his bundle of waylaid clothes barely visible in the partial darkness. The clock seemed to shorten its hourly beep and it blinked at him from the corner. He lay there motionless, observing the sounds, the low drone of the neighbours' television set, the sound of a dog barking outside, the gentle hum of the traffic in the distance. Somewhere around midnight, while watching the movie of his dismissal for the last time, the images began to swirl and he found himself dropping gently into a sleep.

That night while he slept, Norman's life changed forever.

THREE

I am standing in front of the bathroom mirror performing my daily cleansing routine. In my reflection I notice that my front tooth has come loose. I begin caressing it back and forth with my tongue tip. Applying my toothbrush to other areas of my gum line I suddenly realise that even with the slightest pressure, teeth would slide right back. There is no pain whatsoever. It is as if my gums have turned to jelly.

I flick one of the teeth with my finger and it pops right out and rattles off the mirror into the sink. My astonishment peaks when I sneeze and spit out my entire two rows of teeth into the sink, turning them to powder on impact. Searching through the little hill of dust, I am surprised to note there are no fillings among the debris. Then it dawns on me, 'I must be dreaming!' At that instant, I experience an unbelievable sense of clarity and perception that becomes incredibly exhilarating. It feels...

***

Norman sat up in bed, bemused by the brightness of the vision only seconds before. A few minutes later the alarm rings and without any of the previous grogginess that clouded his recent awakenings, he walks over and turns it off. The shouts of his mother below eventually snapped him out of a stream of thoughts prompting him to get dressed. Habit dictated the rest.

"You OK, honey? The milk hasn't gone off has it?"

"It's fine, ma," he said and, rising from an untouched breakfast, kissed her cheek.

"You haven't kissed your oul ma in years! You sure you aren't running a fever?"

"I'm good. Honest."

He left the house and slipped into his car. Norman drove around the town without any real purpose and, after ten minutes, eventually decided to park along the kerb of a quiet housing estate to rest up, close his eyes and have a nap. He flung his blazer jacket on the passenger seat, loosened his neck tie and unbuttoned the top button of his shirt, then began to recline his seat into a flat position.

While fidgeting with the stiff dial, he noticed a sign erected in the ground on his left behind a small brick wall. To the side was an open gate, with a path leading to a long bricked building with large open windows on its front. Inside someone was busy fastening the curtains to either side, allowing the sun to beam into the room.

He looked at his watch and then read the sign again.

Shaysburg Community Library
Opening Hours
9 a.m. - 6 p.m.   Monday to Friday
10 a.m. - 7 p.m.   Saturday and Bank Holidays
CLOSED   Sundays

Encouraged by his watch face and too early for a morning siesta, he propped the seat back up and left the car. As Norman approached the building, he could see bright fliers glued to the window pane beside the door. He hovered in the doorway casting a quick eye over them – monthly jumble sales, computer classes organised by the library and help wanted with babysitting duties. Neither of the adverts flicked Norman's interests so he walked inside and approached the counter.

"Hi, can I help you?"

The speaker was quite plump, about as high as she was wide. She was teetering on a small step reaching for a book from the shelf above, when Norman entered. Her cheeks were flushed red, a spider web of broken capillaries, and she was just catching her breath.

"I hope so. I was wondering if you had any books on dreams?" Norman asked while also scanning the room for a coffee machine.

"Let me just check."

The woman stepped off the stool, moving to the circled desk counter, easing into her chair before letting out a sigh of relief, pleased to be seated again.

As soon as the computer had loaded, she began typing on the keyboard with fixed concentration. Somewhere north of sixty years of age, with limited IT skills, she punched the letters with a choice confined to either left or right index finger. Her face clouded when, after several long minutes, she looked up from her keyboard.

"I'm afraid we don't have any books on sleep," she said.

Her eyes magnified through thick lenses that seemed to cover half her face.

"No. I'm looking for books on dreams," Norman repeated.

"OK. Let me check that for you."

She went back to typing again, selecting one key after another with careful thought. Hesitating at one moment, with hands poised over the keyboard, she mumbled, "M. Where's M?" Finding the offending key after an eternal struggle she struck it harder than was necessary, before her eyes left the keyboard and scrutinised the screen.

"We seem to have a couple of books in stock. I'm not sure if they are in our branch though. Can you give me a second?"

She was gone without waiting for a response, moving into a dim room behind and Norman could hear her talking to a colleague within, repeating the request. During their discussion, Norman took the opportunity to walk around and noticed there weren't any other visitors at that early hour. Nor any coffee machine it appeared.

"This is Mr Breagal who will assist you."

Standing alongside her now was a tall, thin man, piercing blue eyes commanding attention under a brow wrinkled deep by a lifetime of reading. With a practiced smile that seemed anything but welcoming, he extended his hand to Norman. Breagal seemed to take a moment to scrutinise him, which made Norman feel like a bug being examined under a microscope. Although younger than his colleague, his gait and actions appeared to age him, as if he had spent too much time around older people.

As Norman followed the beanpole man, he was surprised at the size of the hall they entered. The library had appeared smaller from the outside but he felt miniscule here, surrounded by shelves that rose high to the ceiling, laden with books threatening to topple over. Their footsteps echoed in the hollow corridor, bouncing off the marble surroundings. As the assistant led him through a maze of bookshelves, a heady smell of old dusty books enveloped them.

"This section is where we archive all our books pre-dated 1900s," the librarian fired over his shoulder, as they continued to journey deeper into the jungle of books. "You won't find much of use here anymore, everything being barely legible and moth eaten."

They had to sidle along the shelves now, with space becoming more cramped. Twice, Norman was struck in the ribs by the spine of a sharp hardback that edged out from its resting place. He was beginning to feel claustrophobic, looking up at the cases of books on either side that loomed over, threatening to drown him in a sea of pages. They were approaching what appeared to be the furthest corner of the building; the lighting dimmer here, making it a little more difficult to read the titles of the books as they passed. *'Ayahuasca and Shamanic Hallucinogens'*, *'A New Model of Witchcraft 1845-1889'*, *'Psychical Phenomenon in Tribal Cultures'*, just some of the gold lettered titles that grabbed his attention.

"Are you sure this is where I can find books about dreams? It seems a little…"

"Demonic?" Breagal replied.

"Well you could say that!"

Norman detected a smile curl on the face of the assistant as he half turned, but it vanished as quickly as it came.

"I could show you some of the more mainstream books we have about dreaming, but they are of relatively little worth, adding nothing new to the subject. To be honest, you might find some of the original texts and manuscripts that we have considerably more interesting because they have escaped censorship and some are still considered taboo even today."

"How could a book about dreaming be dangerous?"

The assistant paused for a moment, his back still to Norman. He seemed to deliberate over his next sentence.

"Let's just say that, for some people the world of dreams is much more than a playground for a fertile imagination."

Satisfied that he had encapsulated the point he was trying to make, he began walking again, with Norman keen to stay close behind and eager to initiate the conversation again, intrigued by the man.

"You seem to know quite a bit about dreams Mr Breagal."

"Please call me Stephen," he responded, turning to shake Norman's hand for a second time before continuing down the corridor again. "Yes, you could say it is a passion of mine. Might I ask, what piques your interest, Mr...?"

"I'm Norman Adams," he answered to the librarian's back as they continued to walk. "I had a strange dream recently, last night actually, that I'd be keen to find out more about. It was a dream that I've had before, but this one was slightly different."

Norman's voice wavered, recalling again the strange clarity just before he woke that morning. Breagal must have detected something in his voice, for he stopped suddenly and turned to him with a serious countenance.

"Different? Different how?"

Composing himself, Norman looked up at Breagal and felt his intense gaze bore through him again.

"This may sound a bit odd," he said. "Have you ever found that some dreams feel more real than others?"

"It would appear that we both share a common interest," the man said and smiled. "Please. Tell me about your experience, Norman."

Explaining the events of that morning's dream and the panic at seeing his teeth fall out, Breagal continued listening in rapt silence, face narrowed downward and rubbing the light stubble of his chin until Norman had finished.

"This is not at all a curious dream. It is in fact very common, and tends to occur when one is at a crossroad in their life. Symbolically speaking, the act of losing one's teeth is said to mean that the dreamer is currently lacking self-confidence, or feeling impotent in their life. This is one point of view. There are others, but this would tend to be the one considered most plausible."

Norman thought about this for a moment. Breagal was correct in his diagnosis, but that still didn't account for his abrupt awakening or even the vividness of the experience.

"What do you make of the dream ending? When I woke up, for a second it felt like I was still trapped inside my dream."

"Trapped or liberated?" Breagal replied, and then set off again with his hands clasped tight behind his back.

"You see Norman, for countless centuries man has been captivated by their own nocturnal explorations. Few have actually cultivated the awareness to delve deeper into this journey of the mind. Did you know that the Chinese, for many years, believed that a dream was the soul's journey from the body to another world?"

Unsure if this was a rhetorical question, Norman remained silent but attentive to Breagal's lecture, who was speaking now with added enthusiasm.

"The purpose of the dream, they believed, was to connect to the ether with gods or spirit beings helping to educate the voyager, ultimately preparing him for tribulations in his waking life. This theme of drawing upon dreams for advice was a common thread linking Ancient

Civilizations, yet even after all these millennia, most of us still appear no closer to discovering their true value."

"Most of us? You mean to say that some people believe dreams mean something?" Norman asked.

Breagal either chose not to respond or did not hear, continuing instead to steer their course around a stack of books in their path. They had reached their destination and he turned back to face Norman, looking embarrassed.

"You must forgive my ramblings! It's exceedingly rare I get the chance to involve others in my passion for such matters. My wife always tells me there is a reason why I was given two ears and only one mouth! It's just that when you came into the library just now, I figured that given the early hour and your request, you must have had a particularly intense dream experience."

Pausing, his cold blue eyes scrutinized Norman once again.

"But, clearly I was wrong. This is where you will find all the information you need," Breagal said and signalled to the row of aligned books in front of him. "Co-incidentally, this is also where I store and look to build on my own private collection. You are free to select any of these books. Please let me know if I can assist you in any way."

Passing, he gave an encouraging nod and smiled as he zigzagged his way back through the rows in the direction they came.

Crouching, Norman picked out one of the heavier tomes at random and began to inspect the text on the spine, unaware that in the bookshelf behind him, a lone figure stood in the shadows, watching his every move.

FOUR

It was quiet, even for a Tuesday. The old reliables were still propping up the bar, bathing the half-digested home cooked meal in the familiar sparkling beer bath, but it had been the distinct lack of new customers that worried him. Watching the same faces drink themselves into a stupor each night the owner had slowly grown accustomed to his new life in the pub, and found he enjoyed it and the personalities. The new highway hadn't helped matters, shooting out-of-towners right past his watering hole, meaning fresh customers were few and far between. Tonight he had the rare opportunity to serve one and he slipped out from the conversation with those at the counter and looked over.

Clean cut, jet-black hair with a short back and sides, he sat in the corner, by himself, crushing the melting ice-cubes in his drink with a straw. The man was pale, anaemic looking or at the very least suggested he wasn't on first name terms with many vegetables or greens. A little twitchy mouth shifted on his face as if he was trying to tie his tongue in a knot. Eyes hadn't raised off the table as he sat staring into space, oblivious to the noise of chatter and football commentary from the TV in the corner. Propped on the chair beside him, sat a bloated school bag bulging at the zips from the contents inside. Norman had been there for an hour now, suit jacket flung over the adjacent chair. It had been a long day and he looked forward to some respite, meeting his friend who had suggested the local bar.

Victor entered, spotting the forlorn figure at the opposite end of the room, strode up to the pensive man with a great big beaming smile and gave his friend a bear hug before sitting down opposite.

"You found a new job already?"

Norman looked at him confused.

"You're wearing a suit! It was only yesterday they let you go, or are you still in denial?"

They both laughed, and Norman's mood lightened for the first time that day.

"I figured my parents wouldn't be too happy if they knew I wasn't working there anymore."

"So you decided you'd play dress up and carry on like nothing ever happened. Brilliant!" Victor's laugh was so infectious that Norman couldn't stop from joining.

"And how long are you planning to get up each morning and play accountant?"

"Well, until I get another job."

"How long will that take?"

"A few weeks, maybe a month."

This produced more fits of laughter from Victor, finding it harder to control himself now.

"Honestly Norman," he said, swiping away the tears. "I love you like a brother, but you have to learn to grow a set. How else are you going to stand up to the Walter Richmond's of this world?"

"Never you worry about me," he said. "Come on. I'll get the drinks in."

He walked to the bar counter where a bored looking owner was stocking the pint glasses. When he returned to the table with two fresh drinks he found Victor with a book open on his lap.

"Hey! You went through my bag!" he said, planting the drinks down.

"Yeah, sorry man. I was just curious what you were smuggling in there. It looked fit to burst." Victor closed the book and handed it back to Norman, who slotted it with the others. "Any use?"

Norman looked at him now, trying to detect if there was a genuine interest there.

"That book you were just looking at is a good read. That's where I've spent most of today. At the library."

"Why?" he said bemused, as he stifled another laugh.

Norman began to recount the morning's dream and the subsequent visit to the library. After Breagal had given him a tour, he had spent several hours reading about dreams, first to satisfy his curiosity but then getting more fascinated the deeper he delved into it the subject material.

"And that's what you've been doing all day? Spending your time with some loony talking about dreams?"

"Well... pretty much," he replied. "But Breagal vanished before I had the chance to quiz him on what I found."

With some difficulty Norman pulled a small leather bound notebook from the bag and plumped it on the table between them. It was as thick as a fist, with no discernible title or signature on the front. The smell of dust was still strong, and he wiped the remainder off its taut skin.

"I found this hidden inside one of the books I was reading today," he opened the book and turned it around so Victor could read. "It's someone's journal. The handwriting is a bit sketchy in places, but you can make out a lot of it."

Victor flicked through the pages, careful not to tear them; the paper looked quite old and crisp to his touch. The writing was in fact very neat; the author taking considerable pride in his work. Some of the pages were illustrated with detailed pencil drawings, text woven around the intricate images. There were tiny pictures of various fantastical creatures, of a dragon or winged variety, adorning each page corner. A gifted artist drew them with a deft precision to completion.

"Look at the next page," Norman instructed and watched his friend's reaction as Victor turned and looked at the illustration before him.

It depicted a man staring at his own reflection in the mirror. The image appeared ordinary, the character dressed in morning robe, back turned to the reader. At the centre of the image, however, the mirror appeared to distort the man's face. The reflection's skin sagged at the corners, giving the impression that it was melting. The toothless mouth was agape, longer than seemed natural and drawn, contorted into what looked like a scream from the other side of the mirror. The eyes were hollowed out, two deep black holes scorched onto the page by the artist, emphasising the darkness staring back which seemed to add to the haunting image. In the reflected mirror at a distance a forest of bare pine trees sloped up the hillside out of view. Emerging from the nearest trees, several odd shaped figures still cloaked in shadow appeared to be advancing on the reflection.

Victor read aloud the short text entry that accompanied the drawing.

"Number 15 – Through the Looking Glass – Attained lucidity. Dream signal – crumbling teeth. Too frightened to revisit."

"Well?" Norman asked him, eager to share his own thoughts.

Victor took his eyes off the image, and slapped the book closed. He took another swig from his beer and handed the journal back to Norman, looking him firm in the eye.

"Well what?"

"What do you think of it? Don't you think it's weird that just this morning I had this dream and this person drew it? He also mentions something about crumbling teeth."

"Your dream sounded fairly tame in comparison to this one mate. You didn't have these things crawling out of the mirror? Or a face like a melted candle?"

"Well no," Norman replied.

"Exactly. You said yourself that this Breagal guy told you it was a common enough dream. Christ, if I think hard enough, I'm sure even I've had it too at some stage. The drawings are pretty good. A little too macabre for me though."

A waitress approached, smiled at the two men and collected their empties. Victor's eyes traced her hips all the way back to the bar.

"Another scoop?" Victor asked.

"No. You know I get indigestion if I drink more than two Cokes."

"Rock and Roll."

Norman slumped back in his chair now, a little deflated that his friend didn't share his enthusiasm. Victor polished off the rest of his bottle before signalling the waitress over, flashing his best smile as he ordered another two drinks. They waited until she returned and Victor gave her a hefty tip before picking up the thread of conversation again.

"Sometimes I worry about you, man," Victor said and shook his head. "How long ago were we back at Uni?"

"Three years?"

"Christ," Victor said and blew out his cheeks. "But in all that time, I've never seen you socialize, talking to new people."

Norman was trying to interrupt but Victor held up a head to suggest he wasn't finished.

"Fair enough, when we were back in the city," he continued, "people are a bit tougher to get through to, which should make it even easier now we're in Shaysburg."

"This is my hometown Victor. You don't really want to get to know the people here, trust me."

"Nah, that's not it," he responded. "I've seen a few peeps here since I moved. More than a few I could think of that I'd like to get to know better. Come to think of it bro, I've never even seen you chat up a bird your own age before. Aren't you interested in that kind of thing? 'Cos I got no bones with it if you're gay. Just saying."

Norman blushed and fidgeted with the straps of his bag, untying then tying it again, unable to face his stare. After a few awkward seconds had passed he found the courage to meet Victor's eyes again.

"Of course I'm interested in that kind of thing," he whispered, "But some people are, I guess, just better at these things than others. It's OK for you. This is a new town for you so you've had to get out of your shell. You were forced out of your comfort zone. You had no other option."

Victor took a sip of his fresh beer, contemplating this fact and then his composed face broke out into another grin.

"What's so funny?"

"All of us need a little push sometimes. That's why I've arranged a little get together this weekend at my house. Some of my old friends are coming up from the city and I've told them all about you."

"Our University crowd?"

"No, no. I'm a culture vulture mate. I swim in more circles than one. I'll say something though. Some of the women especially are keen to meet you."

"Why would they be keen to meet me?" Norman asked. "God, Victor. What have you said?"

"Relax!" Victor said, a beaming smile flashing to calm his friend's fears as he gripped his tense shoulder and massaged it. "You're my best mate! Some of my city friends are single and I've told them how you helped me settle into the town. So naturally they're keen to meet you."

"I don't know. I just…"

"Here we go. What excuse is it this time?"

Norman began spinning the half empty tumbler around on the table between his forefinger and thumb, ice cubes sloshing against the wall of the glass.

"OK."

"OK what?"

"Let's do it!"

"Yeah?" Victor said and almost choked on his beer, sending suds down his nose.

"You're right. Time to get out more."

"Great! You know it makes sense! Just remember to bring your costume."

FIVE

The remote dangled between the fingers of his outstretched hand, hanging limp over the edge of the chair. His head had rolled back again, exposing a sharp Adam's apple that danced along his neck with each swallow. Mouth drawn open, a long guttural snore boomed throughout the house, loud enough to be heard above the din of gunfire from the TV set showing the Thursday night matinee. The other two occupants of the room didn't seem perturbed by the sleeping man – it seemed to be a regular occurrence and they were both distracted with their own thoughts.

Norman was preoccupied with an open book that rested on his lap. His mother was looking through the TV screen at some future moment that only she could see. Mr Adams continued to sleep, unaware of his promotion to chief breadwinner of the household, supporting both wife and adult son. Not that Norman had plans to reveal that sordid little detail. They hadn't spoken in days. Not through spite or animosity, but because of a social awkwardness that seemed to start with his son's puberty and which they had never quite evolved from. Two negative ends of a magnet in natural repulsion, virtual strangers despite their blood link.

Arriving home that night like every work night before it, Senior would sit passive in the living room, vacuum formed to his favourite seat and glued to the TV set. In an effort to unwind he paid more attention to it than his wife's probing questions. His demeanour was suggestive of someone returned from battle; victorious in vanquishing the hidden enemy but expending so much energy in the fight that he is unable to muster enough energy to even talk.

Lying prostrate like a huge slug waiting for something from the TV to jolt him to life, Mr Adams' primary movements involved shifting a colossal frame an inch here or an inch there to open a vent. A dinner plate as big as a shield would be served up by his wife and parked on the man's lap. An hour later as he dozed, the food fairy would return to collect it, trading the plate for a beer which sat on a table by his side. As the contents of his swollen belly began to churn, a reluctant audience with front row seats shook their heads and complained as the prone conductor regaled them with a variety of noises. The accompanying smell continued the daily battle with the fragrant potpourri cups and scented air freshener dotted around the room until inevitably they were all beaten into submission.

As they sat around the TV, neither Norman or his mother was interested in an encore from Mr Adam's who seemed to have burned up his reserves and energy as he dipped in and out of sleep.

"Honey, you're snoring."

Mr Adam's awoke with a start, looking around confused. Wild wide eyes surveyed the surroundings then glanced at his watch. He mumbled something incoherent back to his wife before shifting position. He reached out a hand for the beer by his side but noticing it was empty, parked it and eased back to sleep again.

Norman had watched his father struggle to stay awake for a few minutes now. Eyelids becoming too heavy to hold up, Mr Adams tried to catch himself before sleep had taken him entirely. This little inner battle persisted throughout the film, until he finally broke free from the spell to accept the challenge from the comfort of his own bed.

Mrs Adams sat across from Norman watching the film so he decided to return to his book. The spine was weak and pages were now loosening from the middle seam despite his careful attention. It had been only two days since its discovery and he had devoured its contents whole.

The book appeared to be a collection of dreams in both written, pictorial and symbolic prose, with the author charting a range of personal experiences over the course of an eight-year period. There were over seven hundred dreams documented in painstaking detail, each dated with an outline of characters and plot summary. A title was attached to each story such as 'General Jigsaw', 'Bobby and the Banshee', 'Earthen Veins', and 'Hairy Palms'. The last title described the author's memorable first date experience with a childhood sweetheart. In the story, the dreamer was horrified to discover that the palms of his hands had begun to sprout hair. For the duration of the date, the young lover went to great lengths to cover up his predicament, inventing all sorts of excuses to his date for why he couldn't show his hands.

A large portion of the stories were only several lines long, appearing rushed and written without the same attention to detail granted others. Such stories spanned several pages in what the writer described as his most 'lucid' state, seeming to dwell a lot longer on these, revelling in them with incredible clarity, the emotion colouring the written prose.

Norman noticed that as he read further into the journal, the dreams began to assume a darker tone. The underlying theme seemed to revolve around sickness and death of loved ones or animals, mirrored in the text by a much more fearful tone. This shift had been gradual, appearing like a dense fog that eventually seemed to cloud the world of the author. Some dreams repeated over and over again, spawning many sequels; one in particular entitled 'Shadow Men' appearing every night in disturbing detail over a three-week period. Norman began reading the text curled around the eerie looming figure on the page.

"OK, son. Switch everything off when you're going. I'm off to bed."

Mrs Adams jerked her stiff body out of the chair, ambling her way out of the room.

"Honey, did you hear what I said?" she asked, but still received no response from Norman whose head was buried in the book.

She flicked the lights off and on to get his attention and he looked up at her with glazed eyes.

"I don't know what you're reading, pet, but you've been reading that book every minute of the day lately. Maybe you should take a break."

"Sorry, ma," Norman answered. "I didn't mean to be rude. I know what you're saying. I'm actually going to a party this weekend."

"Oh. Is it anyone I know?"

"Yeah. It's Victor's. Just a few of his friends from the city and I figured I'd tag along."

"That's good, son," she smiled. "I always said you should be getting out more. See you in the morning."

It was getting late, and Norman knew he would still have to get up early. The deception would have to carry on a little longer until he found another job. Each morning he had visited the library reading the section Mr Breagal had guided him to, but found himself returning to the journal he now held. The contents of it seemed to burn into his mind, and he tried to imagine the dreams of its author in detail. His own dreams had increased in frequency and colour, and he found some of them shared by the author.

In possession of the book now, he considered that the real owner might have been missing it. Dismissing the idea, Norman reasoned that given the last entry of the author had been several years ago, and without a name attached to the scribe, there was little he could do to reunite it with its owner. The librarian hadn't appeared since their original meeting days earlier. The other assistant was no use at all with his queries, but had assured him that Breagal would return before the weekend.

Flicking to the back of the journal he noticed the blank pages again. The last dream entry was scribbled in disjointed shorthand. Norman could only make out the date of '24/10/13', and a name in the body of text underlined by the writer and written in bold letters – 'KROLLSON'.

He closed the book, and lay it on the table rubbing his dry, weary eyes. He retired to bed and soon drifted to sleep, his last woken thoughts ruminating on what had happened to the author and why the entries had stopped so suddenly.

SIX

There was a smile on Breagal's face as he dug deep in his mind vault, found the old memory, and blew off the dust before carefully handing it to him. The librarian's description of the incident made Norman feel like he was there also, a passive observer, transported to a time, decades earlier.

Norman followed the man's narrative and saw in his mind's eye the girl of Breagal's past. She stood rooted to the spot like a pillar, transfixed by a romance book in her hands, unaware other people were swerving to get around. Tightness in her calves suggested distributing the cramp, so she began rocking from foot to foot.

It wasn't the first time Stephen Breagal said he had spotted her. At fourteen, she was a couple of years older than him at the time, which posed a problem not least because she was one of the most beautiful girls he had ever seen in his short life. In those days Breagal said, he looked older than his years, thick glasses making him look more mature. Since first noticing her a month earlier, he had come back every day hoping to see the girl again and described how his heart felt a flutter that glorious day as he caught sight of her golden mane peeping out over one of the bookcases.

"I had it all mapped out," Breagal said to Norman. "I would walk straight up, nice and confident, natural stride and complement her choice of book. She would smile back surprised at my boldness."

"I'm guessing that's not what you did?"

"You guess right," Breagal said and continued the narrative, painting the scene for Norman.

The younger Breagal had watched as she returned the book to the shelf, picking up her schoolbag to leave. Summoning courage from his bootstraps he had paced up to the girl before his mind had a chance to give him pause. As she turned her body to walk away, Breagal had felt his mouth open but the words stuck in his throat. He watched her leave the library that day, and never saw her again.

Recounting that memory some thirty years later, he still winced at his cowardice. Norman sat opposite listening with a mild interest as the man then explained his career path and decision to become chief librarian.

"You see Norman. I honestly don't think I could have become involved with books if it wasn't for that girl."

"What do you mean?"

"Well," Breagal said and smiled. "I came to this library every day for three months after that episode, hoping to see her again. Slowly, as time passed, I fell out of love with her and in love with books. I was never much of a reader back then, but I found solace in stories; stories that could distract me from this slip of a girl I should have spoken with."

"So you think your life could have been different had you opened your mouth that day?"

Breagal blew his nose hard into the handkerchief, swollen nostrils becoming more inflamed.

"Absolutely! You need to realize that every day, in every decision, we face a fork in the road. Whilst these choices may not appear absolute, their cumulative effects create the life you lead today."

It was just after 10.30 a.m., and they were both sitting in the small café section near the entrance of the library. Breagal had insisted on coming to work even though he was still battling the flu, which had explained his absence that week.

"So did you ever find out what happened to the girl?"

"Of course. We married and had many, many wonderful years together."

Norman looked at him in such confusion it made Breagal laugh out loud with the few visitors present looking in their direction with stern faces.

"But I thought you said..."

"Yes, Norman, but the imagination in dream form is incredibly stirring and can create a world as rich as this one."

"So you dreamt you met her again?"

"Not dreamt. Lived!"

Norman sat back in his chair bewildered.

"Let me explain. Have you ever had an erotic dream?" Breagal asked, pouring the contents of a third sachet of sugar into his already diluted coffee.

"I can't see what that has to do with-" Norman started.

"I don't expect you to make the connection just yet. What I'm trying to tell you is that the mind sometimes has a way of mistaking thoughts, more specifically images we create in our minds, as reality."

Norman's silence prompted him to continue.

"I'm sure you're aware of the popular visualization technique," he said. "Where you imagine plucking a zesty scaled lemon from a tree, feeling its texture and smelling the citrus aroma. Imagine biting deep into this and the sticky juices oozing out all over your fingers."

"OK," Norman commented. "I can see how that could get a reaction."

"Good, my boy," he said, taking off his glasses and dipping a leg into the coffee to stir the sugar around. "What we visualize the mind can't tell apart from 'reality'. Visualize the lemon hard enough and it will be as realistic as if you had experienced the real thing."

His eyes widened incredulous, creasing a thick stack of lines across the centre of his brow, that looked like the symbol for a Wi-Fi connection.

"Regarding my earlier inference I'm sure thousands of teenagers can attest to the lucidity and seemingly very real nature of some of the 'wet' dreams that frequently accompany puberty. The body acts in very much the same way as if the sexual act itself were taking place. In truth, everything was visualized with no external stimulation."

The librarian now spoke with more passion, becoming somewhat too animated for the setting they were in. Sensitive to this fact, Norman couldn't prevent himself from blushing, especially since the topic of conversation had drifted. Wary of other people eavesdropping nearby, not least engaging in sex-talk with a relative stranger, he feigned interest and diverted Breagal's attention back to the original point of his visit.

"It sounds interesting," Norman lied. "I'd be more interested to hear your thoughts on whether you think it's worth keeping a dream diary to catalogue your dreams for better recall?"

The librarian looked at the man opposite in surprise and clasped his hands together before rubbing them in glee.

"My, my! Someone has been doing their homework!"

Norman shrugged his shoulders, uncertain how to answer, prompting the librarian to laugh again.

"Excellent. I'm glad that you have been making use of the library section. In fact, sweet Casey has informed me that not only have you been an ever-present here all this week, asking after my good self, but that you've been enthralled, seated for hours at length reading the texts. Admirable my boy! Perhaps I have found a younger kindred spirit in you after all."

Breagal reached out a hand and stroked the other man's arm, causing Norman to bristle.

"Alas. To answer your question. Yes. It is highly recommended."

"I'm glad you say that. I've actually started to document some of my own this week. They've definitely been memorable. Do you think I should keep journaling? Would it help get deeper into my dreams?"

"Absolutely. How else could we remember unless it was written down? Our brains have erasers of a sort that delete such dreams within hours, sometimes in seconds. However, an intense dream can stay with us for life. But, to keep a dream diary is a very personal item," Breagal said. "A thing that one should not be frivolous with. After all, some believe dreams to be the key to the soul. Were a man's thoughts to be documented accurately from a platform of higher consciousness, or dare I say it, even lower consciousness... well it would be a very dangerous thing to share."

There was a silence between the two men for a moment, and the librarian's stare was arrowed downward as if contemplating something. Norman waited for a moment, unsure if he should break the sudden spell. A child nearby began crying, which brought Breagal back all of a sudden, and his face again took on a cheerier visage.

"Again! Babbling. Pray, Mr Norman Adams, with your interest and growing passion, I'm probably preaching to the converted. Please, tell me how I can help. Casey informs me that you were interested in a specific book? Oh, speak of the Devil and she shall appear!"

Suddenly the older library clerk that had greeted Norman on the first day approached them, excused herself and whispered into Breagal's ear. He looked pensive for a moment, and then dismissed the clerk. Pausing a moment, his face clouded in uncertainty. He looked like a mathematician working out a complex puzzle in his own head, eyes darting back and forth groping for an answer. His face jerked up, scanning his surroundings as if for the first time, and turned back to Norman.

"I've got to leave momentarily my friend, but I hope to be back in the early afternoon, if my schedule permits. Feel free to reside here a little longer."

"But I haven't had a chance to ask you about-"

"My able colleague will answer your requests in my absence," Breagal cut across.

"Is everything alright, Stephen?" Norman asked.

But Breagal didn't respond, having already risen out of the chair. Taking the coat and hat passed to him from the clerk behind the desk, he strode out of the library.

Through the double windows, Norman stood and watched as the librarian exited into the rain and ran across the length of the car park, busying a tweed cap on his head. He walked beyond the entry gates to a parked blue car, windscreen wipers beating away a thin pattering of rain. Entering the passenger's side, the driver of the car sped off, rounding the corner out of sight. The driver seemed in no mood to hang around, leaving Norman alone with his confused thoughts once more.

SEVEN

"Slow down Margaret, or you'll get us both killed!"

The driver eased off the accelerator by the merest of touches as they approached road works. A workman in bright orange overalls stood by the side of the road holding a stop sign, directing traffic. The rain had opened up his long ponytail which trailed to his waist. From the breast pocket of the luminous jacket two wires exited leading up to the man's ears. The aggressive head bobbing, which whipped the pony tail from side to side suggested the choice of music wasn't Country and Western. Their car slowed to a grinding halt directly before the sign, annoying the driver who cursed under her breath. There was no oncoming traffic.

"Jesus. We just need to keep calm. I have things under control."

"Under control?" she replied with a mock tone.

Her body was arched forward, muscles tensed around the wheel, gripping it with both hands as if she intended to rip it off and throw it at the offending workman.

Their attention was drawn to him again as he reached behind for the lank ponytail and began to wring it. Without warning, the sign flicked around in his hand and the driver shot from the blocks, skidding loose gravel. After several minutes of weaving in and out of the traffic, they peeled off the narrow busy streets and onto an open road. The fields of the countryside zoomed past their windows with driver and passenger shielding their eyes from the streaks of light filtering through the wooded area.

Breagal allowed himself to relax a little.

"Come on dear. Deep breaths. Nice and easy," he patted her thigh, and she seemed to soften under his caress.

"This is the second time in a week, Stephen. The second time!" she said but without the earlier bluster.

She shifted the stick to a lower gear, easing around long country bends, which in other circumstances would have been an enjoyable drive, with the rainstorm subsiding and opening a path for the sun to illuminate their way.

"I know. I know," he muttered before looking at her. "I just feel it's my responsibility."

"No Stephen! It's gone beyond that now. He's a liability and needs professional help. There's no knowing what he'll do next," she argued.

Breagal's hand curled into a fist and he noticed the blood change the shade of a scar around his knuckles, as if coming to life the closer they approached the source - like Tolkien's Elf blade that signalled that orcs were near. The scar had long since healed but they were both aware that the man's mood swings were becoming more violent again and unpredictable. Reasoning and logic worked up until a point, but that point was lodged in the past when they were different people.

"We need to call her," the driver said, looking at Breagal who remained silent and looking down at his hand.

Slumped in his seat, he lifted his head and met her tender gaze.

"It's the right thing to do, honey," she said, reaching across and holding his hand; it felt cold and wet in her own.

He looked out the window, seeing the sharp turn off to their house, a kilometre ahead. A thin gravel lane traced its way up the hill where behind it hid a small white cottage, with a tiny greenhouse at the back. An uncertain wooden fence laid a wide perimeter battered by the high winds above ground but it still stood, undeterred and unbroken. Painted four summers ago to prevent critters from their rhubarb patch. Jam for the nieces on family occasions. He enjoyed the memory and it played on his lips before it was stolen, imagining the scene before them in a few moments.

"She needs to know the whole truth," Margaret said, as she pulled the car sharp into the hill rise on her right.

"OK, dear," Breagal replied and pressed his wife's hand for comfort. "I think it's time."

EIGHT

Rifling through her satchel, Moira Hart fished out the thin folder and placed it on the foldout train table to let it breathe, then leaned back in her seat which despite her best efforts refused to give an inch.

The train rounded a sharp bend, sending the manuscript sliding across the smooth table surface and onto the floor of the gangway before her dulled reflexes could grab it. The train conductor passed at that moment and reached down and picked it up, then passed it to her and she placed it on the table again and smiled.

"Thanks," she said.

"You're very welcome Miss or should I say Doctor?" the man replied, noticing the profile badge clipped to her suit lapel which she had forgotten to pocket. "Rough night?"

She looked up and into his cheery face with a surprised expression. He pointed to the blind that was pulled down, shielding her eyes from the early rising sun.

"That's why I'm on the big bucks. You get good at spotting hangovers in this job and yours looks like a corker! Here take this."

He reached into his back pocket and unearthed a little can of energy drink which she accepted.

"Second best cure I know."

"What's the first?" she asked.

He leaned in so close that she could smell gin on his breath, which almost made her gag again.

"Never sober up," he smiled. "You can keep that."

The man continued walking and whistled a tune as he passed. Moira weighed the can in her hand, uncertain what to do with it.

"I wouldn't drink that if I were you."

On the opposite aisle, a woman was watching her movements closely. Her lined faced looked like withered bark and betrayed a stylish bouffant that rocked with the movements of the carriage. Her eyes were narrowed above a thin pointed nose.

"You're probably right," Moira said.

She could do with the liquids but it was warm, feeding off the body temperature of the man and she had no intention of drinking it.

"My Jeffrey's a doctor. What is it that you do?"

Moira inched open the window blind and hoped that the sun would temporarily blind the other woman or at the very least end the conversation.

"I'm a psychiatrist."

"I see. Frightfully young though," she said and angled her body toward the younger woman who smiled by way of courtesy.

Moira swallowed a deep breath and tried to relax. When she opened her eyes, she looked across and was disturbed to see that the woman was staring.

"Been practicing long?"

"Around four years now."

"I studied psychiatry myself back at university. Back when you had to earn your stripes. Unlike now where they give out distinctions and decorations to anyone that can spell," she sneered.

The woman shook her head free of the thought before considering whether to continue.

"I trained under Frederik Masteau in Paris no less. I don't expect you'd know who he was. You're far too young," she said without waiting for an answer.

Moira was rolling the full can around in her hand now with half a mind to throw it at the woman, but decided to store it out of arms reach and tucked it in her bag.

"A genius in the field. A luminary of his time. Above his peers. He described psychiatry as a death of sorts and emphasised the need to detach completely from the patient."

Peering over the back of a seat, Moira looked around to see if there was a vacant one nearby or a bathroom she could escape into until they arrived at their final destination.

"The key is to disconnect and remain impartial. Cocooning oneself, killing your emotional responses which go against our natural instinct as human beings but it's the only way to survive in this profession."

The headache pulsed inside her skull and the sun was scorching her skin dryer than a bone and, worse still, the woman's voice seemed to shape into a drill and bore into her brain.

"You don't say much for a psychiatrist, do you?"

Her patience had long since expired and now Moira picked up her bag and moved to a seat at the far end of the carriage, avoiding the look of the woman's face.

She sat back down, pulled out the folder from her bag and placed it on the table in front which sobered her thoughts. At the centre, emboldened words marked 'CASE FILE – 207535 – 15/9/11'. It might as well have been called Case #1. The memory of her first patient still as vivid as the acrid taste of vomit in the back of her throat.

She flicked open the file and scanned to the symptoms. Memory loss. Insomnia. Hallucinogenic fantasies. Depression. Distorted view of reality. Paranoia. Self-harm. Violent tendencies. The list of items was longer than most family's weekly shopping lists. Hell, she thought, I've dated most of these.

Lapses, although not uncommon, varied in how far the user regressed and the duration, but this sounded serious. Certainly serious enough that Breagal felt the need to call her out of the blue after a three-year hiatus. Confirming the appointment that morning, their conversation had been brief. It was the message from last night that had alarmed her. She withdrew her mobile phone from the bag and replayed it again.

"Dr Hart, this is Stephen Breagal. I hope you don't mind me contacting you on a Friday night like this, but we have no one else to turn to."

There was a faint voice in the background, barely audible that she hadn't heard in last night's listening – perhaps because of the fact she was still inebriated. Increasing the volume, she pushed the phone back to her ear.

"You helped my brother Saul several years back. Things were under control until he relapsed for the first time over two years ago."

The sound of a woman shouting in the background caused him to pause.

"The truth is, other psychiatrists I've consulted haven't been able to help and you are the only one who has been able to get through to him in any way so far."

As Moira listened she could pick out several sharp hard knocks in the distance.

"Stephen, I need you here!" the woman shouted.

"Please call me when you get this. I urgently need to speak with you and can collect you at the station tomorrow. The first train arrives at 9.30 a.m. I realize it's short notice and the weekend but please. For my brother's sake, please."

Breagal was not prepared to go into any more detail over the phone. Again, his insistence to meet in person had made Moira curious. The train speaker suddenly sprung to life with a woman's comforting voice. "The next station is Shaysburg – please ensure you have all your belongings with you."

She placed the file back in the satchel along with her mobile phone and, as the train slowed, she rose and approached the carriage exit furthest away from the other woman. Ahead of her stood a well-dressed man and a little girl holding his hand. She looked no older than five or six years old and was styled in a pink floral dress, with sparkling studs along the length of the sleeve. Blonde pigtails tied by red ribbons spilled out onto her little shoulders. The man was tall and slender, dressed in a grey well-pressed suit, neatly ironed and designer. In his free hand he was confirming the existence of his laptop bag at his side with a gentle tap, strap slung around his shoulder.

"But I want to go to Jenny's house tonight Daddy!" the girl pleaded. "Jenny's mum says they have a horse in the field next door. I want to ride a horse!"

The suited man crouched down to level eye contact with the girl who was stamping her feet. His face pulsed red and Moira could see the whites of his eyes bulge. The little girl was afraid to look at him but he yanked a pigtail back so she had no choice to hear him.

"For the last time, you are not going to Jenny's!" he said through gritted teeth.

Suddenly aware of other passengers on the carriage, he relaxed his grip on the back of her head and smoothed a strand of hair off her face.

"I don't want you wasting your time with fool's errands. I want you to come home and do your homework."

The man stood up and grabbed her hand again. The little girl tried to pull away just as the carriage doors opened but the man was too strong.

"I don't pay for the benefit of private school education to have my girl grow up to be a horse rider."

They left the carriage and the man's giant strides off the platform had the little girl scurrying to keep pace. Moira caught her reflection in the glass pane as she readied to exit and sighed.

"Come on, girl. Showtime."

NINE

The traffic of people inside the small train station almost swept Moira Hart away in the current. Trying to adjust to her bearings she edged against the railing and scanned the sea of faces for one that stood out. She hadn't seen the librarian in years, but figured the tall figure would be easy to recognize above the rushing commuters in front. Her headache was beginning to throb again in the heat and noise of the bustling hall. Spotting the exit sign, she weaved her way through the clusters of bodies and stepped out of the station at a side entrance where a row of cars parked.

"Taxi, Miss?"

"No thanks, I'm waiting for someone," she answered to the young porter.

He frowned and retreated inside the building to find another customer.

She was about to dig into her bag and pull out a cigarette, when across the street she noticed a man standing, looking in her direction. Screening the sun with her hand, she could see he was well dressed, wearing a long navy coat that trailed the ground, somewhat out of place in the growing morning heat. Below it he wore a woollen grey jumper housing a red and white striped tie.

She watched the man with curiosity as he played Frogger with the traffic. A gap opened up and Breagal skipped across the road, holding up a hand to wave. His hair was cropped shorter than their last meeting, fused grey at the temples. As he approached, she could see that his smile was nervous, but greeting her with a hug he brightened and expressed his gratitude for her prompt arrival at short notice.

They walked a short distance to the car park where he had only just arrived and left the motor running in one of the bays, and began a scenic drive to the librarian's small thatched bungalow in the country.

"You look well, Moira," Breagal remarked. "Definitely blossomed since we last met."

Unsure how to respond, the psychiatrist smiled back. She screwed down the window and let the country air blow away some of the staleness she felt on her skin. It felt cold but energizing and she took deep breaths to calm her headache.

"How is your brother?" she asked.

"In truth, I wanted you to see for yourself. My dear wife is scared to her wits thinking that he might do something."

"Has he given any reason to suggest he might?"

Breagal twitched in his seat like he had just sat on a pebble, and his mouth screwed up into a grimace.

"Well..."

"Tell me, Stephen. I need to know."

"You remember how we agreed that the best way to control and deal with his mood swings would be to make him comfortable, provide him with his own room and supply him with toys?"

Moira remembered only too well. Saul Breagal was a man in his late forties when she had met him for the first time. During one counselling session in those early days, she had observed him staring with fascination at the toys in the corner of her office. It so happened that the previous patient that morning had been a young boy, only seven or eight years old. The boy had suffered physical abuse from his stepfather, and Moira had used the toys as a way to help him open up. Not only had they helped make the boy comfortable around her, but they had also allowed her to build a connection and bond with him. On impulse, following the stare of the older man, she had asked if he wanted to play with some of the toys.

His eyes had opened wide like moons and she had watched his face transform into a bright smile. Approaching with some trepidation, as if it were a trap, he had paused and looked back at her.

"Go on!" she had insisted.

Saul had reached into the pen and picked out a toy and brought it back to the couch where his brother was sitting. He had held the toy pirate in his hands, bouncing it on his leg, running it along the armrest of the couch. For the remainder of their session that day, the man had been in bliss with his little figurine. The result had been nothing short of magic, and he had been inseparable from it in subsequent sessions.

"Yes, I remember. Has anything changed?"

"Well," Breagal deliberated. "At the start of this week, I could sense a certain restlessness in him. That was soon announced when he decided to leave our abode while I was at work. On Monday morning, he decided to go for a walk around town."

"But, he can't be let out without supervision."

"Yes, I know that of course," Breagal answered. "I've tried my best to keep him out of harm's way, and it has been a testing time for my dear Margaret these past few years. I considered this, and to take some of the responsibility off her shoulders, I decided that I would take him into the library next day, just like old times."

Dr Hart looked across at him now. Breagal took his eye off the road for a moment and saw in her face a look of disappointment.

"I know. I'm sorry," he said. "I didn't know what else to do."

The car eased off the main road and ascended a gravel lane cut into the hill, crunching the stones below.

"We agreed that it would be best for Saul's wellbeing if he be kept out of the public eye," she said. "At least he hasn't harmed anyone."

A silence hung in the air which unsettled Moira. She looked at the driver who hadn't responded, focusing instead on crawling the car up over the hill.

"Stephen, please tell me nothing violent has happened to anyone?"

He slipped one hand off the steering wheel and pulled the car to the edge of the gravel path alongside a little wooden fence in desperate need a new lick of paint. Up ahead, they could see the roof of the small house peeping over the hill. Breagal pulled up the handbrake. His head dropped onto his chest and he let out a long sigh, before taking a moment to study the face of the psychiatrist.

"This is what I wanted to tell you. Why I asked you to come here."

"Go on."

"Since Tuesday, his behaviour has become agitated. Yesterday, I was pulled away from the library. My dear wife had the shock of her life when she found my brother in hysterics screaming the house down. He was tearing everything down in his room. Throwing toys, chairs, anything and everything against the walls. Kicking in the doors."

"My God!"

"My poor wife was so scared. She had to get out of the house and drove straight to the library to get me. Fortunately, when I arrived he had calmed down again, barring a minor blip last night, which is when I called you. Ever since Tuesday, he's been different. More detached. We don't know why, or what to do. You have to help us Dr Hart."

The eyes of Breagal began to tear, and she reached out a hand to the man and rubbed his shoulder.

"I'm going to help as best I can, Stephen," she said. "Now let's go and see your brother."

Breagal lowered the handbrake again and the car pulled off the grass bunker and up over the hill with the white walled house beginning to lower into view.

"What on Earth?"

In front of the house, a trail of broken glass winked under the sun's rays. Tracing it to the wall, they could see the window had been smashed from inside. The front door burst open suddenly and a woman in a silk white nightdress ran toward the vehicle as it approached. Her mouth was locked in a scream and the hair wild and slapping around her face. Margaret Breagal slammed her hands onto the trunk of the moving car and implored them to help.

It all seemed to happen in slow motion with the driver and his guest leaping out of the car, following the outstretched hand of the hysterical woman. As she entered the house they could see that it had been ransacked, paintings and portraits ripped off the walls, torn and battered on the floor. It was silent except for the sound of the agitated woman outside who refused to enter as they crept inside.

"Saul?" Moira tried and received no response.

A path of debris spilled from the room on her right, half way down the corridor. The door closest to her, on her left, remained closed and she pressed her hand against its surface before reaching for the handle.

"No," Breagal scolded.

He had left his wife and had quickly joined her at its entrance.

"Check Saul's room," he said and pointed to the opening on her right.

She continued down the corridor until she reached the room. Pushing the door open, she saw bright crayon loops daubed on the wallpaper, ineligible and drawn without attention. Toys lay broken around the foot of the bed in pieces. The occupant wasn't there. Breagal pointed toward a door further along the hallway and she could see from the aperture a longer room. As they approached, she again eased the door open, seeing furniture assembled at the far end - warm browns against the azul walls. This section of the house at least looked untouched.

In front of the sofa and partially obscured, she could see a large open fireplace. It had been cleared of firewood and tinder, which lay on a bundle to one side. Beside it was a tin drum which had fallen over. The top was missing, and it looked like the container was empty. The bright blue and yellow colour of it reminded her of the starter fluid needed for BBQ fires.

Moira was about to turn back to Breagal in the doorway and suggest looking elsewhere, before a spark of light drew her attention. Her mouth opened in horror to see a man she recognized, although the face was scratched deep in fresh lines as if from uncut fingernails. The oily shape was curled up inside the alcove of the fireplace on a bed of newspaper. He was naked and shivering, tears flowing free from his face. In his hand he held a lighter and was flicking it in desperation.

"No!"

Moira sprinted across the room, jumped over the couch and slapped the lighter out of the man's hand where it slid across the wooden floor. The stricken man let out a gut-wrenching cry of pain and closed his eyes as the figures of his brother and shaken wife joined Moira in a circle staring down in amazement at the helpless figure.

***

They were seated in the living room which was now darkening with the setting sun. Stephen Breagal and his wife were both sitting on the couch cradling cups of coffee that Dr Hart had prepared for them. Their eyes looked at the firewood, which Moira had been trying to ignite. She continued to crouch by the fireplace trying to light the tinderbox, until suddenly the air caught it and breathed the flames over the wood and pile of peat.

Three refuse bags sat bloated against the wall near the entrance to the kitchen, the fruits of their labour after two hours of clearing broken ceramics and toys. The broken window in the front room was managed by Breagal - cardboard boxes sliced and sealed to the gaping hole with sticky tape.

The only sound in the house now was the shallow snores of Saul who could be heard through a baby monitor in the living room. The psychiatrist was quick to administer some benzodiazepines to calm him and had it not been for Breagal's constant pleading, the police would have arrived hours earlier. The librarian had carried his stricken brother into the shower and washed off the oil before guiding him to bed where he had remained all afternoon.

Dr Hart picked up an antique poker from a prop stand and began to prod at the blazing sticks, little orbs of light swept up and away through the chimney. She replaced it, and sat back down beside the distressed couple who had been quiet for too long, and studied their faces. Breagal had removed his glasses and they sat on his lap reflecting the bright glow of the hearth. His eyes were distant and glazed, watching the fire consume the bundle of wood. By his side sat his motionless wife still holding her mug full of coffee; untouched it had now gone cold. She too was in deep repose following his gaze.

"I think it's time we spoke honestly and rationally," Hart began.

She studied their reaction but they remained still, staring straight ahead.

"What we've seen today isn't an isolated event. By all accounts, it seems that recently things have gotten worse," she said. "Stephen, are you listening?"

He turned to her now, and put on his glasses. The smile was weak and apologetic and he cleared his throat, which startled his wife.

"Sorry Moira. As you can imagine, it has been a lot to take in," he said with a voice that was thin and raspy, spoken in a quiet whisper devoid of strength.

"I understand," she said and nodded but continued undeterred. "You called me here for a reason, and thank God you did. Who knows what could have happened had we not been here on time, or calmed him down."

"Yes," Breagal stuttered. "Thank you for your help."

He left the empty cup down on the ground and clasped his hands together, thumbs fidgeting.

"Listen," Hart said. "I know it's been tough for you both. But if you want my professional opinion your brother needs to have proper medical care and assistance. Facts are facts. He is a serious risk to both you and your wife."

"I can't let my brother be sent off to some institution. You made him right before. You can do it again!" Breagal entreated, emotion rising in his voice.

Dr Hart's stare remained fixed on the librarian, seeing the pain swell there.

"Stephen," she started in a soft tone. "I've known your brother for a few years now."

"And I've known him for forty-two!" he fired back, voice trembling.

"I realize that. I have to use my professional experience here, and everything is telling me that you are in danger if you continue to have him under this roof," she said, directing the words to both he and his wife.

"She's right," Margaret said.

Breagal looked at her, desperate.

"But, my dear…"

"No Stephen. We've had enough trouble. Your brother is a problem we just can't manage. There have been times these past few days where I've feared for my own life. I don't want to feel like a victim in my own home."

"But Margaret," Breagal replied and tried to placate his wife by putting his hand around hers, but she slapped it away.

"No! It stops now. You have to choose either your brother or me."

Dr Hart watched the exchange, grateful that the woman was showing some sensibility in the matter. Breagal's face crumbled before her eyes and she watched the life force drain out of him. He was slow to turn to his wife and held her hands in his own, before kissing them.

"I love you, Margaret," he said and smiled.

"I love you too, Stephen."

They kissed each other and it turned into a loving hug, tears beginning to flow for one another. After a few moments, they unhooked and sat back up straight, a mote embarrassed at the sudden show of affection in front of the patient psychologist who couldn't help but flash a smile at them.

Then her thoughts returned to Saul, considering the eventual next steps. She would need to do a full psychoanalysis with him in her office, followed by a physical exam. Results of which, coupled with the events of this week, should lead to her findings being examined by a panel which should pass judgement that he be summarily sanctioned for his own health. These thoughts went through her mind, as she watched the couple in front of her holding hands like love-struck teenagers. It was a touching moment and the gentle orange, dancing glow of the fire basked them in its warm embrace. Her attention turned to the noise there, sticks crackling under the heat of the blaze, the only sound in the room seeming to add to the ambiance.

Suddenly she stood and moved to the coffee table propped alongside the wall. The Breagal's looked at her perplexed, watching the woman kneel down and observe something below the table. Immediately she jumped back to her feet and sprinted past them and out of the room.

"Moira?" Breagal exclaimed. "Where are you..."

The couple turned around in the couch and heard her running along the corridor. They stood up concerned and Mrs Breagal flung her arms around the waist of the librarian who was tensed. He looked to the table and could see under it the baby monitor. The living room door opened again, and in it burst the panicked and breathless psychologist, the look of shock on her face.

"He's gone!"

TEN

The commander exercised caution when steering his craft through an oncoming thin sheet of sleet, eyes narrowing directly ahead. Clumps of low-lying fog made navigation more difficult but he had traversed this passage before, confident in his ability. The weather had descended quietly on the land, foreboding and hugging the contours of the objects as they glided past.

    He guided his vessel with elegant ease and consummate experience, the wheel a living extension of himself, master crafted, tuned with his emotions and thoughts. His smile was one of contentment. Venturing forth into uncharted territories and new adventures, he sucked in the cold, sharp air and let it wash over him, exhilarating and raw. Tonight would be a good night.

    He adjusted the mirror to catch his reflection. A manic grin stretched tight across his face, exposing a gap of blackness where two front teeth would have stood. Long black hair dangled from the scalp, concealing the fresh pink scars across his forehead. Smoothing the strands behind his ears he became conscious of the second set of eyes observing. The parrot's claws gripped his shoulders, body bobbing back and forth with the sway of the vessel. Its colour had faded over the years. The once electric blue dazzling feathers and sunshine yellow breast were replaced by a blotchy lighter shade, with pale specks of caramel down its front. The parrot looked as well-worn as its owner, with hairless spots blighting its head but its eyes still carried the same lustre as ever.

That was one of the lines that the shopkeeper had used. Clearly eager to shift stock, and given the short notice, Norman had been happy to oblige.

Besides, he reasoned, the alternative costume of a Power Ranger wasn't conducive to this weather and skin-tight mesh emphasised every bulge and curve.

There was a faint itch at his neck, and he snapped the mirror back down again. A beady eye had popped out from the stuffed parrot - stitching loosened through wear and tear, dangling free from its orifice. Norman tried to pop it back into place but without the requisite glue had little success. The body limped forward each time his raised arm signalled the indicator as if to peck at his neck.

When the eye continued to dangle on its optic nerve, tickling his skin, Norman pulled it out and stored it with the coins in his dashboard; his own little veritable treasure chest. As the traffic unexpectedly congested around a set of lights, a glance at the clock offered reassurance and he eased back in his chair. Sweat dampened the bandana wrapped around his head and, removing it, he refolded it once and then twice and rotated a fresh sheet on his brow. Norman wound the window down an inch, welcoming the fresh air in spite of the few drips and drabs of pelting rain, which by and large were unable to make the gradient into the car.

He pulled the mirror down again, carefully fingering the scars on his face, feeling for the ends and openings and satisfied they were flush to his cheek. Next, he fiddled with the collar underneath the seat belt. He unbuckled it and inspected the inside lining abrasive against his thin neck and fanned it open further. The clip-on ear decoration, a plastic loop with chipped paint that looked more like a curtain rail ring, bit into his lobe and he removed it and assessed the small indentation, until a car behind honked its annoyance.

The traffic continued to splutter and cough until his car finally cleared the bottleneck and sped off down a quieter artery away from town. Gradually, the buildings by his sides became fewer and spaced apart, until he could see the fields and countryside beyond.

He fished into the bag beside him on the passenger seat and, although it was dark in the car, his groping hand still managed the inventory check.

"Deodorant? Check. Aftershave? Check. Eye patch? Check. Hook hand? Check. Bottle of rum? Check."

On the ground he noticed the thick corner of the library book and he reached down, picked it up and pocketed it inside the bag, tightening the rope cord around the top.

His car slowed to a halt behind a road works' sign just out of town, where a young man in orange overalls was dancing to the rhythm of his own beat, using the parked sign in his hands as a stripper pole of sorts. His hands were snake heads wiggling through the rain, long arms carrying the fluid movement. Trailing down his spine was a long, dark ponytail which Norman half expected to be charmed and lift up with the workman's spell.

The chorus of honking horns either displayed their frustration or humour at the sight, it was hard to tell but Norman's own car beeped in support with them. The sudden noise seemed to distract the man mid-trance and he flipped the sign around, signalling the cars to go. When Norman passed the smiling man, he opened it up into fourth gear and veered out from under the procession of cars. He began to trace the familiar route to Victor's house in his mind, beginning with the natural wonder that was the Jones' Road.

A short winding corridor of one kilometre, the road was lined on either side by a procession of old, vine trees. The trees leaned into the road and created a natural tunnel. No one was certain if it was because they were initially planted on uneven ground or if it was some curious quirk of nature. Claustrophobia was a common emotion felt, not least because of the narrow road and remoteness of the location, but also because the branches overhead wove perfectly together creating a ceiling to shut out natural light.

Fields surrounded it, and the ghost stories of farmers with pitchforks were common in the town. Children were regaled with tall tales of hitchhikers and broken down motorists being seized upon, never to be seen again. It was an intimidating prospect for any motorist, with winding roads preventing an opportunity to see oncoming traffic. Anyone with the misfortune to have broken down on that stretch of country lane would have no choice but to take cover in the marsh lands on either side, blanketed by the thick fog or run the gauntlet through the tree tunnel.

The tunnel crept out from nowhere, but Norman was prepared and had cast his full light beam ahead. A flurry of bugs danced in their spotlight, basking in the rare illumination. A little further ahead on the side of the road, two glowing eyes stared back, startled. The car's bright beam had caught a scurrying fox dead in its tracks. Blinded for a moment, it suddenly darted back across his path, dropping a small object from its mouth. The subsequent crunch below the tires turned the fox's hearty dinner into a meat pancake.

After a succession of meandering corners, Norman saw the tunnel exit ahead. He shifted up a gear again, pushed down on the accelerator, stealing a quick glance at the mirror. A sudden movement in the road ahead caught his peripheral vision. Under the line of trees, a figure stepped out onto the road. Norman's breath froze in his chest. The car was travelling too fast to brake as the silhouette loomed larger in his windscreen. Tires screeched with the acuteness of the angle as he hauled the car to one side, whistling past the figure.

The vehicle jolted off road, hitting the grass embankment hard, throwing the driver inside against the roof. The hit dazed Norman, as the car sped through the undergrowth. Branches cracked against the windscreen and the faint headlight beam blinked to avoid the pain. Slamming the brakes hard had little resistance against the slick grass underneath, bouncing off unseen bumps in the terrain. He was tossed around inside like a rag doll as he battled to gain control of the wheel. With sudden clarity, he sensed the road above on his right hand side now, as the car continued hurtling downwards.

Objects from the undergrowth shot past his window, tearing the side mirror clean off. He tried to inch the car towards the right of the embankment. His best bet at this speed was to somehow catapult back onto the road into safety. Visibility was made more difficult by the drunken light beam. Mud and bug smears stained the windscreen obscuring his view, but the meandering road suddenly came back into sight and he could see a break in the trees. The vehicle made a final violent dip at speed, before it surfaced at an angle, throwing the car off direction in mid-air.

It came to a crushing halt smashing head first into a tree, spitting the bloodied driver through the windscreen. A single headlight flickered upward out of the ditch, catching the broken body of the driver several yards ahead, lying face down. His twisted torso lay motionless beside the road, illuminated by the beam which flickered one last time before darkness swallowed him.

ELEVEN

He was flying. That much was certain. Whether it was a dream or not, it was difficult to know.

It wouldn't connect. The pieces didn't fit. Not yet anyway, but it gave him pause for thought and helped to block out the pain. A distant beat of a drum that he could choose to listen to at any time.

He felt a tear trail its way down the bridge of his nose, ticklish and he moved to wipe it dry but his arm wouldn't follow his command. He felt somehow disconnected from his body.

A point of light in the distance appeared. His thoughts which had whirled now seemed to collect and considered his new frame of reference, and the surroundings. There was darkness all around. Or perhaps he was unconscious. Norman felt incredibly tired, and the pain in his body seemed to grow by the second. His garbled cry brought the light closer. It flashed in his eyes before moving beyond. He could see now that the figure behind the light had moved to a wreckage nearby. Was there something connecting him to the mangled car that flashed in the man's torchlight? Propped on his side, he saw the figure reach inside and pull something out just beyond his sight.

Norman strained to move around to see what it was, but the pain shot straight up his back, immobilizing him. All his senses were engaged now. The figure turned back toward him, casting the light into his eyes again.

"Please..." he heard himself mouth.

His jawbone clicked and slid together roughly, like two tectonic plates that pre-empted an earthquake. The pain was all consuming but he persevered.

"Please…help…me."

The figure hesitated. Light still dazzled Norman, and the pain flared again in waves. He felt like an ant caught in a magnifying glasses pinpoint of sunlight.

The searing pain raged once more and he clenched his broken teeth together to prevent slipping into unconsciousness. The figure suddenly shone the torch beyond him and ran away toward the tunnel of light it carved into the darkness beyond.

"Please don't go!" Norman begged, as the footsteps became fainter until finally they were out of earshot.

He began to cry in the darkness. Tears stung his face, slicing across the open cuts. When they had frozen to his face he noticed the chill of the cold night air. It was welcome relief to the red-hot searing pain in his back which had contorted into a position which disabled his movement.

He listened to the wind as it howled through the trees, jangling the twigs like broken bones on a skeleton. He heard the traffic in the distance, the murmurings of nocturnal creatures surrounding him that seemed to encroach further the longer he lay. His parents, he thought. He imagined what his mangled body must look like and he began sobbing, the tears which had salted dry his wounds opened fresh again, stretching the cuts wider and deeper.

Suddenly he felt the pain rise again. This time he was sure it would take him, and he fixed his attention on the image of his mother and father as they flashed in front of him. His father was slim like when Norman was a boy, reaching out his hands to scoop him off the ground and throw him high into the air. His mother was young and beautiful, a face that showed no sign of age or pain. She crouched down easily, looked up at her husband and then toward Norman, smiling as he ran towards them. As soon as he accepted the agony, the pain washed over him and he felt at peace. His parents beckoned him closer. Reassured, he smiled back at the vision and reached out for their hand.

TWELVE

Noreen and Frank Adams were sitting beside each other in the centre of the doctor's office. In front of them was a small unoccupied desk, behind it a chair that had just been vacated. Their hands locked tight together, fingers intertwined reminding Frank of twenty-four years earlier when she had squeezed his hand during a long and painful childbirth. It evoked powerful memories of a better time, taking on the mantle of father. Guardian. Keeper.

He felt his wife trembling in her seat. Her uncontrollable sobs made him feel powerless, somehow less than a man. Frank caressed her hand in his, and turned to face her. His lips moved to speak but he couldn't utter a sentence. Instead, the emotion broke through and he collapsed against his wife's shoulder, unable to hold back the flow.

"He'll pull through," he said though his breathing was strained. "We'll get the best team of people, and we'll…"

The last sentence trailed off.

Paramedics had arrived at the scene of the car crash just after midnight after being alerted by Victor James. Trying to reach his friend by phone, he had become worried, knowing how tricky the roads were leading to the house especially given the weather conditions. He had parked up in a safe dirt road along the Jones' road and seen a light flickering off-road in the distance, and there he had found his friends sprawled body. Norman was in a critical condition and had suffered a spinal break, several broken ribs, a cracked skull and a broken leg. Considering the length of time, spent out in the open cold, there was also a risk of pneumonia.

Overall the prognosis was bleak, with a strong chance that he would never walk again. The doctor had explained that given the severity of the brain trauma specifically, that an induced coma would be best for their son, given the huge shock to the body and head. The large swelling in his brain was of their utmost concern, the result of which, he had explained may "incapacitate the patient".

"What does that mean exactly?" He had asked.

"It means, Mr Adams, that your son may struggle to regain consciousness."

Frank had been silent as he considered the judgement. The surreal conversation had felt like some sort of role-play or out of body experience. It had been difficult to make the connection between what the doctor had said and tie that to his son. Were it not for the plaques and framed certificates on the wall, and his white coat and name badge, they might have been in the more familiar setting of a conference boardroom.

By his side, Noreen had slumped forward and had buried her head in her hands. She had let out a gut wrenching cry of pain and burst into tears. Shaken from his thought stream, Frank had looked across at her in confusion. With a deep intake of breath, composure still in check but a torrent of thoughts that had fought for attention in his mind, he had asked the one question that he could think of.

The doctor had looked down at his table in brief thought, splayed his fingers wide and looked at each manicured fingertip. He had been careful to choose his words, and they still rang in Frank's ears now as he sat with his wife alone in the room, holding her in his arms.

"Physical injuries will heal. But with brain injuries…" he had said and let out a sigh before continuing. "You may not recognize your son if he wakes up."

THIRTEEN

The faint hum of traffic outside carried through the room. Her attention diverted to the clock on the wall. 8.45 a.m. – the school run. Frantic parents weaving in and out of a dotted line to gain an extra yard and she remembered the little girl on the train from a few days earlier, wondering if she was caught in the traffic somewhere.

The man lay motionless on the couch to her side, in a deep hypnotic trance. His face was a cold mask. She was amazed at how much he had regressed. The case file was parked on her knee. She opened it, flicked to the back and removed a card, which brought a smile to her face.

On the front, a picture of an attractive blonde curvy nurse took the temperature of an excitable young man. Sweat dripped from his forehead onto a soaking bed and a caption in the top corner read, "Thanks Toots!"

She opened it and read the first of two inscriptions on the inside.

> Thank you for saving my brother.
> Stephen.
> PS. He chose the card!
> November 2012

Then she looked at the second inscription – a short sentence drawn in a different hand, and smiled.

"Saul," she began. "Do you remember when we last met in my office?"

He gave a monosyllabic grunt, but she noticed something stir behind those closed eyelids.

"Do you remember when we were with your brother and you gave me a card?"

Again another grunt, as he squirmed in the couch, flicking his head away from her.

"Your brother Stephen said that you wrote the message inside. Do you remember what you wrote in that card Saul?"

He remained impassive, unwilling to participate in the conversation.

Hart looked at the tape recorder. The red light glowed, recording the conversation. She returned her stare to the strained face of the man. She could sense something swimming below the depths, something that required all her experience to tease out.

"You wrote the words, 'You wake me.' Wake you from what Saul?"

He suddenly arched his back against the couch, pelvis thrust in the air. Fists clenched by his side, head thrashing against the cushion, teeth gnashing so hard that she could her them squeak.

"Night. Mares," he cried in a barely audible whisper, as if afraid of who would hear.

Hart moved the recorder to the edge of the table, closer to the agitated man. Her immediate concern was that the trance would be broken, not uncommon when the subject experienced undue physical pain or distress.

"Calm down, Saul. Deep breaths," she said.

She exhaled, long deep exaggerated breaths for effect, and soon enough their breathing aligned and his body relaxed, sinking back into the couch.

"I would like to talk to you a little bit more about these nightmares."

He flinched and missed a breath, but otherwise remained unperturbed, which she took as a sign to continue.

"When did you first start having them?"

"Eight years ago."

Breathing had become fixed now and she could see he was completely under.

"How often do you have these dreams?"

"Lots."
"Do you still have them?"
"Yes."
"Do you dream every night?"
"Yes."
"That's a lot of dreams."
"784."
"And, how do you know it's that many?" Hart asked.

She looked up from her notepad at Saul when he paused, and asked the question again, noticing some tension in the response.

"I... keep... a book."
"You recorded every dream in a diary?"
"Yes."

Feeling a renewed confidence, she decided to take a dangerous path.

"You're doing great, Saul. Do you have any particularly memorable dreams? Dreams that stand out or feel more real than others?"

No response.

She saw the muscles in his neck tense again, lips beginning to curl back over his broken teeth. Again, she persisted.

"Yes," he exhaled, as if it caused great pain.
"Can you tell me about them?"

His breath quickened again and Hart saw him unravel in an instant, living the nightmare.

His already pale complexion turned translucent white, perspiration licking his brow above eyes scrunched tight, blocking out some unseen terror. The little body began to spasm in front of her, and the breath was catching, suffocating the voice inside. Hart stood and moved quickly to soothe him, whispering in his ear to evoke a calm that melted through his body until he finally returned to a resting state again.

After a few minutes, and when breathing had returned to normal, she tried again.

"Where is this dream book, Saul?"

The breaths had become so deep and relaxed she couldn't tell if he had inadvertently fallen from trance into sleep. She asked again.

"Safe," came the soft spoken response.

"Safe from who?"

"The pirate."

"The pirate?" Moira asked again to make sure she had heard correctly.

With a reflex movement she turned to the corner of the room where the little playpen had once stood.

"The pirate," Saul confirmed.

"What would happen to the pirate if they got the book?" she asked.

Saul suddenly began to cry, as if his resistance had completely broken. Big tears rolled down his cheeks onto the soft pillow below. He wiped the trails clear with a palm and sighed in resignation, pointing a finger at his temple.

"He would be in here with me."

FOURTEEN

"How's our little star doing today?"

He looked up at the pretty nurse in wide-eyed wonder, smiling a perfect row of pearls.

"I'm doing fine thank you, though Norman's the same," Victor replied.

"I was talking about Norman, you joker!" she said, a broad smile filling her cherub face.

"I swear you spend more time with me on your shifts than you do with your own patients," he teased. "If you want to ask me out Nancy, then all you have to do is ask, you know."

"Not short of confidence are we?"

"Here for a good time, not a long time. That's my motto."

She pulled the curtain around the bed, giving them privacy and he watched her slip away from sight, footsteps fading down the hallway.

"Don't say it. I already know what you're thinking," he said, looking down at the patient. "'Same old Victor. Here I am, hooked up to this bloody machine, pumping air into my lungs, tubes in more holes than I'll openly admit and here, here of all places he has the cheek to flirt with the nurses!'"

His laughter felt good, a human voice amid the electronic beeps.

"You know fine well what a woman in uniform does for me, mate. Why do you think I threw the fancy dress party in the first place?"

His smile soon sloped off his face, looking down at the lifeless body of his friend who remained passive.

"There will be plenty more nights like that ahead bro, don't you worry," he said, clasping his friend's hand.

Victor studied the breathing apparatus connected to his friend, pushing air with a whoosh, filling Norman's chest in a strangely hypnotic fashion. The equipment filled the little conclave, a walled curtain separating the other patients in the ward who he hadn't seen, but had heard in the quietude of night, soft sobs cursing their existence.

In this state, Norman was barely recognizable from the man he had sat beside in work. The figure in front of him was a cloaked skeleton. Hollowed cheeks and sunken eyes against a skull that looked bulbous propped on thin shoulders. A deep purple scar snaked its way from his ear to lower jaw. A neater scar crept out from below the bandaged head, a necessary action to access his frontal lobe to relieve the pressure, the doctors had said. The bruises were healing better. Victor had watched them fade over the last three weeks, from black to purple to their current hue of yellow. During those tense few weeks the patient's face had showed more colours and shades than a painter's palate.

Victor stood and walked around the little enclosure, timing his slow steps with the metronomic beat of the heart monitor.

He stopped just above the prostrate patient and looked down at him. Placing a hand on the brow, he caressed it, cold to the touch. Sliding the cover up closer to Norman's neck, he heard something drop and hit the ground, making a strange tinny sound. Cursing himself, Victor looked down to see what had fallen. He crouched down, peering underneath the bed and groping around for the object. Extending his hand, he managed to hook it and looked at it, puzzled.

He rubbed the object between his fingers, at once noticing the sharp contoured edges and tiny imperfections in its surface. Holding it up to the light, it blushed in a purple haze, colours ripening near the base. In it he could see the deep complexity of the crystal in its fragmented layers, and it seemed to evoke a sense of serenity and soothing effect as he studied it.

The sound of plimsolls at the end of the corridor echoed in the foreground. Victor exited the curtain just as the nurse was passing.

"Nancy?" Victor said.

"Victor, I really have to get to-"

"No, no," he broke in. "I just wanted to ask you something real quick. Honest."

He held the crystal up to her face in his palm, colours appearing more vibrant with the warmth of this hand.

"Any idea where this came from? It fell out of Norman's covers, and I think someone might have tucked it in there."

Victor placed it in her hand and she rolled it around with her thumb, before handing it back.

"Sure," she said and nodded. "A visitor came in yesterday and asked if he could place it near him."

Victor's baffled expression made her laugh.

"But I was here yesterday."

"Don't I know it," she replied. "You're like a dog on heat. Us girls can pick that scent up, you know?"

"A dog on-"

"Look," she interrupted and glanced her head over and beyond his shoulder. "You can ask him yourself."

Turning, Victor's eyes narrowed on the tall man at the far end of the room. He was standing still but as soon as they locked eyes, the man turned and fled.

"Wait!" he shouted.

Victor chased the man down the corridor, bursting through the double doors and an emergency exit. He found himself back outside in the parking lot, the sun temporarily blinding him. Looking around he saw the man lurched against the wall beside the exit. Victor's concern began to dissipate, watching the middle aged man doubled over and breathing heavily.

"What the hell were you running for?" Victor asked, moving toward the man who had planted his head in the crook of his arm, still fighting for air.

The large overcoat he wore hung from his frame, weighing him down further. He took it off, and folded it over his arm.

"Well?" Victor prompted.

"I ran because you were chasing me!" he replied through several gasps.

"How do you know Norman? That's who you were coming to see, right?"

The man nodded, breath beginning to return.

"Did you put this in his bed?" he asked, holding the object up between forefinger and thumb.

The man stood up fully, hands on his hips as he looked at it and smiled.

"That I did, sir."

"Who are you?"

"My name is Stephen Breagal. I knew…" he said and flushed suddenly, correcting himself. "I know your friend Norman, and we became friends in recent weeks."

"And the crystal?" Victor asked.

"That my dear boy is a rare Amethyst crystal. It has certain healing qualities which can help with rest and peaceful sleep. It is also a great protector against various ailments and unclean spirits."

"You can keep your crystals and your spirits," Victor said and tossed it at the chest of Breagal, where it bounced and fell to the ground.

He turned toward the door and was about to pull the handle but it froze on hearing the man speak.

"Wait!" Breagal said. "I'm here to help. I think I know how to bring Norman back!"

FIFTEEN

The man shoved the gun into his hand, closing his fingers around it, pushing him toward the staircase. The new owner hesitated, fumbling with the object, trying to give it back but the man was insistent. There were tears in his eyes, as he helped lace the reluctant fingers around the barrel of the gun but it hung limp on his wrist.

There was the noise of a siren, somewhere outside, distant; it's constant beat finding a place inside their little dwelling. By the gun owner's side, a small boy was watching, looking up at the two taller faces, not comprehending and broke into tears. The older man bent down and kissed him on his forehead before addressing the other who was staring down at the revolver, weighing it in his palm.

"If they break through," the older man said. "It means it's too late. Don't hesitate. Not for a second. Like I showed you before. For you and your brother."

His eyes opened wide, nodding to make sure the instructions were understood.

"Do you understand what I'm telling you?"

The gun owner wiped away the tears that were beginning to form and looked to the woman who was sitting nearby at the table. She seemed lost in thought. Unmoving. Still like a photograph.

"Please Norman! You need to understand," the older man said.

Norman finally nodded.

Light filtered into the room through cracks in the boarded windows. A thin streak illuminated the older man's tear stained face. A shadow quickly ran across the window flickering the light on the man's face. Norman noticed it, drawing his attention back to the front door of their house.

"You have to go now," the older man said, voice lowered but revealing more urgency. "Take your brother's hand. There's no time."

The young boy, too young to understand, was still crying. His head was buried in his hands, trembling with fear. Norman reached for one of the hands which was locked tight to the boy's face, burrowing deeper and slinking away from the two men.

"Now Norman!" the man implored.

Norman pulled the boy's hand away from his face, dragging him across the kitchen and ascended the steep spiral staircase. Just before reaching the upper level, a sudden thump on the door below paralysed them mid stride. The force behind it shook the walls of the house. Tracing a few steps back, Norman crouched to capture an elevated view of the kitchen. They hadn't moved. The man's body was slumped forward, with his back to them. His large frame shook with sobs and he held the hand of his wife sitting by his side, still motionless.

The few shards of light that had filtered into the room were now extinguished. The blows began raining down on the door, booming through the house. They grew stronger and more frequent, the pauses now filled with loud guttural grunting voices on the other side, more agitated with each unsuccessful hit.

Jumping to his feet, Norman scaled the remainder of the stairwell, streamed down the long hallway, dragging the boy into the spare bedroom, locking it behind. They stood with their backs to the door, straining ears to hear.

Constant dull pounding from below shook the room's foundations, mingling with the siren's call in a swell of noise. Norman hugged the boy's head tight to his chest, covering his ears. The boy looked up, frightened but Norman couldn't meet his eyes. They cowered in a corner, holding each other tight. Suddenly a different noise filled the room from downstairs. A huge crack of wood breaking, like it was being ripped apart. Voices became audible. They rose in pitch, shouting and yelling. The babble was quickly punctuated by a woman's piercing scream which was sharply cut off, followed by a deathly silence.

Norman remembered the man's words and took the pistol, kissing the top of the boy's head. He apologised before raising the gun to the boy's temple. His wide eyes looked up at the man searching, not understanding just before Norman pulled the trigger.

SIXTEEN

He watched the man take off the thick-rimmed glasses and stir the coffee with one of its legs, before fishing it out, sucking the tip and replacing them on his head again. Victor blinked away the image and turned away from the man.

"So what did you say you did again, Stephen?"

"I didn't. I'm a collector of books – a humble librarian."

"Of course," Victor said. "Norman mentioned you last time we met."

This seemed to please the other man, as he licked the froth of his top lip and smiled.

"How did you know he was here?"

"He borrowed a number of books which were soon to become overdue. As I do with all customers, I give them a gentle reminder by calling their telephone. It was two days ago when I heard the dreadful news from his parents," he said and shook his head.

"Ah so you're a debt collector too?"

"Goodness. Nothing could be further from the truth," Breagal said. "I came to know Norman after he frequented my library a number of times in the days leading up to his untimely, unfortunate accident. Very intelligent fellow. Very interested and inquisitive by nature. Rare these days to find someone like that."

"I'd say that it was a case of having nowhere else to go to during the day."

"I don't follow," Breagal said, blowing on the surface of the piping hot coffee.

"Well," Victor started. "I used to work with Norman, but for one reason or another, he was given the heave-ho."

Breagal looked at him perplexed.

"He was relieved of his duties."

"Ah, I see. I can't quite see the connection though."

The librarian opened a small cup of milk nearby, which seemed better sized to house a contact lens than it did to dilute the coffee.

"Norman pretended to keep going to work so as not to upset his parents. Instead of going to work, he would go to your library where he could bunk off as much as he wanted."

"'Bunk off'? I don't follow."

"You don't follow much, Mr Breagal. I forget that you prefer to be chased."

Breagal covered his smile with the mug as he raised it to his mouth.

"Apologies for that. Hospitals give me the willies. Heaven knows I've been in enough of them for one lifetime," he said and smiled across at Victor. "I was startled when you started running. I had only visited on account of Norman's kindness to me in letting me regale him with some of my stories. I had hoped to relieve his suffering somewhat."

"By using crystals? You're barking up the wrong tree there. Unlike their more famous namesakes, the Adams' family aren't into any of that stuff, so you're wasting your time with that new age crap."

"Be that as it may, the practices I preach do not seek the approval of the recipient to have their desired effect. They work for believers and non-believers," Breagal said, leaning back and satisfied with his point.

Victor took this opportunity to lean forward, the hospital cafeteria chair hurting his back.

"That may be the case, Mr Breagal, but I don't like your tone. Plus, I don't think his family would appreciate some stranger coming in and planting crystals in his bed without their permission. That's completely out of order."

The librarian shrugged in deference and raised a hand in apology. He was starting to explain until Victor cut him off.

"I don't know what you got Norman involved in, but what I do know is this," he said and stared into the other man's eyes, hoping to emphasise the gravity of the words to follow. "It stops now."

Victor finished his own bitter coffee in one slug and planted it down on the table with finality, before rising off the seat. The eyes of Breagal watched him stand and tuck the chair under the table. He hovered for a moment, rested his hands on the sturdy chair back and looked around the room, confirming that they were the only ones in attendance before addressing the librarian.

"What did you mean when you said you knew how to bring Norman back?"

Breagal looked up at the man and for an instant saw a chink in the tough armour, a solemn reflection and tenderness for their mutual friend.

"Please sit with me, sir. Perhaps we can start again," he said and extended a hand to the empty seat but the man remained standing.

"I'm not what you would call a 'quack'. I'm not a witch doctor. I am but a simple librarian, albeit a well read one, at least in certain topics," he said.

His eyes looked down and he followed their stare with a gentle sigh, as if cursed with the knowledge.

"My dear brother slipped from this world recently. Although he still roams on the physical plane, his mind and consciousness is elsewhere and that is the essence of who we are, my boy. We are merely guiding these vessels we call bodies in an aimless pursuit of the earthly pleasures which delight us, but our true selves, the real 'you', is buried inside. Once you lose that, you lose everything."

Breagal, encouraged that Victor had now retaken his seat, signalled for another coffee before continuing. Opposite, the younger man's arms were folded as he sat in silence, stony faced.

"The reason I tell you this is because I believe that Norman is still reachable. There may still be hope!" the librarian said, looking at him in expectant wonder.

Victor shrugged, and rubbed his tired face. The server returned to the table with a fresh jug of coffee, filling both cups.

"I'm sorry to hear about your brother, Mr Breagal. Truly I am. But this still seems a little bit… off, to me. How do you seriously expect to reach him if the doctors can't?"

"Through his dreams," he replied.

Victor's face was blank as he stared at the man for a few seconds and then burst into spontaneous laughter. Breagal reddened and rose from his chair to excuse himself.

"No, please!" Victor cried through fits of laughter. "I didn't mean to cause offence. Please. Take a seat. I'm an idiot."

He wiped the tears forming in his eyes, and successfully ushered the half standing man back down. Suddenly he felt pleased to have met this strange man who had, at the very least, been an amusing footnote in his day.

"Do you take me for a fool, sir?" Breagal retorted with wounded pride.

"No. Not at all," Victor said and motioned for him to continue.

"I believe, nay, I know that Norman can be reached through his dreams. The Mayan Egyptians believed several thousand years ago…"

Victor sniggered, and quickly raised his hand in apology. The librarian paused a few moments to stir the coffee, waiting until he had full attention again.

"The Mayan Egyptians believed that through shared dream experiences, two or more people could interact on the dream plane. Combine this with the lucid dreaming state, and the possibilities are endless."

"Wow," Victor interjected. "This is starting to sound like the same stuff that he was reading the last time we met. All this stuff about waking up in a dream world?"

"He spoke to you about that?" he said, smiling.

"He showed me some of it – the diary entries, creepy pictures, handwritten notes. It looked like some sort of a cult handbook, which made me wonder why the hell it would be in a library in the first place."

"How odd," Breagal said. "I don't recall there being a book of that nature in my collection. Are you certain?"

Victor nodded in all seriousness, convincing Breagal that he was telling the truth.

"Do you have any idea where I might find it?"

"No. To be honest, I don't even think this was part of your collection. He mentioned that it was hidden away inside one of the library books. It looked like someone's personal journal or 'dream diary'. Yes, that's what Norman called it. Dream diary."

The colour drained from the librarian's face, and he knocked over the coffee, sending it racing across and over the table in an overflow. They both jumped out of their seats to avoid the hot coffee spill, Victor reaching for some tissue from a nearby table.

"Sorry!" Breagal said. "I… have to go now."

"Wait! It's only a spill!" he said to the fleeing librarian, who was already almost half way across the cafeteria.

Breagal turned, face as white as alabaster, a look of terror suddenly drawn. He hesitated before opening his mouth.

"I know this may sound crazy to you, but…" he checked himself. "Do you know anything about a pirate by any chance?"

The librarian's body was half turned, expecting another witty repartee from the man. Instead Victor smiled, which seemed to cause the man even greater distress than a jibe.

"Yes," he said. "That's the costume Norman was wearing the night of the crash."

Before Victor had a chance to ask a follow up question Breagal was already out the door.

SEVENTEEN

The blue sedan slowed down, allowing it to edge the considerable nose through the narrow high gates, emblazoned with the words Elm Hurst Psychiatric Ward on an imposing metallic archway on its face. Successfully clearing it, the road opened up ahead and the car accelerated deeper inside the walled complex.

"Welcome to Alcatraz," the driver joked in bad taste, looking across to her husband in the passenger seat.

He had leaned forward, oblivious to his wife's remark, and removed his spectacles, looking above and around them. His face was filled with wonder, deep wrinkled lines in his forehead that could pick up pencils.

"God help him."

"At least he's safer here," she said. "No more wandering off."

Breagal grunted, not paying much attention to the driver as he continued to scan his brother's new surroundings.

They continued to drive along smooth paved road across the lush plains. As they rounded a corner the building loomed into sight, some hundred yards away; a grand old structure, white walled and bedecked with an orange tiled roof. There was a small car park adjoined to the building, a fleet of cars assembled there. Their car pulled into one of the empty parking bays before the driver killed the engine.

"I can come in with you if you like?" Margaret Breagal said, though without any conviction.

Her husband pondered this for a moment before smiling and blessed her for saying so. She had been through enough already.

"That's fine dear. I don't imagine I will be too long if Dr Hart is to be believed."

"You have doubts?"

"I don't doubt her prognosis, but I suppose I just carry hope in my heart."

"That's always been your problem," she said. "You and your big heart. You're a good man Stephen Breagal, and I love you very much."

She leaned across and caressed the side of his head before kissing him on the forehead.

***

He found his brother standing in his bedroom by the window, looking out onto the courtyard of cars.

"How long has he been like this?" Breagal asked, watching on from the doorway.

The attendant at his side looked at him confused, unsure whether he was asking about the patient's state of mind, or the standing position he was in. In the end she decided the answer satisfied both questions.

"Ever since he arrived two weeks ago."

"Any trouble?"

"Nope."

"Has he wandered off at all?"

"We keep them on a pretty tight leash here Mr. Breagal."

"I'm sure you do. It's just that last time-"

"We know all about the last time. You were very lucky."

"You mean to say you don't get many people wander off in the middle of the night, return a few hours later and go to their bed as if nothing happened?"

"Something like that. Well," the woman said in summary, "he been good as gold. Ain't said nothing. Ain't done nothing neither. I'll give you a few minutes. Be right back."

She left and he heard her footsteps recede down the corridor.

Breagal continued to watch his brother stand guard by the window. His head was as bald as a cue ball, but even with a turned back the librarian could still see the outcropping, big, grey, bushy eyebrows peeping out from his profile like fat slugs glued to his face.

"Saul?" he said and the word broke in his throat.

He tried again without getting a response. Looking around the bedroom he was encouraged to see it was threadbare and empty, liberated of objects that could potentially be used as weapons. The single bed was placed against the back wall centre. The bedcovers looked as tightly wrapped as a Christmas gift. There was a small chest of drawers slotted into the corner by its side and a tiny bedside lamp sat there, no plug attached to the end of the cable. Sunlight shone in from the opposite side, stretching a long frozen silhouette of his brother against the back wall, the only adornment hanging there.

Breagal was slow to walk over to the window, standing beside his brother and seeing his face for the first time. It was unshaven and specked with food remains. The colour in it had disappeared, faded to grey and he looked much older.

"Hey Saul!" Breagal said to the man. "It's your little brother, Stephen."

The man continued to stare ahead, not deviating for a second or expressing any emotion. Breagal swallowed the emotion hard, fighting back tears and tried again. This time he stepped between the standing pillar and the window, gently holding the man's head between his hands. Imploring him to look, the dull eyes dragged their way to meet his, and for a second they found each other again. No sooner had he done this when a long trail of drool spilled from Saul's mouth, hitting the ground. The eyes were completely lifeless.

Lifting a limp hand that sagged from its socket, Breagal kissed it and let it drop by his side again. The attendant had returned and was standing in the doorway watching and the brother shook his head, sharing a look of helplessness with her. Joining her at the entrance he looked back at the man who hadn't nudged an inch.

"Please keep me updated with his…" he hesitated.

"I'll let you know how he gets on," she said.

Breagal started to go, but the attendant spoke again.

"I'm not sure if I should be telling you this," she said, her eyes darting to the standing man at the window. "One of the cleaners was cleaning your brother's bedroom earlier and found this stuffed under the mattress. Lord knows how it got there, but I felt you oughta know."

EIGHTEEN

The boss walked into the offices of Richmond and Regen Ltd, with a tall, clean-shaven, suited man at his side. He hovered about a foot over Richmond who delivered him to the room with a gentle push from behind.

"Guys, this is our new starter, Mick. Please make him feel welcome here," he said, forcing a brief smile which didn't sit well on his little square jaw.

The employees looked up from their computer monitors to acknowledge the new recruit, with some offering grunts as way of introduction.

They moved toward the unoccupied desk at the far end of the room, Richmond scurrying to keep stride with the taller man. On the desk lay a number of thin files bound tight by an elastic band that had been placed there early that morning.

"These are some invoices that I need you to sift through and reconcile to the P & L account of Merger Acquisitions."

He directed the recruit to sit in the chair.

"Some of these invoices have already been completed. Those that have been completed have already been marked with a red star in the top corner, like so."

He removed the band and wore it on his thin wrist where it could have comfortably wrapped around twice. Flicking the first page open, Richmond pointed to a bright asterisk in the corner. Then he picked up a red marker and looked at the seated man who was eye level with him.

"Some of these invoices need to written off as bad debts. Those are indicated with a black star in the corner."

Opening to the next page he indicated what another asterisk looked like. Not finding the offending marker on the desk, he called out to the room.

"Guys who has the black marker?"

This received no response and the boss's glare swung around the room before gradually cooling. Logic seeped through, and opening a drawer he found a fresh pack, which he opened and placed on the table.

"Some of these invoices have not been completed. These haven't been marked with any star." Rifling through a few pages he pointed these out. "These are the ones that I want you to work on. Do you think you can do that, Mick?"

"Mike" he corrected without Richmond flinching.

"Good!" he said, pulling up his suit sleeves at the crook of his elbow. "If you need any help, you can speak with Victor."

Richmond signalled to his neighbour a couple of yards away. Victor gave a little salute to Mike, who when returning to thank Richmond was surprised to note that the conversation had already ended with the little man already walking to his desk. Walter Richmond stretched back in his high chair, turning his newly purchased desk clock around. It showed time zones in six of the main trading capitals of the world.

The new recruit opened up the shelves in his desk, surprised to see a little stationery office of supplies. Victor glanced across and watched the man as he began sorting through coloured sheet pages, folders, wall charts and calculators.

"The last person here seemed like a bit of a hoarder," Mike said. "What happened him?"

"Norman Adams," Victor said and smiled. "Best accountant on our floor. Liked to be organised. That was Norman alright."

Mike noticed the sad expression on his colleagues face and decided not to push his line of questioning. It was the voice of his new boss that brought reality back in.

"OK people. Get to work. Half the day is gone already."

Mike looked up at the wall clock. It was 11 a.m.

***

They waited under the shelter of the front door porch, deciding whether it was going to clear or not. It had just begun raining and Victor and Mike had only left the office.

"Thanks for showing me the ropes today, Vic."

Victor cringed. "No problem mate."

They watched the rain as it started getting heavier, beating a drum against the pavement.

"Are you sure you don't want me to drop you off? My car's just over there."

"No, that's OK. You go ahead though. I'll catch you tomorrow."

The lanky man ran out from under the doorway, narrowly missing his head on the exit beam on the way. Victor watched as he folded himself into the front seat of the tiny three-door hatchback before it sped off.

He stepped out into the rain and breathed in deep, letting the rain smatter his face like little pin pricks. No sooner had he walked out the gate did the window of a parked car roll down; its occupant, with a little panicked face, bellowed out from within, calling his name. Shielding his eyes, Victor looked both ways for traffic before crossing the road.

He walked over to the car and recognized the driver as the librarian he had met at the hospital a few days earlier.

"Breagal, right?"

"Yes. That's right. Can I offer you a ride home?" Victor looked around him, weighing up his limited options.

"I don't normally accept rides from strangers," he smirked.

"Well I'm not sure if I would be classed as a stranger per se," Breagal replied in all seriousness.

"Mr Breagal, you're as strange as they come!" he smiled. "But I'll take you up on the offer."

Victor jumped into the passenger side, satisfied to be seated and sheltered again, but shivering he began to rub his hands for heat.

"So where are we taking you?" Breagal asked.

"Pembroke Road. Three miles south from here if you follow the Durham bypass."

"Certainly."

After the car had pulled away and entered a line of traffic, Breagal broke the short silence.

"I want to apologise for dashing off as I did last time we met."

Victor started to say something but Breagal raised his hand to cut him off.

"An explanation is warranted. Your mention of a diary greatly distressed me. You couldn't have known but my dear brother has been recently institutionalized. His condition has worsened over a number of years, and I'm afraid that medical care, security and supervision are the little respite I can offer him at this late stage. Little solace to a man, prisoner in his own mind."

"You mentioned him last time."

"I did? Oh right. Excuse me."

"That's fine."

"It doesn't get any easier though," Breagal said. "Watching the decline and accepting it as any loving brother must. All I can hope for is for his pain to end."

They continued to bob through the traffic, showing no great pace as conditions worsened outside making visibility more difficult. Breagal opened the glove compartment and took out a small leather bound book, and passed it to his neighbour.

"This is the book Norman found?"

Victor nodded his head in agreement. The driver exhaled and took the book back, before placing it back inside.

"What is it?"

"This was my brother's diary. Before he got sick, he was fascinated by the nature of dreams. He had a voracious appetite for books, and through his early studies he flirted with something called lucid dreaming. Are you familiar with the term?"

"Norman mentioned it. Waking up inside your own dream or something?"

"Precisely. It's a rare enough phenomenon, research in the subject at least in traditional circles is still in its infancy, but with enough patience and practice, one can train oneself to shift consciousness as they slumber. My brother was fascinated by this idea. He figured that if, on average, we spend twenty-five years of our lives asleep, then shouldn't we take advantage of those empty years?"

"Hmmm. I'm not convinced," Victor replied. "If you pushed me on it, I think sleeping is supposed to be a way for the body to recharge itself. I wouldn't want to be active all day every day."

Victor closed his eyes and leaned his head against the window, the cool pane comforting against his temple. Caught in the thick of rush hour traffic, their passage was slow and his mind was already turning to dinner and whether the pizza leftovers from three days earlier had grown legs and scarpered.

"I'm not disputing the therapeutic benefits of sleep, sir. What I'm positioning is that there can be a practical aspect that can be derived from it."

"Go on," Victor said.

"Imagine learning an instrument, like a guitar during the day, and then in the dream state, being consciously aware enough to again practice those same chords while you sleep, perhaps playing in front of an audience to help with stage nerves."

"Hmmm. Bit of a Jimmy Hendrix are we?"

"No. Music isn't something I'm interested in."

"No?" Victor said and yawned.

"I'm more interested in developing hands-on techniques in my dream state. Learning how to hunt, capture animals and develop survival skills."

Victor looked across at the librarian, shook his head and laughed.

"What?"

"Don't think you'll catch many hares or rabbits in this town Breagal."

"Maybe not, but you never know when it'll come in handy."

The traffic started to move again, the librarian slowly moving up through the gears. Victor looked out through his window and watched the water pool along the kerb, pedestrians huddling under little umbrellas giving the line of cars a wide berth as they drew nearer.

"Even if you take away the practical applications, there is still scope to entertain ideas that wouldn't be suitable in our daily lives."

Victor was still staring out the window, mind wandering and barely listening to the librarian continue his ramble.

"Frustrated with your boss at work?" Breagal asked. "How about the thrill of killing him in your sleep? Homosexuality would almost certainly be cured overnight, individuals living out these secret dark fantasies safe in the confines of their own constructed world. Paedophilia would be deleted from society. No more causing unimaginable pain to the victims and having to live with the shame."

"Homosexuality would be cured? Did I just hear you say that?" Victor asked, staring at the driver in disbelief.

"Exactly!" Breagal continued. "Think of the endless possibilities."

"Unbelievable," Victor replied and shook his head, rolling his eyes up and out the window.

"Isn't it just?"

"Anyway, it sounds like you're talking about some sort of virtual reality."

The traffic had now dispersed, and the rain had eased off making conditions easier to drive, but the car still crawled along owing to the driver's pace preference.

"Yes I suppose it does. However, in my brother's experience he got so involved in creating this alternative reality that the lines began to blur between it and his waking life."

"Hold on," Victor argued. "How can there not be a clear distinction between the two? I can tell a dream from reality."

"Ah! therein lies the rub! He who tastes, knows. Lucid dreams are as real and vivid as this experience right now. How do you truly know you are not dreaming in this very second?"

"Because," Victor paused, trying to find the words. "I can think clearly and can influence things around me."

"Quite. Anyway, I digress. My brother's confusion with reality obviously had a devastating effect on his waking life. This is chronicled in the dream diary from his very first lucid dream experience. Digging deeper into the subconscious he lusted after richer experiences that made his waking life pale in comparison. I've read through many of these dreams and it becomes clear that he was digging in quicksand. Eventually he found himself sinking and couldn't escape."

Breagal's voice stuttered, thinking back to his brother standing at the window, detached and distant. Alone in some horrible reverie.

"My concern for him now is that his pain is lessened. His dreams became waking nightmares toward the end of the journal and for him to be trapped in one of those for the remainder of his days would be unthinkable."

They had turned off from the Durham junction now, and Victor interrupted the silence and directed the driver to the row of terraced houses lined on the right. Victor guided him to a small house where the gate swung back and forth on a broken hinge. Beyond it, the rectangle patch of lawn was overgrown and weeds sprouted out from the paved stones leading to the porch.

"I'm sorry to hear this, Mr Breagal. Truly I am. I hope your brother manages to find peace," he said and squeezed the librarian's arm.

He was about to leave the car when the driver placed a hand on his shoulder, preventing him from rising.

"Don't you see what this means, Victor?"

"I don't follow," he said, suddenly realizing the irony that he sounded now like Breagal.

"What if Norman has slipped into a similar state of purgatory? He was reading the diary. We know that he'd already had some lucid dreams. He was exposed through this very book to some of the warped images my brother painstakingly detailed," Breagal argued. "What if, given his accident, the solitude and damage to his brain has caused him to seek peace in another plane of consciousness? What if he is dreaming right now? What if he finds himself in one of these nightmares?"

"I think that's a stretch at best."

"Perhaps. But if he is, don't you think it's our responsibility to rescue him?"

"Rescue him? You make it sound like we're the SAS Mr Breagal! Listen, what you're saying is..." he couldn't think of a polite way to dress it up. "Ridiculous."

Breagal's hand dropped from his shoulder, and he recoiled back in his seat as if he had just received a blow to the gut, face sinking.

"Ridiculous?"

His voice was raised now, and he felt himself trembling with anger. Victor shrunk away from him.

"Try telling that to my brother, though you wouldn't get a response," Breagal said, staring out through the window. "He wouldn't know you. He doesn't even know me. Don't you dare tell me that it's ridiculous after the things I've seen."

The librarian's hands made a squeak on the leather steering wheel and Victor looked from the clenched grip it and up to his face. There was a fire in the man's eyes.

"Invisible demons putting me and my wife's lives at risk," Breagal continued. "There are horrors that you and I can only imagine, and I pray that we never will. But if Norman doesn't pull through, you'll have to live with it."

"You done?"

They stared at each other for a moment, before Victor opened the door and stepped out of the car.

"Goodbye Mr Breagal," he said and slammed the door shut before kicking the garden gate off its hinge.

NINETEEN

He brought some refreshments from the vending machine, anticipating he wouldn't be alone and was correct in the assumption. Thirty minutes later the cans of soft drink still lay on the table top unopened.

Victor looked at Norman's parents. His mother had wrapped rosary beads around her hands and her mouth twitched in a soft silent prayer as she rocked silently back and forth on the chair. Her eyes, which were red raw, continued to stare straight ahead. There was a bedside dimmer lamp casting a solemn glow within the enclosure.

The morning sunlight had already begun to brighten the ward and Victor moved to the lamp to switch it off.

"He doesn't like the dark," Noreen said, eyes never raising from the expanding chest of her son with each breath.

"I can turn it back on if you want?"

Mrs Adams turned around and surveyed the scene. She squinted her eyes to adjust to the man's face.

"That's OK," she said, her voice monotone and without emotion. "It's bright enough now."

Victor sat back down again by Norman's side, on the opposite of his parents. He looked at Mr Adams whose large frame spilled over the small plastic chair; its sturdy metal legs splayed a fraction more than his wife's, inching him lower to the floor.

"You remember when he was little? You used to leave the door open a crack at night?" Frank said, smiling. "What was it he used to say?"

"Two fingers, Ma," his wife replied.

"Two fingers!" Frank laughed, the sound seemed strange in the enclosure. "That's right. It had to be just right and only you could do it."

Victor looked away from the couple and stared down at his feet. The image of his friend had long since been printed in his mind, lying in the bed prostrate with a mask fixed over his mouth helping him to breathe.

Looking at his watch he gently rose from the seat. As he did so, the curtain was drawn back and a doctor of Indian ethnicity entered. He wore a tightly bound navy turban, jet-black eyebrows dancing underneath and a long dark beard, with strands of grey neatly clipped in place.

"Good morning Mr and Mrs Adams," he said, but they never lifted their eyes to acknowledge him.

Lifting a chart from the front of his bed, the doctor moved toward one of the machines connected to the patient and scribbled a few notes against it. Victor observed him from the corner of the room and heard the soft sigh escape his lips. The man paused and scratched an itch underneath the turban, before returning the chart to its original place.

"Hello Norman," he said in a cheery but artificial tone. "How are we today? Your mother and father are here to see you."

Suddenly realizing there was a third guest, the doctor apologized.

"Excuse me," he said, offering a hand. "I'm Doctor Tawia."

"Nice to meet you. Victor. I'm a friend."

"You see. Even your friend Victor is here to see you."

The body of Norman Adams still slept in peace, unaware of those in attendance. Dr Tawia turned to address the parents, glancing at the litter of Styrofoam coffee cups stacked beneath their seats.

"Mr and Mrs Adams. I wonder if we could have a quiet word."

Frank Adams responded first, looking up at the doctor and then to his wife, who was still staring straight ahead at her son, ushering a rushed silent prayer that was growing in volume.

"Noreen," he whispered in her ear and gently placed a hand on her leg, prompting her to jerk suddenly like a hot coal had touched her skin. "Dr Tawia would like to speak with us."

She turned to face him and then looked at the doctor standing on the other side of the bed.

"If I can, I'd like to have a word with you to discuss your son's condition. Can you come with me, please?"

Frank reached for his wife's hand and standing, he raised her from the chair. Her tired bones unkinked and cracked audibly, the curve in her spine more pronounced than ever. She suddenly resisted and pulled back on her husband's hand.

"No! I won't leave my baby here alone," she said, defiant eyes peering out from sockets as dry as sand beds.

"Victor is here. Look," Mr Adams responded. "Besides we're only going around the corner."

He tried comforting her with an arm around a shoulder, but she shook free and looked at the doctor.

"Whatever you have to say, Doctor, I want to hear it now. I'm not going back to that office, and I'm not leaving my boy."

The doctor paused in thought and then nodded, motioning that they should take their seats. Only Victor remained standing. Tawia looked at him and then to Norman's parents for assurance.

"Victor is like part of the family now. He should hear this too," Frank said, pulling the chair closer to them before Victor sat back down.

They all looked up at Dr Tawia in expectation, and he moved across to join them on the nearside of the room.

"I've been monitoring your son since he arrived here four weeks ago and, whilst he remains in a comfortable state, there has been little improvement in his actual condition."

He spoke slowly, as if measuring the weight each word had on their respective faces.

"My concern is this. The cerebral cortex covering the outside of his brain has experienced significant trauma, to the extent that he has been unresponsive to external stimuli."

"What does that mean exactly?" Victor asked.

Tawia took an empty chair, placed it in front of them and sat down. He was bent over at the waist, and his large hairy hands grappled with the concept like a balloon artist to shape it in a way that they could understand.

"It means that whilst Norman is in a comatose state, we have no way of communicating with him, and the longer this goes on the more likely it is that he will stay in his current state. The machine behind me is essentially keeping him alive."

Noreen slumped into her husband's chest, muffling a painful cry of despair. He held her tight, fighting back fresh tears from a reservoir that he thought was dry. Victor felt the colour drain from his face.

"I can't imagine how difficult this must be for you. All I can say is that the best we can offer right now is to make your son as comfortable as long as you wish," he said before standing up, and placed a reassuring hand on Victor's shoulder.

A hopeful smile touched his lips and he exited the room, leaving behind the grieving family.

Victor rose on unsteady feet and caught the railing of the bed for support. The room started to swim around him and he closed his eyes and battled his breath back to normal.

"Mr and Mrs Adams?" he interrupted. "I... need to go back to work."

Frank Adams turned his head around on its thick neck, which was wet with tears from his wife. His eyes were slits on his pained face. The best he could offer was to nod in Victor's direction, his throat constricted with an emotion that rose deep in his chest.

"You're a good lad, Victor," Noreen said, muffled by her husband's shoulder. "Norman's lucky to have a friend like you."

Her voice trailed off and Victor pointed his stare away, the convulsions that had now taken the couple were beginning to infect him.

As he opened a door in the curtain he gave one final glance toward them and then back at the patient and froze.

"What's wrong?" Noreen asked, confused by his expression.

He flung the curtain to one side and ran from the ward shouting for help. Each patient room he entered was empty until one of the nurses grabbed the hysterical man and calmed him down.

"You've got to help us!" he panted. "It's Norman!"

TWENTY

His head pressed tight against the door, desperately trying to track the footsteps within, but the siren continued to blast its noise through the house. It seemed to create a sense of panic in the room and he found it difficult to string together any coherent thoughts. For now, the footsteps seemed distant. Somewhere downstairs, but difficult to place with any certainty. His ears still rang from the gunshot.

He reached a trembling hand to the gun at the corpse's feet. The pathetic limp body lay in a heap on the floor, head covered in shadow by the emerging night. The thickening red pool enveloping him oozed out from under the shade, advancing slowly to the centre of the room. Norman stepped over it, breath frozen in his chest, crossing the floorboards with pained carefulness. He continued to the corner of the room and sat down, staring at the door, back propped against the walls.

"There was only one bullet," he stammered half in a daze. "Only one bullet."

***

He couldn't tell how long he had been sitting there, rocking back and forth. Minutes. Maybe hours. The empty gun lay between his feet. He wasn't sure how it had gotten there. Wiping the tears dry with a dirty sleeve Norman scanned the room, eyes adjusted to the dim light. It was bare, save for the prostate body, crumpled in a heap by the door which looked like it might have been sleeping.

The noises hadn't yet made it to the second floor, the ground floor still holding their attention. He listened for them now, hoping for the familiar voice but resigned to the fact that he was alone, especially after he had heard her scream. Without the gun, they would have been defenceless. What use was one bullet in any case, except to grant the small mercy as the man had requested. There was no way they could have…

There was a loud crash directly below him; he felt the floorboards underneath vibrate from the explosion. A muffled gaggle of pleasure followed it, just audible above the clicking of heavy boots on the wooden surface. Closing his eyes, he pictured the interior of the house; listening becoming more tuned. The voices carried beyond the kitchen into the living room now. Despite the initial breach they were advancing slowly, savouring the contents of the house. Soon they would be on him.

Looking up and against the wall confirmed his fear that the windows were boarded up. Anything that resembled a tool or lever would be downstairs in the kitchen, the source of the breach. There was no way he could go back to the ground floor, so his options were limited and there was no telling how long he would have left.

Heavy boots struck the staircase. He stood rigid to the spot; breath caught, air around him electrified. The footsteps climbed slowly upwards and he could hear a solitary voice growing in volume, incoherent snarling with an animal quality. The siren continued its beat, banging a drum in his head, puncturing his stream of thoughts, encouraging him to shut his eyes to regain focus, which was the last thing he wanted do.

Panicking Norman jumped up and looked around the room, unable to discover any way out. Running to the window, he began to pull at the wooden beams barring it. They were nailed shut and he couldn't prise it open. He grabbed the gun and began banging it against the beams. The clanging noise brought the marching footsteps quicker down the hallway. It was no use. He couldn't open it.

His eyes raced around the smooth walls in desperation, catching sight of a rectangular hollow in the low ceiling directly above him. Positioning himself directly below it Norman leapt high, pushing the wooden lid up through the roof with outstretched fingers, but it fell back onto itself into place. The footsteps were growing louder now, and he heard them approach. Norman paused, listening as they stopped outside his door. He could hear the heavy rasping breath of whatever lay beyond it and he observed his own breath, careful to remain quiet. After a few seconds, the footsteps traced their way back down the hall again. He jumped once more, stretching higher, the lid toppling over this time and falling back into the attic space with a thud.

Suddenly, a fist burst through the door panel, turning him to stone. Through it he could see a snarling darkened face. Seeing the man, the face contorted grotesquely into an open-mouthed furious scream. A high-pitched deafening shrill, forcing him to cover his ears. A troop of heavy footfalls from elsewhere had now collected and were pounding the stairwell. The figure at the door screamed again, beckoning. This time the choir, closing in on the room quickly, answered it emphatically.

The door was being pummelled from all sides now, with panels snapping like twigs. Norman sprung upward again with all his might, grasping; body stretched and managing to touch the edge of the skylight, he was unable to hook his fingers around the sides. He couldn't find the necessary leverage to hoist himself up and crashed back to the floor. Desperately he looked around the room for something to step on, finding nothing. He tried again, springing upward from a crouched position. Again falling short, growing desperate, inches from reaching safety.

The door heaved inwards, jagged wood snapping and splintering off. Heavy boots now broke through the bottom panels. It barely hung on its hinges, and a gang of bodies jostled around it to inflict the next pounding that would ensure their entry.

He saw the limp body a few steps away and rushed to grab it. Doubling it up on itself below the attic, he stepped on the shoulders and leapt for the opening. Just as he did so, there was a final barrage at the door and it flew off its hinges.

Norman caught the inside of the attic space, and heaved himself quickly up into the inky darkness above. Just as he swung his body up and over, a sudden sharp yank on his ankle jolted him back through the opening. Losing grip momentarily his nose hit the frame hard dazing him, but somehow managing not to affect his grip. The firm icy hand held the ankle fast, and he tried yanking it free, but it wouldn't budge. Norman desperately scratched at the floor of the attic space to secure a stronger handhold, which was weakening by the second, but couldn't find any.

Digging his other foot in the angle of the opening, he lurched his body upwards with all his might, but whatever had a hold of him was stronger. By degrees, he began slipping gently back through the attic door. He could taste blood in his mouth which ran freely down his face. This summoned something primal inside him and with a sudden burst of energy, he kicked the hand with his free foot with all his might. An icy hand wrapped around the second ankle rendering him completely immobile. Crying desperately his last image was a cloud of blood spat out from the exertion, as his arms spasmed from the massive effort, trying to maintain the grip. They were too strong, he realised, and his body pulsed before he resigned himself and let go.

The moment he did, from the attic darkness, a set of hands pulled under his armpits and dragged him closer to the surface.

"Come on, son. You need to work with me here!"

Summoning his last sinew of strength, he finally kicked off the hand around his left foot, and then the right, as his liberator hauled him over the side and Norman collapsed in an exhausted heap on the floor.

Hands leapt up from below, snatching at the open edge. Norman withdrew his feet quickly, scrambling away from their grasp. His rescuer, a tall shadow standing above, stomped at the fingers and hands with a heel, snapping bone, the shrieks of pain from the shapes below. The mob stopped jumping allowing the tall man to replace the attic lid again.

Looking up, Norman saw the figure moving a short way toward the end of the small room. A match was struck and he could see the faint silhouetted outline of a large well-built person with his back to him. He turned around carefully with a small stumpy candle which illuminated his worn, lined face, giving it a wizened worldly glow.

"Lucky for you, I found you when I did," he said, tossing a rag in his direction, which he applied to his bloody nose. "Bet you didn't know you shared an attic with old Yenjin?"

The man approached with the candle to the edge of the attic space carefully and opening the lid up a crack, peered down, face becoming grave. Norman crawled over on all fours beside him but Yenjin laid a firm hand on his shoulder, preventing the approach.

"Please!" Norman pleaded.

Yenjin conceded, shook his head almost in apology before removing the big hand that barred his way.

He looked back down through the attic opening, seeing a ring of black figures in the darkness bent over. They were ripping the clothes loose from the boy's body and flashes of his pale skin could be seen through the thrashing, frenzied mob. The pack began tearing his arms and legs from their sockets, the dull pops punctured by snaps of bone as they crunched on hands and ribs, yanking them with brutal strength from the torso. Limbs, organs and plump stringy intestines all competed for within the group, as the delirious pack squealed in delight, intoxicated in an orgy of lust.

From the weak candle illumination, a figure stood separate from the pack. He was dressed like the others in khaki, seemed uninterested in ravaging the corpse and stared straight up into the attic space crack at them. A metal green helmet firmly attached to his head bore a bright red cross on its front. On his chest was a blood spattered metal tag sewn into the garment. On it, Norman thought he could read the name 'Krollson', before looking into its face. The eyes shone orange and luminous in the dark room, raging at him, sharp teeth tightened into a menacing snarl and flashing like glinting daggers.

"Come on, son," Yenjin said, lowering the lid back down. "There's nothing you can do for him."

The lid closing severed the stare between Krollson and Norman who looked around at his surroundings now and saw the flickering candlelight throw quivering shadows on the walls. The siren stopped suddenly and the beasts downstairs fell silent. A few moments passed before the savages cried out in union, a fitful, angry roar of triumph cutting through the air. Norman cupped his hands over his ears and stared at Yenjin, unsure how to react. Without warning, they heard them run out of the room, their boots thudding heavily on the wooden panels in the hallway, echoing around the house. The sound of something being dragged accompanied their hasty exit, mingled with their footfalls. The load bounded off each step as they made their stairwell descent.

"No!" Norman cried out.

Yenjin crept over to the opening, pulled the lid up again, looked down and returned to him with a sombre expression.

"He's gone now, son," he said, planting a strong hand on his shoulder. "You did the right thing."

Norman began to weep, burying his head in his hands before rolling over onto his side. He let the tears dry without his help and became vaguely aware of a thin sheet being placed over his numb, shivering body. His last conscious thought floated up outside the attic, into the night sky until finally, exhausted, sleep rescued him.

He heard the booming of their fists on the door in his sleep, and wakening from a fitful dream he saw Yenjin looking closely at a panel in the attic roof. Hearing him stir, he motioned for him to come over.

"Look," he said, pointing to a space in the wall.

In the dim flickering light, he saw a small peeping hole carved in the wood. Pressing his face tight to it, he could see, from their elevated position, the layout of the street that lined their house.

There was a procession of them, marching in a straight line. They were like those that he had seen earlier, but now there were dozens of them. Their shapes were distorted by the thin silver moonlight overhead. Some he could see nearby, carrying heavy loads weighing them down, dragging them without concern. As they continued to watch in rapt silence, they noticed that toward the tail of the group four of the walkers shared the load of a large single boxed object propped up on long beams.

Although their passage was more careful and deliberate than the others, the object continued to sway from side to side, threatening to break free from the ropes that secured it. It was a wooden structure the size of a telephone box, with thick sturdy bars enclosing the treasure safely within. Squinting his eyes, Norman tried to make out the object that lay within it.

"Is that...?"

No sooner had he said it, when suddenly from the cage, a thick arm escaped, hand reaching skyward seeking some higher source. The savages continued on without giving a moment's notice, ignoring the man's screams from within.

Norman recoiled in horror, turning away from the opening and threw up by his side.

"It's OK," Yenjin said. "You're safe now."

He patted the man on the back as he continued to vomit violently. A wretched string of acid, with his stomach expelling the final remnants. Gasping for air, his convulsions finally stopped and he wiped his mouth with the back of his hand.

"What are those monsters?" Norman asked, minutes later after regaining some composure.

"Didn't you see?"

Norman looked at him perplexed. It hadn't occurred to him before. The khaki uniforms, metal helmet, steel-capped boots. Yenjin turned away, moving again toward the hole.

"Son," he said. "the military were sent here to police and protect us. Now, I don't know what happened, or why they turned like they did, or if those things are even human in the biblical sense anymore, but I do know something."

He looked back at Norman to ensure that the man was listening.

"They know there are still survivors. Not only that but they know where we are. When they come back, and I assure you they will come back, we best not be here."

"But we are supposed to be protected. Protected!"

Yenjin looked down at his feet and shook his head. It was propped on massive shoulders that, despite their strength, were now slumped over in resignation and he met Norman's imploring eyes one more time.

"That was before. But now we're the hunted."

TWENTY-ONE

Two giggling boys with blazing red hair ran round his legs before darting off down one of the aisles. He watched them shoot off through the maze of bookshelves. The older one leaning against a tall column, holding his head in his palms and counting to ten. The smaller one removed a few books from the bottom shelf of a row several aisles across, and hid within then replaced the books with great difficulty.

"Can I help you, sir?" said the bespectacled woman behind her desk.

"I'm actually here to see Mr Breagal?" he said, collecting himself despite the strikes to his feet.

Two young girls with copper hair slid books across the carpeted surface and with each successful hit on Victor's feet, they high-fived one another. The woman left and entered the back storeroom, saying a few words to the man out of sight.

Breagal came from within and approached the desk, stopping short of offering his hand or raising a smile.

"You might want to do something about your pest control problem," Victor said.

A little yelp from across the room brought Breagal's attention. As he moved closer to the front of the desk he looked down and could see the cluster of books around Victor's feet.

"Fionnuala! Aisling! Come here this instant."

Busted, the girls crawled on all fours to the desk and looked up at the librarian.

"Some parents are starting to use our library as a dumping ground for their kids," Breagal said to Victor, before bending down to address the chuckling girls.

"I want you to behave yourselves now. You don't want me telling your daddy what bad girls you've been, do you?"

"No Mr Breagal," they said together and stood up quickly.

"Good. Now, be good girls and pick up all those books," Breagal said. "And apologise to that man."

"Sorry that man," the smaller one said.

She hadn't meant to be funny but the older one giggled and, sensing that she had done something funny, the little girl joined in too.

Victor smiled at them both and patted their heads. He stepped out of their way so they could collect the books.

"Everything OK?" Breagal asked, analysing his face.

"Mind if we grab a coffee?"

***

"So now you know," Victor said. "The sight of all that blood gushing from his nose made me want to try something. Anything."

He looked away from the image his memory had conjured. Breagal was watching closely and pushed the coffee cup towards the younger man, which he lifted and sipped.

"I don't know if you're a raving psycho, delusional, eccentric or just plain weird, but given what I've just told you, if there is anything we can do to help Norman... I want you to know that I'm game."

Breagal's cup trembled in his hand, and he steadied it with the other one and placed it back on the saucer. He removed a handkerchief from his front pocket and dabbed a perspiring forehead.

"I'm deeply troubled by your report Victor, and it is grave news indeed," he said, body suddenly quivering like a bow. "If what you say is true, and I believe it to be, then we can't waste any more time. But I need you to do one thing for me."

"What?"

"I need you to suspend judgement. Please, even if you think it folly, if there is a slim chance that what I say is true, then surely that is a risk worth taking, agreed?"

"You have my word, Mr Breagal," Victor replied and nodded.

"In that case, let us begin."

He took out a small notebook from the inner lining of his tailored jacket, a stubby pencil dangling from it by a cord. Opening it to a fresh page, the librarian drew two circles which intertwined at their edges, and wrote above each one the two words DREAM and REALITY. The small portion carved out by the two circles was shaded in grey. Victor watched him draw an arrow pointing to it with a word circled and, turning the book around so he could see, read the word LUCID.

"It is impossible for us to predict to what extent the brain damage has affected his unconscious mind. But let us surmise that he is dreaming in this instant in a lucid state. We must enter into this dream and pull him from that realm into this one."

He drew a second arrow connecting the lucid piece to the reality circle.

"OK..." Victor said with a degree of uncertainty, rubbing his face and trying to understand. "How do we know he is in a lucid state?"

"Ah, you see, Norman described to me on our first meeting how he had inadvertently opened this portal. You need to understand that once that door is opened, anything can cross over. Exposure to my brother's dream experiences would have weaved more hypnagogic imagery and auto-suggestion into his mind which..."

"Hold on there. Lot to take in at once!" Victor said, holding his hands up in a mock defenceless pose.

"Yes. Sorry. What I mean to say is that if Norman can be found in his dream, then we need to jolt him back to reality."

"OK, well that sounds straightforward enough."

The librarian made a rueful smile, fidgeting with the cup in its saucer.

"If that were the case Victor, my brother would be seated here right now instead of a psychiatric ward two hundred miles away under 24-hour surveillance."

He tucked the pencil inside the ringlets of the notebook and returned it to his jacket pocket.

"Please listen to me carefully. A lucid dream world is an unstable place. Under the right conditions it can be a great breeding ground for creativity and learning, but in the wrong conditions it can be a prison that can trap the dreamer from ever escaping. This is an exceptional case and we won't know how ambitious our plan is until we start digging."

"OK. So how can we rescue a man from his own dream? It sounds very farfetched," Victor said.

"I told you to suspend your beliefs. The practice itself is not well known, at least not in the West, but it was a tradition among certain tribes in Central America led by pioneering Shamans several generations ago. Knowledge which has since been forgotten."

"But not by you, of course."

"Precisely," Breagal answered. "Spiritual teachers would enter the dreams of their devotees and connect them to astral beings, tapping them for knowledge and wisdom, which in essence was really their higher consciousness talking."

"Breagal, you're doing it again."

"I'm sorry. It's hard for me not to get carried away sometimes, which is why you should be the one to rescue our friend."

Without delay, Victor nodded his head in agreement.

"Just tell me what I need to do."

"Exactly as I say."

TWENTY-TWO

The dawn light had crept into the attic space slowly giving shape to the room. They watched the savages walk west in a straight line, observing their foot trail until they became specks on the horizon. The path they tread led toward the base of a tall jagged mountain which they rounded before disappearing from view. Norman didn't realise he had been holding his breath until they had gone. Yenjin turned around, his eyesight taking a moment to adjust to the dim room. He walked over to the candle and blew it out.

"Never know when we might need it again," he said to Norman who pulled back from the aperture.

Yenjin removed the candle from its holder, rubbed the wet wax on a trouser leg and juggled it between his palms until it had sufficiently cooled. Satisfied, he finally put it into his jacket pocket, patting it for good luck. He signalled for the other man to join him and they walked the short distance to the other end of the attic, floorboards squeaking below them.

"Careful where you stand," Yenjin warned. "It's around here somewhere."

He slid his foot around a darkened patch where the light had made a shadow, and they heard it hit something metallic.

"Bingo."

He crouched down, and Norman saw him curl his fingers around a metal loop fixed to the ground, heaving it upward. Bright yellow light burst from within, illuminating the room as the attic door swung around on its hinge; the man allowing it to flip over completely. The light from below bathed Yenjin who remained crouched and shielded his eyes with a hand, taking a small hop away from the door.

"Skye, you down there?" he spoke into the opening, cocking his ear for a response from below.

Norman took a moment to study the man. He was dressed in blue slacks and a checked shirt, rolled up at the elbows. His forearms were as thick and hard as baseball bats, the muscle tweaking as he cupped his ear listening for a response.

The deeply lined face, expressionless and grey showed no emotion as they waited. What may have been strawberry blonde hair in his youth had now receded to a wispy pale colour with the consistency of cotton balls. The grey fuzz on his cheeks looked more than a few days old, a sprinkling of iron filings, dense and sharp on his face.

"Come on," he said and crawled to the edge of the opening, dangling his legs over the side. "I'll go first and scan the house before coming back to get you. OK?"

"OK."

Yenjin leapt down, landing softly below with the poise of a big cat. Peering up, he gave the thumbs up sign to Norman, who nodded in response before the man jogged out of sight. A few minutes later he reappeared and, standing below the opening, he beckoned Norman to join, which he did, although not with the grace Yenjin had demonstrated. He needed the strongly built man to steady his fall forward, as he placed his feet on his wide shoulders.

"Welcome to my humble abode!" Yenjin smiled, more gum than tooth.

Norman looked around the tiny room, which measured about one by six strides wide; a quarter of the size of the room he had escaped from the day before. It looked too small to be of functional use which was evidently the case because there was nothing in it, save for a single chair at one end beside a narrow door.

"Come this way and I'll give you the grand tour."

Yenjin approached the door and opened it. The opening was tight and the man had to enter sideways, lowering his head on a neck that was just as thick, to tuck his body inside and along the narrow corridor. Norman followed closely behind and entered the passage with ease, tucked in behind the shadow of the man mountain as he shuffled through and came out the other end into a much larger space.

"Watch your step son, as you come through," Yenjin said and turned to look back.

The warning came too late as Norman tripped forward and fell through the other side of the door. When he had recovered, he looked around the room. It was bigger with a bed in the corner dismantled almost beyond recognition, sheets ripped and shredded into pieces. The main door lay splintered in the centre of the room, broken into a hundred pieces. The floor was covered with torn book pages, large dirty footprints imprinted on them by thick muddy boots. They stepped across the room observing the scene of destruction in panoramic view. Norman turned and stared at the wall where they had just come from.

"They couldn't find it either," Yenjin said. "Easy enough to spot if you're looking for it in the right place, but at night I guess it's more difficult."

He moved toward the white drape that hung from the bleached wall, and pulled it to one side. Inside was a hollow where several garments hung from a pole above. They flowed all the way to the ground, and Norman approached and, parting them, looked beyond at the black background. A crack ran down the length of one side of the wall, which Norman pushed. It resisted, but getting closer into the hollow he pressed his full body weight against it, and it finally gave way, revealing the corridor chamber they had walked and the smaller room ahead.

"Pretty neat, eh?" Yenjin said. "I designed it as an escape route in an emergency, not thinking that it would actually work. Just so happens it saved both our lives last night."

Norman closed the door back into place and pulled the clothes together on the line again. He looked up and offered a weak smile to his neighbour.

"I can't take you next door yet," Yenjin said, reading his mind. "We can stay here a little while until we work out a plan. Those savages didn't get what they were looking for, and if they do decide to come back, we won't last a second."

Norman looked despondent and Yenjin came and wrapped an arm around his shoulder. He was about a foot taller, and the thick arm weighed Norman down.

"Let's see if we can find something to eat."

They left the room and walked through the long hallway, ears tuned for a noise other than the soft steps of their feet on the landing. Reaching the staircase, they looked down into what looked like a kitchen. It was completely gutted, landscape jagged with wooden table and chairs splintered and snapped with inhumane force. Plates, cups, cutlery, every last kitchen utensil or instrument lay broken on the floor.

Suddenly, a movement from below diverted their attention, knocking over a piece of the debris. Yenjin's arm involuntarily tensed around Norman's wrist as the man narrowed his eyes to the source of the sound. All was still again for a few moments, barely a breath passed between them before the man nodded Norman back in the direction of the room. Norman hesitated, terrified although Yenjin's glare made him softly retreat. As he did, he looked back at the man whose hulking frame began to edge quietly down the staircase, until the thatch of his head had left his sight. Norman waited, breath quickening, coiled like a spring ready to leap back into the bedroom and scramble back into the secret annex.

Another noise from below, louder this time with something crashing to the ground. Yenjin cried out. Then it became deathly quiet. Not a stir in the air.

Norman panicked and shouted out for the man in angst. There was the sound of steps on the stairwell, slow and deliberate and he felt himself freeze. He stood rooted in the doorway of the bedroom, adrenaline coursing through his veins, unable to fire his trembling legs to take flight again.

The steps were getting closer now, almost at the top of the stairwell. Norman closed his eyes, hoping that he was hallucinating.

When the steps stopped, he opened them again and saw the large bulk of his neighbour approach, soft steps on the landing and cradling a bundle in his arms. A pink smile stretched across his face as the man slowly lowered the blanket over the bundle to reveal a puppy. It looked up at Norman, just waking and gave a big yawn.

"Skye, meet Norman."

TWENTY-THREE

The incessant mouse clicks began to irk him. Smoothing the lapel of his finely pressed beige jacket he approached the front desk again. A young lady barely in her twenties with bolt-on braces remained transfixed by the animated monitor screen, which threw a series of flashing colours on her pock marked complexion. Breagal gently coughed into a balled fist, which received little response.

"Excuse me, Miss?" he tried, barely containing his frustration.

The receptionist threw a fleeting glance in his direction before scowling at the screen. Hitting a button on the keyboard, the colours stopped dancing on her face. Her hair was a thick bushy mane scraped back into a tight bow. It pulled her expression upward and looked unnatural, exposing a massive brow which Breagal thought looked quite like a movie projector at that moment.

"I'll try again for you, Mr Pringle," she said, and clicked a button on the side of her headpiece attached to an ear already weighed down with the best part of a chandelier set, clinking against the plastic as her head moved.

"Breagal," he corrected too late as he was drowned out by her nasal whine.

"Dr Hart, I have Mr Pringle still waiting here to meet you. Shall I have them continue to wait?" she asked, as she lifted up a badly chewed biro lid and began to pick her nails with it. "OK, I'll send them through."

"Main door, second door on the right."

The woman hit a button and again returned her attention to the screen.

Breagal glanced back at Victor with a look of astonishment, but found his companion preoccupied, flicking through a glossy woman's magazine that had been laid out on the table.

"Let's go."

The psychiatrist and Breagal warmly embraced as they entered the office. They exchanged a few genial pleasantries as Victor hung back in the background waiting for an introduction. He took the opportunity to quickly scan the woman and was surprised at not only how young she was, but that she was also rather attractive. By no means a Hollywood starlet, but she had a girl next-door quality, mousey brown hair and freckled nubbin nose that hinted at a mischievous side. A wisp of hair had freed itself from the little bob on her head, and danced like a ballerina on her rosy cheek. She tucked it back over her ear and smiled at Breagal, nodding as he spoke.

Her posture suddenly opened, cognizant of the stranger behind the librarian. He continued talking at her for a few more moments while her eyes flicked over his shoulder for the first time to acknowledge Victor, which gave him the impulse to introduce himself. Stepping forward, he put a hand on Breagal's shoulder, startling the man for a moment. The woman smiled at him, nodding her thanks for breaking in when he did and relieving the awkwardness.

"Our friend here seems to have forgotten me!" Victor said.

A flustered Breagal apologized and curled an arm around his companion to welcome him into the conversation.

"Better late than never I guess," he smiled, looking into the woman's soft grey eyes. "My name's Victor James."

"Moira Hart," she said, a smile still fastened on her lips as she extended a hand for him to shake.

"No hug for me?" Victor teased.

The cockiness caught the psychiatrist off guard, and she felt the heat on her cheeks. Quickly dousing the flames, she straightened and turned to address Breagal.

"Please take a seat. Can I get you something to drink? Some water?"

The men accepted gratefully and she left them sitting on the couch.

As soon as the door closed behind her, Victor turned to the librarian with a wide-eyed expression and open mouthed. Looking at him, Breagal smirked and shook his head slowly.

"Keep focused," he said. "I need you to close your eyes and open your ears."

Victor sulked in mock exaggeration, sticking out his fat bottom lip to show his disappointment.

"OK, so remind me why we're here again?"

"Dr Hart has been treating my brother on and off for the best part of five years. There is no one better equipped who knows the inner workings of his mind. If we can decipher some of his thoughts, and understand the catalyst for his mental deterioration, then it might be able to aid us as we reverse Norman out of his current state."

"Sweet. I didn't see a wedding ring though. Can you confirm?"

"Victor. Please."

"OK. Only messing. I still don't get how we're going to get inside his dream."

"Leave that to me. For now, I just want you to listen and learn. There might be something we can pick up here that you can use in your journey."

"Journey? You make it sound like I'm going hiking in the Himalayas."

"The greatest journey of all is the one within."

Victor rolled his eyes skywards, just as Hart returned to the room with their glasses of water, which she placed in front of them on the table.

"So," she said, after settling down in a comfortable chair opposite them. "Sorry for keeping you both waiting."

They both raised their hands in a dismissive gesture.

"Thank you for seeing us at such short notice, Moira. I'm most grateful."

"Not at all, Stephen. Please, bear in mind that I am between appointments so I won't have too long with you today. On the phone you mentioned that you'd like to learn more about Saul's condition, and specifically the early stages where he first showed signs of the fantasies. Did I get that right?"

"Absolutely," Breagal nodded before adding, "I want to know if there was anything specific that could have triggered the onset of this illness in him, and ultimately if it was in anyway preventable."

"And…" she replied, leaning her head toward the other man, hoping that the librarian understood her none too subtle prompt.

"And my friend Victor here is studying behavioural psychology for his post doctorate thesis. I thought it would be interesting for him to hear first-hand. I hope you don't mind?"

"Not at all," she said and sat back in her chair, crossing her long legs which attracted the attention of the budding student who shifted in his seat. "Where to begin?"

"Anywhere you like," Victor suggested and received an elbow prod in the ribs from Breagal, which quickly removed his smile.

If the psychiatrist noticed, she didn't make it known, still staring up into the memory halls of her mind to access her earliest encounter with the patient.

"When Saul originally arrived at our clinic, he was already in quite a state. A lot of the paranoid delusions and somatoform disorders had become progressive, and we tried to pin that back with a mild blend of drugs and psychotherapeutic sessions. Over the months and then years, the layers became more complex and those treatments no longer resonated, so we tried alternative remedies."

Breagal turned to his colleague at this point and explained that the alternative therapies had been a medication called Profanol. Saul had been one of the first people to be involved in the clinical trials. It had been labelled as a wonder drug when it first entered the market.

Originally it had been administered to the patient to deal with his symptoms of sleep apnoea and fatigue, but they had found that his immune system became more resistant, eventually adapting to the drug even with higher dosages.

"Does that sound about right?" Breagal asked.

"Absolutely," Hart replied. "The drug was actually discontinued because it was known to have side effects."

"What were those?" Victor asked.

"Profanol made the patients', Saul in this case, dreams incredibly visual. Not only that but we discovered that the dreamer could spend longer suspended in this state, which naturally made some patients nervous, fearing they wouldn't wake up."

"I see," Victor said without seeing.

Breagal decided to change topic.

"Can you tell me what a typical catalyst would be for the degradation like that experienced by Saul?"

"Current thought suggests that it could stem from massive mental trauma, like the sudden death of a loved one, or in some instances extreme stress, paralyzing the victim and creating a hormonal imbalance that could cripple their conscious thought process."

"So," Breagal said, "this isn't something they are necessarily genetically wired to experience. Environmental factors can throw the brains functionality out of synch, if you like, and create a chain of events that could ultimately lead to such symptoms as paranoia and delusion?"

"Yes. That's what I believe. But that flow of events can happen much quicker if the person encourages it."

"What do you mean?" Breagal asked with interest, as he took a sip from the glass of water.

"I mean to say that, when I studied your brother under hypnosis at least in the beginning, he was lucid enough to converse and seemed knowledgeable in the nature of consciousness. In fact, we engaged in lively conversation a few times about the merits of Freudian psychology and its relevance today."

She smiled recapturing a forgotten memory.

Meanwhile, Victor was feeling lost and watched the conversation ping back and forth like a game of tennis. Dr Hart turned to him, noticing his unease.

"I hope this is relevant to your studies, Victor?"

"Absolutely," he answered and turned to Breagal who was silent in repose.

A few seconds drifted past, stillness heightened by the clock ticking in the corner, before Breagal picked up the thread again.

"Are you saying that my brother's downfall was that he knew too much?"

"No, not at all," she assured him. "He had a great thirst for knowledge. I've never seen anything like it. I feel that we only scratched the surface there, but he revealed enough to convince me that there was enough truth that I could tease him out of the fantasy he had created."

Breagal remained unmoved and continued to watch her. Victor had already finished his water and swapped his empty with that of the librarian.

"Look," she said. "Think of knowledge like a loaded gun. Powerful but in the wrong hands, it can have devastating consequences. I think that Saul was so wrapped up in his own journey, that he never considered the direction it would lead him. Ultimately the fantasies fed his fascination, and the deeper he dived, the tougher it became to resurface for air. Not even in his dreams."

She sat back, watching the reaction of the librarian who began to nod as if the pieces were beginning to slot into position.

"By the way, did you ever find out anything about the diary or the pirate?" Hart asked.

It was Victor who perked up and was about to speak, before Breagal cut across him suddenly.

"No," he said. "I don't expect we ever will."

"He did have that little toy figurine for a while. That might be the pirate connection," Hart suggested.

"You're probably right, Moira. As for the diary. It's a mystery."

The desk phone buzzed and Hart excused herself before moving to the other side of the room to answer it, back turned to the guests. Breagal looked at Victor and nodded, trying to placate his colleague, as if to say that he knew what he was thinking.

"OK Suzie. Give me a few moments."

The two men stood up, anticipating the psychiatrist's words that their time was over.

"We were about to go anyway. Thank you so much for meeting us again," Breagal said as he embraced the psychiatrist.

She shook the hand of the other man again, who held it a heartbeat longer than necessary and walked them to the door. Victor stopped just short of the entrance and turned to her.

"Is there any way to pull someone from this unconscious state, for example if their mind is still active and hasn't disconnected from reality?"

She leaned against the open door and thought for a second, before shaking her head.

"Virtually impossible given the speed of deterioration and complexity of the brain's neural pathways and processes. You would need to walk a tightrope to manage it. I tried with Saul, but couldn't find the keystone."

"Keystone?" Breagal asked.

"It's an expression we sometimes use to describe the key piece that ties the delusion together. Once you locate that, then the constructed world can be influenced. Only then can there be any hope of recovery."

They thanked her again and left the clinic, returning to Breagal's parked car.

"Why didn't you tell her that we had the book?" Victor asked, buckling on his seatbelt.

Breagal started the car and drove off at a snail's pace until they had left the car park.

"We don't need Moira to be poking her nose into our affairs."

"Hold on. I thought she was on our side? Surely it would have been good to get her take on some of what your brother wrote?"

"Academic smarts aren't as valuable as book smarts."

"What does that mean?"

"It means she's a little short sighted when it comes to discussing the merits of dreams and the possibilities that lie therein."

"Might have been worth a mention though."

Breagal shook his head, dismissing the suggestion, carefully slotting into the dotted line of traffic.

"She's limited to her academic programming. I'm almost convinced she would have rejected the scribbling at face value. It's her job to be critical and rational. The last thing I want is for us to be dissuaded from the task at hand, regardless of how well intentioned her meaning would be."

"You seemed to have changed your tune fairly quickly, Breagal. Not ten minutes ago, you were hugging her like a long lost friend!"

"Don't get me wrong, she's very skilled at what she does, but a part of me just feels that she gave up a little too quickly."

"With your brother?"

"Exactly. Perhaps I'm just angry with myself. Maybe I didn't do enough. You know, in the early stages of his illness, at Saul's request, I opened the library for him after hours."

"Was that wise?" Victor asked and his mind cast back to the image of the man a month earlier walking the streets in the storm with the broken umbrella, wide smile on his face.

"Probably not but he begged me. I left him there at dusk and found him still sitting in the same spot at dawn when I opened in the morning, a stack of read books piled high on the desk. And so it continued every night for months. I don't even know if he slept at all. Maybe it is my fault."

"You did what you thought was best," Victor tried to assure him. "You got him the help and support he needed like any brother would do."

"And to what end?" he suddenly snapped and banged the heel of his palm against the steering wheel. "No, that isn't good enough. That won't happen again. Not on my watch. It might be too late for my brother, but it isn't too late for Norman. I'll go to the ends of the Earth if I have to. I won't fail this time."

The driver's white knuckles tightened around the wheel and the car began to climb in speed. But it was the sudden mood change and distress in his face that made Victor uneasy. The librarian's lip quivered, his breath becoming more rapid as he changed up through the gears. If Victor didn't know better, he looked like a man hell-bent on revenge.

TWENTY-FOUR

They were downstairs. A makeshift table engineered from a cupboard door was erected in the corner. It was propped up by two towers on either side of various junk, which they had unearthed from the pile of rubble. Norman had managed to find a three-legged chair which served its purpose, provided he didn't lean back at an angle. He was preoccupied by the dog that lay on the floor in front with its paws in the air, getting its swollen belly scratched, big doe eyes and fat lolling tongue unable to contain the ecstasy. Behind an upturned table was a man crouching on all fours, searching through the debris with focused attention. His forehead was mopped with sweat, which he swiped clear with a fat finger and dried on his bicep. He paused for a moment to sit up on his knees and looked around.

"Still nothing?" Norman asked.

Yenjin shrugged his large shoulders in defeat before smiling, creases around his eyes paving a new path for the sweat to seep through. His shirt was now glued to his considerable frame.

"Well," he said, standing up and dusting clean the trousers where he had knelt. "We can find some supplies nearby I'm sure. Isn't that right Skye?"

Hearing its name, the dog jumped to its feet and did a running jump at the owner, who caught it mid-flight with a deft swoop before holding it up to his thick barrel chest. The dog began to lick the sweaty face, much to the amusement of Yenjin, who bobbed his head to avoid the long sticky strokes before dropping the dog gently back to the floor.

"Come on. There's got to be food somewhere."

"What if they took it all?" Norman said under his breath.

"Listen, we've only just started. They can't have taken everything. As long as we're together then we'll be fine. OK?"

"OK."

"Let's get going."

Norman followed the man out of the building, slow and heavy steps until they were back on the mud track. Outside, they took a big breath of air; Norman pushing his hips forward to try and provide some relief to a lower back which had been locked in a bent position for most of the day. Yenjin seemed unaffected by the physical labour, looking strong enough to continue if there had been more houses to search.

They stood and looked up and down the track that divided a row of loosely congregated wooden houses on either side, all searched, all unoccupied. The first house they had entered was Yenjin's. The second had been Norman's. Yenjin had insisted going in alone, leaving Norman to wait outside, playing with the dog to distract his mind. When he had returned thirty minutes later and just in time before Norman's impatience had spurred him to action, the look on his face had shown that there was nothing inside. They had spent all morning visiting various buildings, up and down the dirt path, finding neither sign of life or more importantly source of food.

The same destructive force had touched all the buildings leaving its unique thumbprint - a tornado sweeping through, plucking families from shelter with brutal strength leaving behind no-one, except them.

Yenjin looked skyward at the afternoon sun that had just been swallowed by a cloud, casting a gloomy shadow on the land. Had Norman been looking at the man, he would have noticed a frown shape the hard leathery skin of his face, but he was looking at his own shadow yawn as the passing sun was peeping in and out. Meanwhile, the dog had left them, running across the track and into one of the huts they had entered earlier. It began barking and looked back at them, before creeping into the opening inside.

With a motion of his head, Yenjin signalled Norman to follow and they walked along the track side by side.

"What were those... things from last night?"

"Didn't I tell you already?" Yenjin said, continuing the slow pace, squelching through the muddy walkway. "All I know is what I saw Norman. Two weeks ago, those soldiers were deployed here to police this area. Now something happened to turn them into the savages you saw."

"What happened to them?"

"Your guess is as good as mine. I have a friend…" Yenjin checked suddenly, and took a deep inhalation of breath pushing out his great barrel chest before exhaling gently.

"You lost someone too?" Norman asked.

Yenjin nodded, biting into his lip and he looked down at the ground as they continued walking.

"There were some rumours that the soldiers had been injected with some sort of chemical or implant that would make them more resistant to pain. I don't know if that's likely, but I've seen villagers with my own eyes defending themselves against these soldiers, shooting rounds at them point blank, and they treat bullets like they're swatting flies. They just keep on coming."

They passed a couple of abandoned buildings, both men peering inside as they walked, hoping for a flicker of movement that they had missed earlier. The windows on each home had all been boarded up at some point, but the openings now were fractured holes penetrated by boot and fist. In the doorway of the approaching house a red trail, as if marked by bloody entrails, coloured the opening, losing its colour on the mud outside. Norman looked away. Yenjin noticed and held him closer, stroking the side of his head gently.

"Come on. Let's see what Skye is barking at."

The little bungalow was smaller than their most recent searches. Yenjin had to lower his head to avoid hitting the doorframe on entering as they passed through into a small living room; it was entirely empty, expect for a matted rug on the floor, spoiled by mud.

"Skye?" Yenjin called out, and received a sharp bark in response.

An opening in the corner led through to another room, which Yenjin walked through. The kitchen area was desolate, with the counter broken into pieces on the floor, mangled with broken cutlery. In the midst of this, Skye was pawing desperately, looking up at the owner, who pulled the heaviest piece out of its way. Uncovered, the dog rooted her nose into the bottom of the pile and, finding its target, promptly latched its teeth around it and dragged its prize away into the adjoining room. Yenjin couldn't resist a laugh, and looked around to share the humour with Norman, who was no longer there.

Looking into the next room, Yenjin saw the dog chomping on the oversized bone. In the corner was Norman with his back to the door.

"You OK, Norman?"

There was a little wall table along the side of the room, no longer than a foot. On it, untouched, was a little figurine of a pirate that throughout the entire destruction had still managed to remain standing. On its shoulder was a little green parrot.

"Yes, I'm fine," Norman said, pocketing the little pirate and turning quickly to him.

"Good, well at least one of us has found something to eat," he said nodding to the dog. "I don't know about you but I'd like to get something before it gets dark. Let's make the merchant's our final stop."

They left and began walking further along the track, which was now steadily increasing in gradient. Shielding their eyes from the low lying sun, Yenjin pointed to a little building about a kilometre away that sat on a mound. Beyond it they could see the edge of a forest of trees densely rooted, through which an impenetrable darkness lurked, ominous even during the daylight.

"That's the merchant's," Yenjin pointed. "If he's there, we can trade something for food. If not, then I'm sure we're bound to find something there. Let's make haste and get back home before nightfall."

Yenjin led the way with big strides, which Norman struggled to match. Skye lagged behind, caught between following them and sitting with her bone.

"What if they come back?" Norman asked.

"I've never known them to come out during the day. They seem to favour the night-time. And that siren? That's what brings them out. When it stops, they go back, so as long as we're not too far from home, we'll be one step ahead."

"How come I don't seem to remember the merchant's place? Or anything beyond last night even?"

Yenjin slowed down until the other man had caught up, and spoke in a soothing tone.

"You've just experienced a tragic loss son. It's only natural that you're blocking out a lot of the pain and memories. It'll come back to you in time, don't worry."

In his pocket, he began to play with the edges of the figurine; he could feel the unbroken tips of the parrot's feathered tail. It was strangely reassuring in his hand and it made him relax.

When they finally came upon the merchant's house the sky overhead had darkened to a grey slate. Approaching, they were surprised to see the door of the property not only intact, but locked on the inside. Knocking and receiving no response, Yenjin walked around the building to look for a lever to wedge it open, but the grounds were sparse. It was a single storey and they scanned the outside in the darkened light without finding any discernible openings. Puzzled by this, Yenjin was distracted by a cracking noise as the dog splintered an end off its bone.

"Sorry girl. I need to borrow this."

He lifted the wet bone off the ground and wedged the fractured end into the gap between door and wall around waist height. The dog made a whining noise, before Yenjin suddenly kicked the bone with a heavy boot. The door snapped open and the bone shattered into a pile of smaller shards. The puppy set upon the biggest fragment, perhaps fearful that it would meet a similar fate and took them it a few yards away from the building.

"Who needs a key to open a lock, when you've got a bone to pick?" Yenjin laughed, and curled his fingers inside the door to pull it open.

Inside was a small square room, with a table top counter dead centre, on it sat a little writing pad and a pencil. A wooden beam designed to separate the customer from reaching the goods fenced them in. There was an open walking space on the outer layer behind the counter where the merchant would freely walk around the edges of the perimeter to fetch items, before offering them at the desk. To their sides they were amazed to see shelves fully stacked with tinned goods, seemingly untouched. Tomatoes, fruit salad, peaches, pineapple chunks.

"We hit the jackpot here, Norman!"

Yenjin jumped over the beam and flung his empty rucksack on the counter and began to scoop dozens of tins into it with his massive arm span. There was a mechanical click in the room, and they looked around at a small aperture that opened up from behind the counter. From it, a barrel shotgun protruded and pointed directly at Yenjin.

"I'm going to give you ten seconds to get out of my store before Big Bertha here paints you a nice colour."

It was a gruff low voice that spoke. The kind that you imitated at home afterwards, to see if you had that bass chord. The window wasn't big enough to reveal what was hidden beyond the shotgun.

"Mr Merchant, I sincerely apologise," Yenjin started, spilling the tins out of the bag and replacing them as quick as he could on the shelves. "We were only hungry and thought this building was deserted like the others."

"I have no sympathy for your kind, peasant. You feel it's right to break into a man's store and bring hell to his door?"

"We both got the same enemies. All I ask is a small bit of food for me and my friend here," Yenjin said, pointing to Norman who stood uncertain in the doorway. "We're all on the same side for Christ's sake."

"You've broken my door. That's a free invite for them. Get out and don't come back."

"But sir…"

"Five seconds and I'll shoot you where you stand, you big dummy."

The gun followed Yenjin around the room as he hoisted himself back over the beam and then picked up his empty rucksack and exited.

"And take your mutt with you!" the voice bellowed from inside.

Norman followed behind as they walked into their long shadows, sun setting behind. Skye had caught up with them now, unimpeded by the weight of the bone, content instead with a single sliver to gnaw on. They walked in silence and their slow descent took them back onto the mud track sandwiched between the rows of empty houses again.

"Why didn't you stand up to that man?" Norman asked.

Yenjin forced a smile and said nothing, instead putting his arm on the other man's shoulder and bringing him in closer. Norman could feel the swell of his bicep against the back of his neck. He looked across his chest and noticed the veins on the belly of his forearm stretched close to the surface and thick as bungee cords.

It was starting to get colder and a wind had started up from the lower plains and breezed toward them.

"The walk ahead is about thirty minutes. Let's try and get back before it gets darker."

They quickened their pace a little, trudging through the mud. Norman's legs tired with the effort as it crusted around his shoes, scraping the skin above his ankle. His legs felt heavier, especially after they had descended and walked on the flat terrain again. He parked himself on a little crumbling wall that had once been part of someone's rockery.

"Can't we rest for a few minutes? We've done a lot of walking today, Yenjin."

The man was about to speak, when from the distance there boomed the noise of a siren, which set their hairs on end. They both looked at each other, eyes wide in panic.

"Run!"

TWENTY-FIVE

I'm in the supermarket, basket in hand walking down the aisles. The Christmas music is playing on the radio, something from the '80s. I whistle the tune as other customers greet me as they walk past. The basket starts to become heavier now, and looking down at it, I notice to my alarm, I am completely naked! In utter panic I grab a cereal box at my side and hold it over my privates, shifting along the aisle carefully, eyes shooting around for a quick exit. I run deftly on my toes to avoid the glances of other shoppers, blood shooting to my head, embarrassment making me dizzy.

Suddenly a chink of light penetrates my thoughts. Why would I be naked in a supermarket? This can't be real; I must be dreaming! With the sudden realization, a flush of energy courses through my body and I feel liberated. I begin to recall what Breagal taught me. This is now a blank canvass where I can become the artist. I quickly clothe myself and walk outside the store. For the remainder of the dream I walk along the sidewalk in delirium, breathing in the colours and sounds, rich and vivid. The dream characters that pass me are my own creation and I engage in brief conversation with them. Stopping at a set of traffic lights, I look up and down for a break in the flow. Then realizing deeply it's all a dream, I decide to step across without warning, and look up just in time to see the bus before it strikes me...

***

Victor relayed the contents of his dream back to Breagal and the librarian smiled seeing the animation in his face. It had only taken a week to learn the art of lucid dreaming, and it had clearly made an impression.

"You know, it was incredible when I realized I was dreaming. It was…" Victor hesitated, trying to find the right words, "the real me. All my own thoughts and experiences. I started to think about what you told me, and how I was able to influence things."

Victor smiled, unable to stop his excited leg from shaking as it bounced on its heel. It was almost midday and they were in the living room of Breagal's house. The walls of the long rectangular room were turquoise, and a series of bright landscape portraits hung on the wall along one side. They were both barefoot under Breagal's orders, the sandy oak wooden panelling averse to scraping easily. Victor fell back into the soft couch that faced the fireplace, a grey and dusty pile of soot still remaining from the fire he had helped nurture the night before.

"I thought to myself, 'if this is a dream, then nothing can hurt me' and that's when I got hit by the bus!" Victor laughed in spite of himself.

Breagal looked at him with pride infected by the man's laugh.

"Of course, that's when you would have woken up," he explained. "The rush and exhilaration might have been too much for your sleeping brain to manage, and as a reflex emergency response, it broke the dream."

"Right. Right," he added before nodding.

Victor had calmed down a little now, but his smile was still there.

"We need to be careful," Breagal continued. "You need to remain grounded in the dream. The boundaries can be pushed but to get where we need to get to, a certain discipline must be observed."

"But we're headed in the right direction though?"

"Absolutely. We just need to reign in your enthusiasm a little bit and focus on the job at hand."

"OK."

"That'll come with experience. The journey of a thousand miles-"

"Please, Breagal. No more quotes."

The librarian laughed and passed the dream diary he was holding to Victor. The first dozen pages were filled, barely a dent in the thick journal.

"We still have some ways to go. Usually when people awaken for the first time they decide to see what it is like to fly like Superman, or make love to a popular celebrity, but you," he smiled. "You decide you want to get hit by a bus!"

"All in good time," he replied. "Just you wait!"

"You've experienced lucidity. As you observed they start as a normal dream, and usually an oddity occurs that the mind tries to justify with excuses. Don't let it trick you! With enough awareness through practice, you can notice these 'bugs in the system' easier, because they tend to recur. Look at your journal."

Victor opened it and noticed Breagal had highlighted certain paragraphs.

"Those are the turning points you need to watch for. This dream," he said and handed him the highlighter, "was actually symbolic of the vulnerability you feel, and with the absence of clothes you feel exposed in front of others. This is a tremendously embarrassing feeling, but to your credit, you saw through the illusion and freed yourself. Make sure you document every dream, fractured or complete."

"So what's the next step?" Victor asked.

"Dream recall is critical. Remembering your dreams and documenting them is the first step to becoming lucid. You've opened the door once; you can do it again."

Victor nodded his head, encouraged by the progress and having highlighted the most recent dream passage, he slipped the book into his rucksack.

"We need to document another dozen or so lucid dreams and perform some tests within them to help manage your fears and anxieties. The longer you stay in this state, the greater the influence you can exert."

"And then beyond that?"

"At that stage, we would introduce you into Norman's world through a shared dream experience. You would lose your influence over the dream landscape, because it is his construction. He is, in all respects, the centre of that universe but you need to convince him that his constructed world is illusory. If you can do that then there's hope that he can return."

Standing, Victor stretched out his limbs. He pulled his work clothes from the bag and lined them up on the couch.

"Again, we have no idea what state of mind our friend will be in and you need to be careful to extricate him cleanly. Are you listening?"

"Yes," he said and stifled a yawn. "I don't think I've slept so much in my life."

"No way around that I'm afraid. We need to build your strength in the dream plane. Are you ready for the next step?"

Victor looked at him blankly and thought about the past week and the exercises he had completed to achieve lucidity. He thought about Saul. He thought about the visit to Dr Hart, and the health risks associated with going too deep. He also thought about his experience in the hospital seated beside Norman's parents, keeping a vigil by his side, faith beginning to recede each day. Finally, he considered his friend and wondered if there was any part of him that could still be reached and whether he was the one to do it under the tutelage of Breagal, who he concluded that despite his eccentricities seemed to have his heart in the right place.

He thought about all of this for a few moments and saw Breagal searching his face for an answer.

"Well?"

"I'm having too much fun now to back down," he said and grinned confidently at the librarian, whose own smile was a little more nervous.

TWENTY-SIX

When Noreen Adams awoke, she was surprised to see that the room was dark. Not recognizing her surroundings, a brief panic came upon her before quietening again, noticing her son lying motionless on the bed. She had still been holding his hand even as they slept, and she looked at it now. It dangled weakly on a thin wrist and it felt cold in her hand. She began to smooth it between her palms to generate some heat, and his smooth skin began to warm to her touch. The heart monitor continued its steady beep, and she watched his chest billow with deep forced breaths.

The memory of last week was still fresh in her mind. The trickle of blood snaking its way from her helpless son's nose had caused in her such a panic that she had almost fainted. Dr Tawia had arrived and soon concluded that there was some residual trapped blood sustained from the head injury. The body's way of releasing the valve and letting it out, allowing more oxygenated healthy blood to circulate.

The gentle purring of her husband's snoring made her look to one side. She observed his heavy frame lying prostrate on the small chair. His body had managed to slide down from it during sleep, legs folding beneath him, barely upright now in a sitting position. She was about to wake him, before deciding against it and observing this moment alone with her son. Sleep had stirred a little strength in her and the darkness was helping to crystallize her thoughts. The flicker of light from the heart monitor cast a grey shade on Norman's thin face. There was an eerie calm in the room, an air of anticipation that was still and comforting. Noreen was careful to move her chair closer to the bed without creating a noise on the polished surface. She held his hand tightly, speaking gently in his ear.

"Hello son. It's your mother here," she said and began to caress his brow in soft, delicate strokes.

She studied his face and could see a slight jerking movement behind his eyelids, or perhaps it was the shadows playing tricks. A fatigue gently knocked from within, given the lateness of the hour. They sat in silence holding hands without the words needing to be spoken. She felt a swell of unconditional love for him rise in the darkness. It consumed her body and she could feel it pass from her fingertips to his hand.

"You know when you were a baby, I would sing to you."

She remembered it clearly now, watching it on the hospital wall as if it were a screen, smiling at the scene as she cradled him in her arms, feeling his delicate heartbeat that beat in tandem with her own.

"Of course, when you got older you grew out of all that stuff. That's fine, baby, but I'll never forget when you were once small and vulnerable. My God, you were so beautiful."

His hand was pressed into her face to stem the flow of tears that threatened to push though.

"All the other mothers would fawn over you, telling me how gorgeous you were, and how we were so lucky to have such a well behaved boy. Your father and I were so blessed to have had the perfect child. You gave us no trouble at all, and I just hope that we did a good job in raising you," she said, voice beginning to break a little, but she resisted. "I want you to know, that I'll always be here for you, baby. But..."

The sudden emotion made it difficult and it welled up again inside her.

"You need to wake up. You hear me Norman?" she said with a sudden steel in her voice. "I need to know you're still with us, pet!"

She lifted their hands back onto his thin chest and could feel the tender ribcage swell with each breath. She began to pray, tears collecting in her eyes. When she had finished, she stood and kissed him on the forehead and smoothed away the stray teardrops that fell on his face.

"Baby, I don't want to lose you. But we can't wait forever," she said, looking down at her son's face.

He looked at peace, and she stroked it again.

"I don't care if I embarrass you by saying it, but I want you to know that I love you so so much. More than you'll ever know," she said and gently embraced him.

Then Noreen Adams looked upwards and said to her maker.

"Please God, make sure my boy is safe."

She sat back down in the chair with some difficulty and propped her head on his bed, feeling the breath still rattling in his body.

TWENTY-SEVEN

His lungs were screaming for breath. Sucking in the cold dry air made him wheeze harder. The already tired legs squealed in pain, churning up the muck until his trousers were plastered in it, weighing him down with each lurching step. Trying to keep to the pace set by the dog was impossible. It had stolen a march on them, barely visible in the distance, its white coat contrasting sharply with the shades of grey and brown of their surrounds. The air that pushed against them, resisting their passage back to their base, swallowed its thin yelps. The larger man, looking nervous, arrowed his face to the west, the siren still drumming there, slicing through his thoughts and vibrating the ground as if the rolling mountains beyond had a heartbeat, deep beneath the Earth.

His focus was narrowed on a thin black line that had begun to leak from the base of the mountain like an oil spill. A trail of ants against the grey landscape, they trickled around the obstacle in a neat curved line before sharpening their formation into a point in the direction of Yenjin's gaze. They were barely distinguishable in the gloom which would certainly blanket them within the hour, but Yenjin noticed that they were moving. Fast.

"Come on, lad. You can do it. Keep going!" shouted the man mountain, encouraging his smaller companion.

Norman was panting and couldn't speak. He slowed his pace and hunched over for a few moments, and Yenjin stopped beside him with a concerned look.

"I can't go on," he managed after a series of wheezes.

"Just another few minutes and we'll nearly be there," Yenjin responded, patting him on the back, which almost collapsed him to his knees.

Norman was still trying to catch a breath that wouldn't come.

"Look over there."

Doubled over, Norman looked in the direction Yenjin pointed; a little curve in the path ahead where the dog sat waiting impatiently with the bone in its mouth.

"From that spot you can see your house. Just a few hundred yards, I promise."

Norman began to lift his heavy feet again, slapping them into the muck.

"Try to run on your tippy toes. The more mud that hits your foot, the more it'll suck you under. Like this."

In the dimming light Yenjin seemed to glide along beside him, barely grazing the ground. Even in his distress, Norman observed and then mimicked the other man's run almost perfectly and they began to run in stride together. Looking ahead they saw Skye, whose coat was now completely matted in dirt, wagging its tail. Above the rooftops, the dark grey mountain was cut into the sky and for the first time Norman saw them.

"Yenjin."

The man stopped and ran back to Norman who had lagged behind.

"Is that..."

"Don't worry. We'll be fine."

Yenjin turned away and practically hauled him along by the collar. Norman gripped the man's big hand after a few strides and tried to remove it.

"Yenjin?"

The man continued running and dragging his companion in an awkward shuffle. Norman tapped his big hand, which didn't rouse the runner. He pulled hard against the hand but its iron grip held firm.

"Yenjin, let me go!" he shouted.

The man turned and saw Norman wrestle with his hand, trying to prise the individual fingers open.

"Sorry," he replied and released his grip, sending Norman crashing to the floor.

He reached down and extended his hand, which Norman took. Pulled back to his feet, which left the sucking mud for a moment, Yenjin planted him down on a drier spot and offered a weak smile which didn't touch his eyes.

Unimpeded, Norman managed to match the quicker pace, dragging his aching body around the curve. The cold night sweat drenched through his clothes, hugging his shirt like a strait jacket. The perspiration began to sting his eyes and he used the bloody rag in his jean pocket to wipe it clear.

Coming off a sloping downhill bend, they slipped past the house where Norman had found the figurine pirate. Encouraged, he mentally located it and felt it press in his back pocket. They were below the plane of the approaching soldiers who for now were out of sight. As if reading his thoughts, Yenjin spoke in an earnest tone.

"Back to the attic. We don't have time to find anywhere else. Up the speed. If we saw them, there's every chance that they saw us. I need to make our getaway clean. Come on!"

Yenjin found another gear and pulled away, Skye running at his side. Norman swabbed the sweat clear again and squinted his eyes in the darkness, watching his neighbour who seemed to hover across the ground, the distance between them increasing with every second. He was about to shout out in desperation before Yenjin stopped suddenly. His large frame made the doorway at the end of the street look smaller than it was.

Signalling back to him with a wave, Yenjin entered and ran inside. Between the squelch of the footfalls, the peal of the siren and his heavy panting, Norman thought he detected a foreign sound on the landscape, one that he had heard before – an army of boots churning up the dirt. It began to grow in volume and he began to distinguish their individual voices. Sprinting to the doorway, Norman pulled himself inside to see Yenjin at the top of the stairwell holding a lit candle. His finger was raised to his lips and beckoned Norman to follow.

Leaping double steps as silently as he could, his aching body reached the top and chugged its way down the hallway. He recognised the familiar room, one of many they had traversed that day, as his neighbour's. Yenjin placed the candle on the floor beside the broken bed. Norman was careful to step over it as he joined the big man at the far end of the room. The illumination revealed the drape that hid the secret passage, and Yenjin slid it across and stepped inside holding it open for the other man to follow. Once he had stepped out the other side into the dark annex, he allowed Norman to pass, before reaching in and sliding the drape in place again. When he whispered her name from the other side, he heard Skye run across the length of the room and slip under the drape. He hushed her barks, rubbing her coat which was thick with mud. The noise from outside had gotten steadily more congregated and seemed to envelop the house.

Yenjin stepped on the chair and flipped the attic door open, which shed a little light into the annex. He traded places with Norman and watched as the man successfully climbed up into the attic space. He looked back down at them, lowering his body to the ground with hands outstretched. Yenjin picked up Skye, hoisted her into his arms, and Norman deposited her to one side, where she sat and watched her owner, looking down from the attic space and offering a soft whine.

"Shush, girl. Daddy's coming."

Finally, Yenjin pulled himself up and over with consummate ease and gently lowered the door until it was closed. They drew a collective sigh and stretched out on the hard surface. Norman's reached his boots toward his chest, groping within the thick Bolognese for the spaghetti strands that would unlock his feet and release him from their weight.

"Do you think we are safe here?"

"Aye lad. Better here than anywhere out there," he said, nodding his chin toward whence they came. "These animals are fairly rudimentary creatures, thirsty for flesh and blood, capturing innocents. Provided they haven't seen us we'll be fine. If they have, I'll beat them off again."

As if on cue, they heard the hurried footsteps enter the longer room below them. A garbled cry and thrashing of furniture was heard before the sound was carried away to another area of the house. Norman closed his eyes and inwardly traced the movement of the group again, relieved as they eventually flew through like a bad odour before being carried away by the wind into the distance. There were soft cries from the puppy, dampened by the strokes of Yenjin.

After a few minutes, she was silent and Norman felt the dog lay down beside him. His hand rested on its belly, feeling it rise with each collective breath. Skye's presence soothed him as she nuzzled her head under the pit of his arm for warmth. Norman felt the weight of his own body sink into the floorboards and the aches in his legs began to melt away as his tired mind began to unwind with sleep beginning to creep in. The noises outside faded into nothing more than background ambiance. He was vaguely aware of Yenjin's movements in the darkness, setting up his makeshift sleeping bed. The small noises he made, barely three metres away, felt like miles as everything around gradually calmed.

Suddenly the puppy bolted from under the outstretched hand of Norman. It stood alert for a moment just outside his reach, before walking toward the trapdoor space. Yenjin's eyes were keen and had noticed its silhouetted figure in the darkness, and rising he followed it to where it had stopped.

"What is it girl?"

The dog began to groan as if in pain, and clawed at the surface of the trapdoor with its front paw.

"It's not time to go down yet. It's not clear."

He picked up the dog and returned to where he was sitting on the floor with his back propped against the boiler, cradling Skye in his arms like a baby. Despite her owner's soft strokes, the puppy continued to whine.

Norman felt the aches in his legs pinning him to the ground. His lower back was pressing against something jagged; he relieved the object from his back pocket and held it in a cupped hand close to his chest. With difficulty he managed to kick his slick shoes off his feet, cursing under his breath the cuts around his ankles which flamed from his movements.

His leg slid them to one side, before he peeled his socks off, cold and filthy and slapped them against the floorboards to free the dirt. Visibility was virtually zero and his hands were already dirty, so he gave up and balled the socks into the opening of the shoes. Content, Norman rolled over onto his side exhausted and held the figurine up close to his chin. The earlier sounds, which had invaded the house, had ebbed away. Like an ocean wave, he could hear them return again fresh in his mind. The more he focused on them, the more animated and closer the sounds seemed to become. So close, they almost appeared to be in the same room. Norman shook his head from the thought and closed his eyes tight.

"Good night."

Yenjin didn't respond.

Norman opened his eyes and looked at the spot where the man had been sitting. The was no longer there. Confused, Norman noticed that it was a little lighter in the room and glancing around saw that Yenjin was kneeling at the trapdoor with Skye at his side pawing at the floor. Pulling on the ring, Yenjin heaved the door silently upward and Norman saw a shade of red flicker on his face, as it contorted into horror. The door hung open like his mouth, which instantly bolted Norman upright into a sitting position.

"What is it?"

"The candle," he said, his mouth opened wide. "The house is on fire!"

TWENTY-EIGHT

I am sitting in the front row of tables in the classroom. The desks are divided to avoid cheating in the exam. The headmaster picks the stack of papers up and begins distributing them to each student. Anxious, I wait, following him as he weaves his way around each student. Those who receive their paper first all wear the same expression – all smiles before launching into the blank pages provided, pen poised. When the headmaster appears before me, he plops the yellow booklet on my table before walking off. Pen in hand, I open it and begin to read the questions.

To my bewilderment, I don't understand the question. It seems to pinpoint a complete gap in my knowledge and flicking through the remainder of the questions my confusion is complete. This can't be the right paper, I think. Looking around, I see the other students busy scribbling their answers and begin to feel very distressed. I begin to question which class I'm in, and suddenly realize I'm an adult and these children around me must be part of a dream! A wave of relief washes over me, and I have complete control again.

Victor addressed the headmaster who had been seated behind his desk, studying the students carefully.

"Breagal, is that you?" he asked.

The headmaster looked at the student before standing up and approaching, face stern and foreboding. Reaching the desk, he bent over at the waist, looked down at the student. He held out both hands and touched the cheeks of Victors face between them as if he was intending to crush his head. They remained like this for a few seconds and then the headmaster's expression began to waver, before bursting into laughter.

"Well done my boy! You've done it!" he said, patting his protégé on the back.

"Wow. This is a bit trippy! So we are both in the same dream?"

Breagal couldn't tear the smile off his face and he pulled a vacant chair toward the student's desk. As he did so, Victor looked around, realizing that they were now alone in the classroom.

"Didn't I tell you it was possible?"

"Yes, you did!" Victor laughed. "So, I know I'm me, but how do I know you're Stephen Breagal? You could still be a dream character?"

"True. You'll know for certain when we both wake up and compare the experience. I can assure you that it will match entirely. Of course, your perspective will be different to mine."

Breagal leaned back in his chair and crossed his legs.

"Tell me what triggered it this time?"

Victor thought about the beginning of it. There was never a neat start, middle and ending. Over the past two weeks, where he had quickly ratcheted up dozens of dreams, Victor had found himself plunged into a sequence of events that had taken careful deliberation to detach from. As soon as he had started questioning the experience and challenging the dream, it had created a little window of opportunity. That tiny gap of awareness would widen until inevitably he would be left to think 'this must be a dream'. He related the earlier events to Breagal and his apparent distress at being unprepared for the exam.

"You're picking up the signals quicker and quicker, my friend. Questioning your surroundings and looking for dream signals is the key to accessing this state. Do you remember what I said about dream signals?"

He did. He had soaked everything like a sponge and his recall seemed particularly sharper in the dream state at that moment. He sat upright in his seat, like a model student, and addressed Breagal.

"Dream signals are those quirks or bugs that run counter-intuitive to logic," Victor began, mimicking the librarian's eloquent tone. "And identification of such are a shortcut to lucidity."

"Exactly! I couldn't have put it better myself," Breagal said, slapping his thigh.

Scrunching up the test paper into a thick ball, Victor threw it toward the bin in the corner of the room; it bounced off two walls before dropping in. They stood up and began to walk around the classroom. It was exactly how Victor remembered it from his childhood, right down to the very detail, still safely stored somewhere in his memory. The tables and chairs looked tiny in comparison and he couldn't quite believe how squashed together everything now was.

They observed the murals and coloured paintings plastered on the wall. Studying one of them, Breagal untacked it from the board and showed it to Victor, who shook his head in amazement. It was crudely drawn and splattered with colour. A box house stood in the foreground with two tall stick people, a little shorter than the building, holding their sausage finger hands together. A smaller stick child was beneath the linked arms, paintbrush not quite deft enough to carve it into the space it looked like a little blob. Above the house, a dollop of yellow hit the canvas shining through a cloud, where another stick figure floated in the sky in grey.

"I had forgotten about this one," Victor said. "This was of my uncle shortly after he passed away. Amazing what you forget."

Pinning it back to the corkboard they continued their circuit, Victor thumbing some of the art that hung from sections of the walls. When he had reached his chair again he sat back down.

"So whose dream is this?"

"Why it's yours, Victor. Isn't that clear from the setting you find yourself in?" Breagal waved his arm around the room to illustrate the point.

"OK, gotcha. But how is it that you were able to enter the dream again? I know I've asked you hundreds of times, but to actually experience it happen is pretty…"

"Frightening?" Breagal offered.

"Yes!"

"Rest assured that I have absolutely no influence over the outcome of your dream," Breagal said. "The key is proximity. By being in the same room, we are exposed to the same external stimuli. In this case, my study where we currently reside. Atmospheric conditions, smells and scents, gentle music, and the crystal formation can help trigger thoughts which lead to certain dreams."

"But how do you enter the dream?"

Breagal picked up a piece of chalk and walked the length of the wall, tossing it from one hand to another.

"Three things. Firstly, you must have complete mastery and awareness of the dream experience and this can only come through practice."

"I feel like I should be taking notes."

"Your memory stores everything. You just need to tease it out."

"OK. Go on."

"Secondly, you need to know the specific dream symbols that affect the dreamer, and be able to tune your unconscious mind to see them. This is a pattern that repeats itself, and once you know the dreamer's pattern, you can ride their awareness into the dream. For example, this is not the first time you have documented this specific scenario, is it?"

Victor realised Breagal was right. He'd had this dream at least a couple of times in the past week.

"Other times you've looked at your pen and seen it turn into a viper that tries to attack you. You promptly asked the headmaster for a new pen, before carrying on as if nothing had happened."

"As you do."

"Absolutely."

"I didn't know you were reading my journal. Isn't that a bit personal?"

"You may consider them unique, but I can assure you they are fairly common. When you've been studying the art for as long as I have, certain consistencies are inevitable. Even parallels between your dreams and my brother's..." Breagal said before trailing off, gaze dropping to the floor.

Victor looked across at him, contemplating what he had just said.

"No offence Breagal, but if there's even a snowball in hell's chance that I could be taken away by the men in the white coats I want out now."

"None taken," he said, forcing a smile. "I digress, but alas we have more work to do. Safe in the confines of our practice room."

"What's the third thing?"

"You need to be asleep to dream, of course! Deep levels of meditation can connect the dreamers but I'm not a yogi, although I have practiced the art with Buddha himself, and consulted with various prophets from many thousands of years ago to try and accelerate my learning."

"So, really it's like tuning into a frequency?" Victor said.

"Exactly. I dream as you dream. You sleep as I sleep. But it is in our dreams that we awaken."

"Poetic."

"Thanks. The frequency band is much smaller when you are fixed on those variables I just mentioned."

"You're frying my brain with this one, Breagal."

The librarian laughed, turned and replaced the chalk on the little tray beside the board and approached the student's desk.

"Listen. We're on the right track. We both need to tune to Norman's frequency. It will be on the same wavelength as that of my brother. I'm confident that I know the way in."

"The keystone," Victor murmured, remembering their conversation with the psychiatrist.

"Exactly! But we're getting ahead of ourselves. One step at a time. Victor? Is something wrong?"

Victor's smile flashed wide at the librarian and moved toward the door. There was a sudden soft knocking, before it opened gently. In the doorway stood Dr Moira Hart wearing a thigh skimming plaid skirt, black sheer stockings pulled up over her shapely legs. A white cotton crop top hugged her ample chest, revealing a bronzed taut midriff. Her hair was raised high in a bow, spilling down over the back of her head. She stood watching Victor, then leaned back against the doorframe, foot raised off the floor and the stiletto tucked under her behind.

"Hi boys," she said, moistening her red lips with tongue tip before smiling at Victor. "You called?"

Breagal looked from her, back to the student and then shook his head unamused by the introduction of this new dream character.

"We'll talk about this when you wake up," he snapped.

Victor watched the man fade away, the blackboard he had been blocking suddenly coming back into view. On it, in tall letters written in chalk was one word. Breagal must have inscribed it during his lecture.

The smile dropped from his face and he shook his head in frustration. He looked toward the doorway and she was no longer there. Victor's thoughts were now channelled again into one goal, and he repeated the written word out loud.

"Norman."

TWENTY-NINE

Stephen Breagal had been sitting in his study for several hours now, feeling a weak strain tugging in his lower back for attention. The room was illuminated by several scented candles that had been placed strategically around the room to spread the glow. The smell of incense had begun to percolate through the air, and he wafted it deep into his nostrils, relaxing in his chair, easing the pain a little. Victor lay still on a soft cushioned mat on the floor to one side in semi darkness, arms crossed over his chest, breathing steadily. A circle of crystals curled around his head shaped like a halo. Breagal glanced down at the beatified figure, with an ironic smile, recalling the dream several nights earlier involving Dr Hart. Not such a saint after all it seems.

Seeing the faint twitching of his eyes behind closed lids, he could tell that the man was now dreaming – R.E.M - Rapid Eye Movement was always a precursor. They had made rapid progress over the weekend and collected a huge quantity of dreams for study. Breagal picked up the page in front of him and looked at the chart. Tracing the wave with his pencil he calculated that the current sleep cycle would end shortly, almost time to collect another dream to document. He yawned and sat in silence for a few moments, ear opening to any sounds in the house but finding none at that early hour. He followed his own conscious breath and focused on the dull ache in his back, which began to gently fade under his illicit control.

He drew a small key from his pocket and opened the lock on a wooden drawer in his table, sliding the drawer out gently. Reaching in, he pulled out the leather bound journal again, and closed the drawer. It felt comforting to hold the warm, smooth surface in his hands. He opened it again, and carefully danced his nimble fingers across the delicate pages toward the back. The new entries were not part of the original journal, but he had found them stuffed there when flicking through weeks earlier, torn from another book and added as an addendum. Norman had signed each entry with his initials at the bottom.

There were fifteen entries in all, tone darkening each time, until the final rushed entry perhaps done in terror or scrawled in shorthand in the middle of a night after waking up from the fitful dream. It was hard to be accurate. Although Breagal had read it many times since, it still sent a shiver down his spine. The nearby candle atop the table gently stirred as if affected by a breeze, the shadow dancing on the wall behind. He read the synopsis again.

Entry 15 - Super Soldier – I'm a child in a war-torn village. A bio-military experiment gone wrong, soldiers injected with a serum that instead of switching off their fear, altered their biochemistry. Rumours abound that they have turned to savages. Fortunately woke before discovering.

POST SCRIPT - Still affecting me emotionally ten hours later. WOW.

N.A.

Breagal then flicked back to the first new entry stark in contrast, a rather mundane description about teeth falling out. Then using the ribbon bookmark as a reference he sliced the book in two and was brought to an entry made by his brother years earlier and read the first lines.

Super Soldier – Turning against us. Super strength. Savages. Murdered brother. Father dead. Mother dead. KROLLSON. Escaped attic. Yenjin.

The parallels were uncanny. The only explanation forthcoming was that Norman had been so moved by the entries written by his brother, that they had implanted deeply into his subconscious. Sensing the vitality, excitement and intensity behind each dream entry, the accountant must have been greatly impressed, desperately exploring deep into his own imagination. The specific path that Norman's dreams had taken flowed like the entries made by his brother.

He began to think about Saul. If anything he had laid out the path of destruction in advance. The same story arc that Norman had seized upon and was following into oblivion. A dream sequence that offered no start, middle and end, but instead slowly wedged its way into the brain until you were trapped in the moment. A moment that had overwhelmed the conscious mind and ultimately warped his brother's sense of reality.

Chronologically, for his brother it had unfolded in a matter of months, the startling element being that the nightmare always picked up where it left off. There was no escape from the terror for him. He was trapped in the web, dangling helplessly in the thread waiting for the moment his fate would be sealed.

In Norman's case and given the induced coma, there was no respite from the dream.

Breagal flicked forward through a few of the entries, noting the illustrations as they became more detailed and sprawling, merging with the text in places, and scored harder into the pages. He shook his head and rubbed his eyes.

"Come out, come out, wherever you are."

THIRTY

It was Skye who reacted first, yelping at her owner who was almost too stupefied to react. The stricken terror scrawled on his face instantly set Norman's pulse racing double. Forgetting all instance of a tired body he jumped to his feet, eyes scanning for his boots. The sleepy haze had vanished and his senses attuned instantly. The noises were growing in volume and seemed to be coming from all around them.

The temporary paralysis that had seized Yenjin snapped and, throwing down the trapdoor in place, he reacted decisively.

"We need to get out of here NOW!" he said, taking big footsteps toward the back of the loft, away from the emerging glow.

Norman could now feel the heat from the floorboards warm his feet as he fixed the boots on tight, double lacing them. A crack from within the loft at the opposite end caught his attention, and from there Yenjin returned holding an object about three feet in length. As he neared, Norman could see sudden gaps in the floor around them, the floor sagging under the weight of the bulky man.

Dark smoke was now billowing up in thin streams, already beginning to collect in the upper corners of the chamber. The light was growing around them now and they felt the heat begin to grow in intensity. Yenjin suddenly used the object in his hands to strike up at the angled roof of the wooden loft. His aim was hard and accurate, aimed at the aperture they had looked through the night before. The missile was a large hollow pipe snapped off from the boiler system and its endings were jagged and wet, with Yenjin struggling with the slippery grip. A column of smoke surrounded him, thicker now and he took one large breath of air before hammering at the spot in rapid booming thrusts; hulking the heavy pipe with brute force, with each hit his lungs squealed for air. Finally, he stopped after chugging a mouthful of the smoke in his efforts. Doubling over, he coughed into a balled fist, gasping for air.

Norman climbed to his feet to approach and help but Yenjin blocked him with a hand motion.

"Down! Air…"

From the outstretched hand hung a large seam of skin that had torn, and blood streamed freely from it onto the floor. The end of the pipe was completely soaked in red and lay on the ground next to the man, whose heavy exertion and oxygen deprivation had him on bent knee.

The house around them seemed to rumble, as if on unsteady legs. Norman heard new cracks below them in the interior, like the sound of firewood crackling. His head remained low to the floorboard, breathing rapidly even though he could feel the searing pain on his cheek from the ground. In his limited vision he saw Skye illuminated mouth yapping in a bark, but he couldn't hear the sound such was the noise inside the furnace. The dog was in absolute panic and, seeing Norman, it came rushing over into his open arms.

They both looked up at Yenjin who was still battling, in considerable distress bent over, head bobbing with eyes wild and searching. Taking a gulp of breath, the ash stained figure struggled back on his feet and delivered another series of telling blows on the same point. Norman watched, trembling with the dog in his arms. Just when it looked like his body was about to give in, a final fatal strike at the wooden ceiling punctured a narrow gap. The opening sucked the fire smoke into the night sky. The aperture was just large enough to fit his head through, and with it Yenjin breathed in the sky air in huge gasps.

"Yenjin!" Norman cried.

Hearing, or sensing the call, Yenjin pulled his head back. The room was bathed in yellow flames which climbed the sides of the walls, illuminating the oblong room. With renewed energy, Yenjin grabbed the metal pipe and inserted it into the opening before heaving considerable weight on the lever. A large portion of the ceiling cracked aside. Blinking back ashen soot against the growing smoke circulating there, he wiped his face clean but left a mass of blood in its place.

"Come on!" he shouted.

Norman crawled along the wooden floor as quick as he could manage. Tongues of flame were licking at him between the cracks from below, and his palms were scorching hot. Adrenaline took over and he staggered to the large man who he could now see up close. The eyes were puffy and red, closed to a squint, on a face that was swollen and pink, with smears of blood and ash across his mouth.

"You need to be my eyes here lad," he shouted above the deafening din which was now building below.

Without another word Yenjin pushed Norman up through the aperture on the sliding angled roof of the house. Smoke continued to gush out from the makeshift chimney.

"See if there is a clear passage away from the house. You're lighter than me. I would slide right off the roof," he shouted. "Hurry!"

Norman pivoted his body away from the pouring smoke, moving in a walking crouch along the length of the side of the house, careful not to be noticed. The fire had illuminated the surrounding area and he could observe figures in the shadows running toward the house from all directions. As they came closer, he had to shield the brightness of the fire with a palm to make out their features in the grey shade.

Squeals of delight erupted from the mob, as they reigned in on the house, attracted like moths to a flame. The first few had arrived suddenly on Norman's near side, as he peered down at the view from some twenty feet above. Beyond them, he could see about a dozen dark shadows running toward the house. Turning back in his tracks, Norman tread lightly across the tiled roof, passing the aperture again where Yenjin slumped through, his body half exiting the hole like the mouth of some great fiery dragon that no longer had the appetite to consume him whole. Norman could hear the desperate barks of the dog within the attic.

"Is there an exit?" Yenjin asked, eyes squinting and face wrung in pain, sweat pouring off his thick chin.

"That side is covered by about fifteen or so."

"Try the other side," Yenjin said and pointed. "The street… we… came…"

He broke off to cough into the balled blood fist.

As Norman passed the small window that housed Yenjin, he could see the room was awash with flames now and he felt the flash of intense heat. When he got to the other end of the rooftop, he could observe by the brightness of the fire that the street ahead had several roaming bodies. The soldiers almost seemed disinterested in the inferno or at least hadn't yet noticed it.

"It's clear this side!" Norman beckoned to Yenjin.

The man looked up at him and smiled in response and nodded his head weakly. His body sagged against the roof, the fallen arms dangling, bloodied and dark.

Norman looked at the possible exit before he turned back to the man. As he shifted away from the edge he placed his foot on a loose tile, which suddenly gave way. Unable to reposition his foot Norman found himself falling forward and instinctively reached his hand out toward Yenjin, whose face was lowered and staring mutely at the scene. Groping desperately for a ledge to grab he found none as his body tumbled, hitting several tiles as his momentum rolled his body off the angled roof.

A pained cry from above, grew distant with Norman in free-fall. It was soon drowned out as the sound of a mob swarmed him.

THIRTY-ONE

It was early morning and Breagal was bent at the waist, looking in the cupboard below the sink when she entered.

"Don't tell me it's blocked again," she said.

He pulled his head beneath the boxes of washing up powder, bottled polish cleaner and window wipers and looked at his wife.

"Have you seen any of these?" he said, and pulled from his back pocket a clear plastic prescription bottle of blue pills.

He rattled them in his hand before handing it to her.

"Isn't that what…"

"Yes. That's all I can find. I'm sure we had more somewhere."

He turned back and searched the cupboard again pulling out containers and tubs onto the floor. When they were gathered in one place, he looked down, sifted through the pile and shook his head.

"What would you be needing that for?"

"Please. Margaret. I'm not in the mood," he said, his voice low.

"Is it for that man?"

"What man?"

"The one that comes over here, the one you spend nights in your study with. Don't think I don't notice, Stephen. If you're doing something behind my back…"

"Jesus, Margaret. Don't be paranoid," Breagal said.

"That's what you said last time with your brother."

She threw the plastic bottle onto the floor where they landed on a set of brightly coloured dishcloths between his feet, jangling like a set of keys.

"Suit yourself," she said and stormed off.

"Margaret. I... Margaret!" he shouted and heard her slam the door of their bedroom.

Breagal was about to rise and follow her into the room, but experience taught him that things were better left to cool when his wife was angry. He threw the objects back into the cupboard until all that remained on the floor was some washing powder which must have spilled from a bag, and the lonely tub of pills.

He punched the cupboard door closed then, picking up the tub, got to his feet and walked the hallway to his office at the front of the building.

When he entered, he locked the door behind and made his way to a little wooden workstation in the corner of the room.

Popping the bottle top, he freed the remaining blue capsules from their plastic prison and spilled them on the table surface.

From a pulled drawer from the wooden bench he drew rubber gloves, snapped them on and pulled the fingered pockets down until it felt like a second skin. He retrieved the instruments from a larger drawer by his shins, and set them carefully on the table away from the flat bed of pills.

The main equipment was a micro lab burner, which was portable and ran on butane fuel. The device which looked like a kettle, had a lever on either side, one for igniting the silver grill in its centre which sprouted like the stamen of a flower, and the other lever to adjust the temperature. Breagal's use of it in recent years had only extended to making coffee which it was more than capable of doing with temperatures that could reach 2200°F.

Shaking the contents of the burner, Breagal could tell that the fuel had long since evaporated or congealed to a paste, so he removed the silver centrepiece which had a small refill valve in the chamber of the pot. As luck would have it, he still had a little tin drum of butane. Its weight suggested enough for at least a few more sessions so he unscrewed its top and fed the liquid into the device.

When he had assembled everything on the lab burner again, he clicked the lever switch and ignited the fuel, the flame long and yellow which he adjusted until it was blue and short.

Breagal looked at the front window which was curtained. Beneath it the double glazed window had been installed over a month before, but the hinge for its top frame to open had been stuck, refusing to budge. He walked over to it now and tried again, hoping that there would be some vent for his chemistry experiment. It opened with great difficulty, but it opened which made him smile.

He returned to the workstation and, taking each pill, the librarian popped the capsules in turn and deposited the contents into a metal beaker, which sat atop a tripod. When the little powder hill was complete, he stored the shells safely to one side.

Making sure the beaker sat centre of the tripod on its heat gauze mat, Breagal moved the tripod carefully across until the beaker was directly above the flame. He observed from overhead as the powder slowly began to melt, the first bubbles forming on the surface. He waited patiently before deciding to take the chair from his little writing bureau.

A modest bookshelf was bracketed against the sidewall above the desk and he walked over to it and traced his thumb across the various chemistry titles. Sandwiched between two encyclopaedias he pulled out the leather journal and sat at the bureau.

There were a number of coloured post-it stamps peeping out from inside, serving as an easy to find reference for specific passages of interest. Thumbing halfway through he opened it on one of the stamped pages, the heading at the top emboldening the dream entry as 'Secret Toy'. There was a short description scribbled below it.

Can't seem to shake off this dream. Strange that I always end up in the same place and the story continues. Must have spent six hours walking around, searching abandoned homes for scraps of food. No fun. On a brighter note, I managed to find a little toy pirate! Hid it from Yenjin. It'll be our little secret.

Flicking the pages of the diary forward to the entries added by Norman, he read the final post again.

'...bio-military experiment gone wrong... affecting me emotionally ten hours later'.

Breagal closed his eyes for a moment, feeling the semblance of a headache pulse behind his temple. Breathing gently, he could hear the flame of the lab burner in the corner as it continued to liquefy the molten contents of the drug, a faint smell floating its way through the room. When he opened his eyes he looked down at the book on his lap and his finger was pointed to a word.

He was pensive for a moment and tossed the word around in his mind until a thought struck that made him catch his breath and sit up suddenly in the seat.

"Ludicrous!" he said out loud and dismissed it, slapping the book closed in spite of its delicate spine.

He walked away from his desk, bewildered by the idea and returned the book to its resting place on the shelf. His smile wavered, uncertain and the first strobes of a headache started to pulse. Rising quickly had made his thoughts swirl. Rubbing the sides of his temple seemed to iron out the tension although the initial thought that troubled him seemed to worm its way deeper until he gave it speech.

"Namastre."

Vocalising the word seemed to give it power, energising Breagal who was pacing up and down the room. He was only brought back from his feverish excitement by the sharp sulphuric smell emanating from the metal beaker. He rushed to it, pinching his nostrils and quickly turned off the flame. Removing the burner, he took a pair of metal tongs from the drawer. Picking up the beaker he swirled the hot solution around carefully. It was a crystal clear pure liquid and pleased with his efforts, Breagal allowed himself to smile.

His mood had brightened considerably.

"Namastre."

THIRTY-TWO

The first thing he noticed was the headache. The second was the searing heat. Third came the bright light. Rolling away from it gave a little respite but now he felt a prang in his side. Shifting a little he couldn't quite get comfortable, wondering what kind of bed this was. Suddenly he felt himself lifted into the air and propped on two unsteady legs, of which he was uncertain who had ownership. A large face filled his field of vision. The swollen pink lips and face that looked like candle wax was almost comical. The lips jabbered but there was no sound. The man lifted him and threw him onto a broad shoulder, speeding away from the scene. The gallop was painful on his slight frame, not least because the man had a vice grip around his waist.

Wincing away the pain he looked back at where they had fled, surprised to see a house in flames. It was now beginning to crumble in on itself. A crowd of excited gatherers closed around the fire, making a circle. Many of them came running out of the burning building and quickly formed a perimeter, backs turned to the fleeing pair. After a few moments of observation, his jerking head stilled on the man's big shoulder and he fell into a sleep.

***

"Norman, can you hear me?"

He awoke and looked up at the man who, in the dim light, was watching him sleep. Pain coursed through his body as he stretched out, feeling it in his sides and at the back of his head.

"What happened?"

He tried to get up onto a sore elbow but was quickly ushered back down. From his position he looked around at their surroundings, covered on all four sides by bare grey walls. From the open doorway he could see it was still dark outside.

"Thank God you're alright!" Yenjin answered, dabbing his brow with a hand.

He suddenly cocked his ear towards the doorway and stopped mid breath, summoning Norman to do likewise. After twenty seconds, he continued in a silent hushed tone.

"I thought you were a goner. I saw you fall from the rooftop and a bush broke your fall. You were damn lucky not once, but twice," Yenjin said and smiled, shaking his head in disbelief. "The side you fell on didn't have any of those troopers around. I think they all rushed into the entrance. A fall like that would normally kill a person."

Norman considered this for a moment, and moved a palm gently to the back of his head. There was a swollen bump, but there didn't appear to be a cut.

"Concussion I reckon is the worst you have," Yenjin said. "In any case, we can't stay here too long."

"Where are we?"

"I ran a few kilometres with you on my back away from the house. I needed to take shelter to see if you were OK."

Norman remembered the last image of his friend in the burning building, his body hung from the opening slowly being burnt alive.

"My God Yenjin! Are you OK? How did you get out?"

Yenjin knelt down beside him and gave a playful knock on his shoulder.

"I guess we are both made of the same heroic stuff, lad!" he said and smiled. "When I saw you fall, I figured you were almost certain to be dead. I thought I was a goner either way, whether I stayed in the loft or fell from that rooftop. I decided I might as well get on the rooftop to see if you had somehow managed to survive. As luck would have it, it took my weight, and seeing you in a bramble bush, I managed to clamber down a side somehow. Not without consequence mind you."

He raised his hands in the air, and Norman saw that the skin had peeled back, pink and raw. The heat almost seemed to emanate from them and some of the fingers were charred ugly and black.

"Live to fight another day though!" Yenjin said.

"My God," Norman said and reached for his hand before the man waved him back down.

Norman lay back down and dug the heels of his hands into his eyes, trying to rouse him from the overwhelming tiredness.

"What about Skye?"

Yenjin made a weak smile and looked away. He shook his head and couldn't find the words. Norman reached over and rubbed a powerful shoulder, the man's weight rocking side to side.

"The siren," Norman said to change topic.

"Yes," Yenjin replied, finding the strength again to look up. "Hasn't stopped once."

"Which means they're still out there looking?"

Suddenly, a sound of shuffling outside drew their attention. Yenjin shifted into a squat position and his open palm outstretched to Norman, pinning him to the floor. The footsteps seemed to hover a moment at the corner of their building before picking up speed and heading away.

"The house really caught fire," Yenjin whispered. "Every one of those things is headed for it. Talk about a diversion. Little Skye must have knocked over the candle on the floor below. Won't be long before they notice we aren't there."

"What do we do?"

"We need to find shelter and food until those things go back to wherever they came from. Come on. You OK to walk?"

Norman stood and leaned against a wall for support. It took a moment before his eyes adjusted to the darkness. He nodded that he was capable of walking and with that, Yenjin moved to the doorway and peeped his head out, before firing back a thumbs-up sign.

"We need to move quickly and quietly."

"Where are we going?"

"To the merchant's."

THIRTY-THREE

The skin looked taut and waxy under the fluorescent light, stretching over a gaunt, hollow face. An oxygen mask was still fastened tight, pumping gallons of air into the emaciated frame of Norman Adams. They stood captivated by each flush of breath filling the lungs of the stricken patient, wondering if it would be his last. Seated by his side were Norman's parents; Noreen still wearing the same clothes from the previous night, Frank unshaven with eyes bleary and bloodshot.

Frank glanced at his wife. Her eyes shone and a flicker of a smile, a nostalgic memory perhaps floated on her face for a moment as she watched her son. Frank squeezed her hand and the sad smile quivered for a moment, as if uncertain whether to stay. Blinking it away, she caressed her husband's hand.

Noreen looked up and noticed the standing visitors hovering in the aperture of the screened curtain. She waved them in and they took their place in the remaining two seats.

Victor introduced Breagal, who shook hands with the parents.

"What's the latest?" he asked.

"He's had a high fever throughout the night," Frank said. "Temperature of 41 degrees. It broke this morning and he's back within the safe zone again."

"Any idea what caused it?" Victor asked.

"They don't know," he said, shaking his head and looking at his wife. "They said it might be the body's way of reacting to his brain activity. Problem is, they don't have the full scope of what's going on in there. Tawia said there are still some channels that are blocked. Whatever the hell that means."

They all sat in silence watching the body's chest rise and expand before dropping, all in the steady metronomic beat of the heart monitor.

"But that's a good sign, right?" Victor said. "His body battled a fever which shows some sort of progress."

"You'd think so. Some of these doctors don't know their arse from their elbow, if you ask me, Victor. You'd think a month on and they'd at least be able to give us something to go on."

"So what do the doctors say is the next best course of action?" Breagal asked, clearing his throat.

Frank Adams suddenly grew quiet, looking down to his feet. Both men looked away from him and toward the face of his wife. Her eyes remained focused on Norman who was sleeping peacefully, and she moved a tousled band of hair from his forehead, which was mopped with sweat. She had found that memory again all of a sudden and it played wistfully on her face. Her response was calm.

"Turn off the machine."

***

Victor left the room, exiting through the building's double doors and found himself in the hospital car park. Finding a quiet corner to face, he leaned against it and hid his head in his hands. A sudden arm around his shoulder curled his wet face into the bulky frame of Frank Adams.

"You've been good to him," the older man said as Victor tried to control his outpouring of grief. "He looked up to you."

This brought more convulsions from the young man, emptying the last reserves of tears that had been untapped for years. After a few minutes they unhooked their hug and Frank fetched a fresh pack of tissues from a pocket and passed it to him.

"Are you OK?"

"I will be," Victor replied, his smile weak.

"Good lad. Now let's go back in. They'll be wondering where we've gone."

***

When the two men re-entered the ward, Breagal was alone at the bedside of the patient, standing over him. His face had clouded but broke with their return.

"Mrs Adams has just gone to get a coffee."

"Sounds like a good idea. I'll go join her," Frank said. "Keep an eye on my boy."

The two guests nodded and Victor walked over to stand beside the librarian whose face had drained of colour as it turned to face him. Breagal nodded in the direction of the side of the bed. Confused, his accomplice looked at the white sheet and almost missed the two small red stains that had soaked through the sheet.

"What are they?" he asked Breagal, who without warning pulled the sheet off the patient's hand.

Victor felt his stomach lurch. Norman's hand was swollen into a bloody pulp. It was balled into a fist, but noticeable was a curved line of deep puncture wounds dotted across the back of the hand, several layers of flesh broken through with jagged precision. The fingers had been sliced around the base and at some junctures skin had been stripped. It was a bloated, blood soaked mess. Victor recoiled in shock, replacing the sheet over the stump and stepping back from the bed.

"It only just happened," Breagal said. "When you were gone. I saw his hand twitching and moved the sheet."

"We need to tell the doctor," Victor said and was moving toward the entrance when Breagal stopped him.

"Calm down. We will."

"Who the hell did this?"

"Not who, but what?" Breagal answered. "I had hoped that our friend's narrative hadn't reached this point, but alas indications suggest we need to act fast."

"Damn right we do!" Victor replied. "How much time do we have?"

Breagal shook his head, stroking his chin as if in contemplative thought before deriving a satisfactory answer from his mind.

"Well, now we have a clear indicator of the peril Norman is in. In fact, given recent news about the possibility of turning off the life support, the battle to save our friend will need to be fought on both planes in earnest – the conscious and the subconscious."

"How do you know all this? How can you know that from looking at a hand?"

"I'll answer those questions later, but we need to get started post haste."

"When?"

"Tonight."

THIRTY-FOUR

The two men shared a cubicle in the gent's toilets, the younger of which was sitting with his arm sleeve rolled up above his elbow. A belt was wrapped around his upper arm, and he made a fist at the end and tapped the veins on his arm. He reached around and dabbed away the sweat with a tissue from his free hand. The older man was standing close above him holding a vial in one hand and a syringe in the other. Holding the vial up to the light, a pale opaque liquid was captured, a tint of blue colour against the cream backdrop of the cubicle door.

"Tell me again that it's safe," Victor asked.

Breagal took his stare away from the vessel and looked down at the seated man and sighed.

"Listen Victor. I will tell you again what I told you earlier. I truly believe that time is against us. I also believe that the tangent that Norman is currently on, that same tangent my brother followed, will lead him to the same fate as my brother."

Victor continued to stare up at the man absorbing every word of the librarian, who seemed to grow in stature with every moment.

"Great peril awaits him and, in all likelihood, total abandonment of his conscious mind. Profanol works."

"Is there no way around this? I don't see why we need to bring drugs into the mix."

"Pfft," Breagal said. "It's not drugs. It's medication. There's a difference. Besides, only Profanol can help you stay longer in the dream state."

"What does Mrs Breagal think about all this?" Victor asked to buy more time. "She can't be too happy."

The librarian paused and took a moment to consider. The smile that followed wasn't convincing.

"She doesn't know. Nor does Margaret need to know. I want to keep her out of this. She had enough stress when I went through this with Saul."

"So what do you tell her we do?"

"Same thing I told Moira. That I'm helping you with your project. Now come on," Breagal said. "You're stalling."

He shook the little vial in his hand, before carefully unscrewing the little metal top. Victor shook his head and looked away, watching the hungry veins of his arm raise to the surface of his skin.

"But, syringes?" he complained. "There has to be another way."

"The safest and quickest way we have of doing this is intravenously," Breagal replied. "Remember, speed is of the essence here, so we need to inject the purest form of Profanol into our basilica veins."

To illustrate Breagal unbuttoned his own shirtsleeve, tensing his hand several times and pointed to a raised vein that emerged from the belly of his forearm. Taking the vial and inserting the syringe, he drew a measure of the liquid. Holding it upwards he clicked the side of the syringe and squirted a tiny amount out, before planting it into the vein. Victor winced but not before he saw the syringe empty its contents.

"Nothing to it," the librarian said and smiled as he began to roll the sleeve back down his arm, buttoning it at the wrist.

"How do you know where to…?"

"Inject? Easy. My brother was on a cocktail of medication to control various ailments. Some of these drugs were intravenous, some oral and some of them were rectally administered."

"I'm fond of you but not that fond of you, Breagal," Victor said.

The sound of the bathroom door swinging open and footsteps entering made them stop their conversation. The person walked past their cubicle to one of the urinals along the side of the room. Still standing, Breagal looked down at Victor who was squirming on the seat, clearly struggling with the idea.

"Can Dr Marshall please come to surgery. Dr Marshall to surgery."

They heard the man curse as he zipped up, walking back past the cubicle door and out of the bathroom again.

"OK," Victor said. "Do it."

Breagal took a second syringe out of a briefcase that was hanging on a hook on the door, and quickly drew a measure of the liquid. Holding Victor's trembling arm in his own, he plunged the needle deep into his vein, the Profanol gushing into the bloodstream of the man who was looking away.

"All done."

Victor looked up, and then to his arm where a small spot of blood had grown from the puncture. He dabbed it with the tissue and smiled wanly at the librarian.

"Now what?" he asked and started to roll down his sleeve.

"Now we wait. Do you have the keystone locked in your mind's eye?"

"Yes," Victor said.

"Describe it to me."

"Pirate figurine. Cutlass, parrot blue and green. Eye patch. Gold medallion."

"Right. Keep it there. Listen to my voice. Tune into the dream. Exactly as before. We'll be under for a longer time, so be careful and save your energy. We won't have the comfort of my lounge to relax. We will be by your friend's side all the time. We can't afford to leave him alone again."

THIRTY-FIVE

They snaked their way around desolate houses along the main dirt road at a careful and steady pace to avoid detection. The cool night sky brought welcome relief, soothing his brow but highlighted the contrasting pain in his burnt palms and the flaked skin on his lower leg that had dried with the mud.

"It's been about twenty minutes already," Norman whispered.

Yenjin seemed not to hear him, the sound of the siren dominating the noise around. The big man paused, and signalled for the younger man to remain a few paces behind, then slid along the wall of the building. Norman stared down at his feet again, stepping on the heel of one of the boots and wincing. Despite his efforts, the wiggling foot still remained locked under the mud crust, sores opening up around the ankles where the lips of the boot had chafed. He turned to Yenjin who was at the corner of the building, head pulled flush to the wall and peeping out. He signalled to Norman, pointing a thick finger to a step behind him.

"Almost there," Yenjin said when Norman had closed the distance.

Guided by a starry and moonlit night, they entered into a crouch run until reaching a stone rock wall. There they slid their bodies low and hid within the stone bunker. Yenjin looked over the low wall and up the hilltop where they had scaled earlier. His eyes scanned the landscape, looking for the next obstacle on the route which they could hide under. He shook his head and rested on his elbow.

"We need to move fast. We're in full view after this point," Yenjin said. "Are you able to run?"

Norman nodded.

"Good."

Yenjin rolled onto his chest and pulled himself onto one knee.

"You still haven't answered me why we're going to the merchant's."

Yenjin stopped, considered the question and rested his hands on his knee. His big shoulders were sloped over eclipsing the moon behind.

"He turned us away last time," Norman said.

Yenjin pulled a loose rock from the wall, rolled it towards Norman and pointed for him to sit.

"Listen lad, that place is the only place we've seen so far that has food, and security. That is something worth fighting for."

"But, he isn't going to give it up without a fight."

"If I was him, I wouldn't give it up either. Listen," Yenjin said. "We aren't looking to take it from him. All we're looking for is to find shelter and, with any luck, a meal for the night. I think any God fearing citizen can understand that. We just need to make him understand. Besides, there might be…"

"Yenjin?"

The man's mouth had suddenly dropped open, and his head was turned. Norman could see the little beads for eyes searching underneath the folds of compacted skin, stretched around his face. His head flicked to the other side as if trying to pick up a scent, and he pivoted on his knee and looked back in the direction they had come.

"Skye!"

Norman turned to look and saw, several buildings away, a small white shadow framed against the darkness, limping along the dirt road. He also heard the wounded cry now, punctuating the siren's high pitch.

"She's OK, Yenjin!"

Norman smiled and stood, slapping the crouched man on his shoulder who remained frozen in his position. He stepped out from the bunkered wall, but was yanked back by Yenjin who sprung to action and began pulling him in the opposite direction.

Norman looked from the man, his face a mask of horror and back to the animal. Skye had now noticed them and had begun to speed up despite the injured leg which hampered her movements. She seemed to kick up a dirty cloud until Norman's eyes narrowed in the dark and realised that the cloud was a movement further down the path.

"My God. Is that?"

His vision sharpened suddenly when the sound of their voices travelled to his tuned ear.

"She's leading them right to us!"

THIRTY-SIX

They leapt over the rock wall and fled from the crying dog and its pursuers. Norman's pace at first was initially leg weary, but he soon found giant strides to match the sprinting Yenjin who had already reached the base of the hill. As they ascended they heard fresh cries of delight from the closing pack, but neither runner dared look back. The noises grew more urgent in the cold night as the black structure loomed into view.

Yenjin got there first, teeming blows on the door with his bloodied fists, pummelling it with all of his strength. Norman arrived, panting and joined the man at the door, looked at its hard surface where no dent had been made. Desperate, his eyes scanned the ground around, searching for a weapon or instrument. Yenjin shoulder charged the door, imploring the merchant to open but there was no response on the other side.

Norman felt the cries getting closer, and turned. The white shadow was still in pursuit just adrift of the group whose faces he could make out, full of anger and spite, snarling at the prospect ahead. The single line they had paved was now a wall, each man picking up their scent and splintering off from the group, eager to reach them ahead of the pack. They sprinted with no sign of fatigue, closing the gap, heads narrowed upward and climbing fast. It would be only a minute before they were on them.

"What do we do?"

The man's head was leaning against the door, eyes closed and he shook it softly.

"Yenjin!"

He looked to Norman then toward the mob in pursuit.

"The forest!" Yenjin said and heaved himself off the door face. "It's our only hope that we can lose them there."

They bounded around the building and from there could see half a kilometre ahead to the edges of a forest, a blackness hidden under its shade, darker than the night sky. Norman managed to pick up speed on this even plain and not only caught Yenjin but also overtook him. Passing, Norman looked into his face. Gone was the sense of urgency, a look of despondency replacing it. The man was crying and his strides were becoming choppier, not the elegant sprint from earlier in the day. He was nursing an arm close to his chest and blinking back the pain and tears.

"Come on, Yenjin! We can still make this!" he shouted above the din that chased. "Skye can still make this!"

With the mention of his pet, the large man suddenly found an extra gear and changed his stride pattern, moving alongside Norman now. Yenjin called back over his shoulder to the white shadow and told her to follow. This seemed to give confidence to the dog because after a few metres it had caught up with the two leaders, which gave real impetus to their run. The hooded cloak of the forest reared up at them only fifty metres away. They could still hear the chasing pack cursing and snarling, keeping pace. Their reserves seemed limitless, whereas Norman and Yenjin were flagging badly.

As they entered under the forest roof one of the troops suddenly appeared on the path in front. Without breaking stride, Yenjin powered directly ahead and met the troop in a ferocious hit that sent him against the base of a tree. Blows rained down on the face of the soldier from the bloodied fists of the hulking Yenjin, each one with such venom it threatened to tear the head from its neck. It was pummelled into submission within seconds and sloped against the tree, lifeless, sprawled in a heap. Yenjin, chest breathing heavy got up quickly and continued running, the noises of the others reverberating around them, the acoustics of the thick forest canopy echoing the voices.

"Don't look back!" Yenjin shouted as he began catching Norman, who had stopped running.

"How did you do-?"

"Look out!" Yenjin screamed too late.

A soldier had cut in from the side again through the mass of trees within arm's reach of Norman. Yenjin saw it stretch out for him, but the dense forest had clotted the path in front, tripping up Norman and sending the trooper sprawling over his body. The soldier was just making it to his feet when Yenjin sprang at him, sending them both cartwheeling down a small hill. Norman watched the shapes tumbling through the under grove out of sight, and then heard a gut wrenching cry. Sensing the pack almost on him, his eyes spotted a hollow log; he ran to it and crept in out of sight.

Shortly after, he heard the remaining pack of troops run past, leaping over the log, some of the heavy boots slapping the hollow bark, propelling them further into the heart of the forest. The hits vibrated the structure and Norman curled into a ball, cupping his hands over his ears. The distant sound of a dog barking managed to pierce through his locked fingers and he scrunched his eyes tight to try and shut all his senses.

Minutes that felt like hours passed, before he noticed the siren had stopped. He lay frozen, listening to the sounds of the forest and heard them return, heavy boots marching in file again, increasing in volume. Norman felt his breath quicken and crept deeper within the log. The wet interior was slick under his feet and he crawled on his belly along the hollow towards a closed end, fearing what was hidden in the darkness there. His hands found wet lichen and leaves as they groped ahead as the sound of footsteps increased, dampened by his hollow base. Turning around and onto his back, he looked down at the opening, between his feet, looking for a sign of moment in the circular window.

Crunching steps beside his log almost made him jump, and he watched, hand gripped to his mouth as legs walked past.

He listened as they made their way back up through the grove and back out the way they came. Finally, when they were out of earshot Norman slowly opened his body, like some animal in deep hibernation. He crawled out from the log and immediately detected a cooler chill in the air.

As he looked up at the night sky he was awestruck by how beautiful it was. The visibility was so clear he could see interlinking webs of starry constellations suddenly making him feel very tiny and alone inside the dense forest. A few flakes of snow began to drop down from up on high, which sent a shiver through him as he bunched his hands deep inside his pockets for warmth. He moved downhill but with some trepidation, careful not to trip over the wild terrain.

"Yenjin? Yenjin?" he whispered without receiving a response.

Continuing the descent, the path became steeper, making footing treacherous. For support Norman grasped several rooted plants that held firm, looking for signs of his friend although the visibility was weak. A few metres to his right he thought he detected a soft muffled groaning sound. Not quite human, it was definitely an animal of some kind, possibly wounded.

Norman's pulse raced as he traced the sound carefully and it took him to a levelled out clearing. Approaching, he noticed a partially visible body behind a boulder, legs parted with torso hidden from view. The feet wore black military style boots. Running now with abandoned safety across the clearing, Norman rounded the boulder. He couldn't contain his smile as he saw the figures of Yenjin and Skye lying beside the dead troop. The sound was emanating from the dog, pawing at the ground in front at her owner's side. Yenjin's gaze meanwhile was away and off to the side. The smile dropped from Norman's face in an instant when he saw his friend's leg. The foot was twisted grotesquely backwards, pointing in the opposite direction and hanging limp at an unnatural angle.

Yenjin, sensing the other man was near, rolled his head in his direction. Flakes of snow started to fall onto the face of the man whose gaze met Norman's. The intensity and fire was gone and had cooled, somewhat distant but peaceful. His hulking frame looked hollowed out somehow and, trying to look away from the obvious injury, Norman could tell that his physical reserves had been spent. The big man still managed a smile and gestured for the man to join him on the floor.

As Norman moved across, he sat down and leaned up against Yenjin, resting his head on his thick barrel chest which was trembling. The big man hugged him closer, with Skye finding a pocket between them to curl up close. The boulder deflected much of the snowfall as it started to become heavier, but the flakes that managed to slip through were still shielded by the giant as Norman nestled in his big arms and cried throughout the night.

THIRTY-SEVEN

As he opened his eyes the first shards of light were poking through the canopy of trees, casting a soothing beam on them from above that warmed their chilled skin. Despite the body heat from Yenjin, Norman was shaking with the sub-zero temperatures, teeth chattering and finding it difficult to move his limbs. The gentle drops of snow gave an almost eerie quality to the scene and all around them the forest was blanketed in white.

His head was still propped on the chest of his companion, who was sighing deeply in his slumber, a cool breath of cloud shooting from his mouth. Looking up at him, Norman could see that the snow had collected on his head and the face was washed clean with freshly melted snowdrops. Snuggled between them lay the small shivering body of Skye, sleep twitching in the cold as Norman began to peel himself from the body of Yenjin. The snow seemed to have grown stronger during the night, but where they slept there was a little cover owing to a fortuitous resting point between the boulder and rooftop of sheltered trees.

Slowly getting to his feet, Norman moved to the snow mound a few feet away. The snow had blanketed the body of the soldier during the night and even though he was sure he was dead, he still approached with caution. Using the bloody rag still in his pocket, he cleared the snow off its face and looked down at the deceased. The lower jaw had been ripped off the skull and Norman observed the layer of upper teeth had all become sharp like razors. Brushing the chest of the man, he could see a small badge pinned to the lapel and reading it, opened his mouth in horror.

"Krollson," he mouthed.

Crawling back, he scooped snow over the exposed features. When the body had been covered again, he stood and surveyed the area, noting the descent from last night which had been tricky. The path back upwards now seemed precarious with the slickened white snow bedding. In the opposite direction however, his spirits sank, the gradient sharply rose creating an almost vertical white wall in front. The trees were scattered haphazardly, no obvious direct path evident and he couldn't tell how tall the climb was as the snow-covered branches betrayed any sense of distance. The snow continued to fall from above, and he closed his eyes momentarily, noticing for the first time the sounds of forest animals around him waking in the morning dawn. One sounded near, and barked. It was Skye.

Walking over to where they had slept, Norman noticed that Yenjin was now stirring from his sleep. The dog continued to bark until the big man slowly stretched out a hand to scratch behind its ear, which immediately silenced it. As Norman approached, they looked at each other before Yenjin pulled his stare away, almost submissively. Between them, they both looked down at the foot which was half covered in snow. The boot was buried but the toe was bent upward revealing the sickening angle of the break.

"I think we can make a sled," Norman began; his voice sounded imploring. "The road ahead looks difficult to climb but I reckon that if we use some of the drier wood from over there, I can pull you to the surface again."

Yenjin looked into the distance at the impenetrable white wall ahead, but his attention seemed to be elsewhere. His movements were slow and careful as he propped his body up into a sitting position, wincing with the pain.

"Or, I could scale it myself and then come back with help. Either way Yenjin, we can't give up," Norman said, reaching down and patting the man's slumped shoulder, dislodging more snow.

The only audience he had was the dog who was staring up now, away from its master. Yenjin's gaze was still fixed on a point far ahead, and a rueful smile came to his lips which worried Norman. The head dropped onto its chest and he shook it slowly. When he looked back up to the standing man, there were tears in Yenjin's eyes which he dabbed clean with a bloodied finger.

"God bless you, Norman," he said, smiling sweetly at the terrified man. "But we both know this is the end of the journey for me."

Norman's heart sank and, approaching his friend, he started to implore that all was not lost, but couldn't find the words, as Yenjin brought him close and hugged him warmly. He felt the man's sure fast grip weaker than before, and the trembling in his body frightened him. They both began crying and the tears brought with it a sudden outpouring of love that strengthened Norman's resolve.

"There is nothing for you back the way we came. You need to go further into the forest. There has to be something or someone for you there. Keep going and don't come back," Yenjin spoke, his voice sounding stretched as if the effort hurt.

"I'm coming back for you!" Norman declared, breaking free from the clinch.

The injured man smiled, and nodded his head, unable to speak with emotion tightening his throat. The lids of his eyes seemed to droop as if suggesting sleep was closing in. Skye watched the interaction between the two, wagging its tail in excitement at seeing its master awaken.

Yenjin motioned to the dog now, looking up at Norman.

"Take Skye with you."

Starting to protest, Yenjin cut across him.

"Please. You can bring her back when you have found help. Besides, she might come in useful."

Norman could see that his friend didn't want to be argued with. The energy seemed to be seeping out of his body with the conversation alone.

"OK," he said. "But hold on. I'm coming back soon."

Yenjin nodded slowly, smiling that the request had been accepted and he eased tired limbs back against the hard surface of the boulder, letting out a long sigh, eyes closing. Norman picked up the excited dog, and started to turn toward the steep incline. Before doing so, he turned back to see his injured friend, his lower half covered in a snow sleeping bag with the heavier fall. Norman paused and could feel Skye wriggling in his hands. It began to whine and its nose was pointed in the direction they faced.

"Goodbye Yenjin," he whispered, before turning and entering deeper into the white forest beyond.

***

There seemed to be no end to the climb, and using a hand to grab at slippery branches only helped to cut through Norman's tender palms as he made steady but slow progress. From his current viewpoint, Yenjin was now out of sight. The task was becoming increasingly difficult given the live bundle that he was carrying. The dog began to squirm like a new-born in a stranger's arms.

"Stop that Skye," Norman said. "Would you ever just sit still?"

Stopping to catch a breath for a moment and get a better grip of the dog, his attention was suddenly drawn to a noise ahead. It sounded like a lump of snow falling from the trees and crashing to the ground. Stillness in the air made his heart race, and he felt like he was being watched. Hiding behind a nearby tree, he peered up through the cracks in the roof canopy for the source of the disturbance. After adjusting his eyes to a glowing sun through the clouds he could make out a shape in the trees. He watched as the shadow jumped from tree branch to branch.

"Do you see it?"

The dog had also heard the noise from above them and had stopped fumbling to cast his keen eyes upward.

They waited for a few minutes before Skye lost interest and started squirming again. Her action compelled Norman to drop the pursuit of the shadow in the trees and continue their climb. With the advancing sun clearing a path, he looked up and noticed that they were near the top of the climb. Beyond he could see thin patches of the blue sky scratched against the dense snow clouds.

"Nearly there, girl," Norman said, patting the coat of the dog which was still a dirty grey colour from the ash.

Smiling, he found another gear and continued upward carefully. The snow was still falling in great clumps, but with the sun's glow, the crunch under his feet on the track became less pronounced. Suddenly, his foot caught a melted slick spot on a rock surface and Norman felt his body slip down. With one hand, he tried to protect his fall, but the other grip dropped from Skye who, seizing her chance, leapt from his arms. Norman hit the ground hard on his side and, turning around to grope for the dog, he grabbed a fistful of her fur coat.

"No. Skye!"

The dog instinctively turned around and sank its teeth deep into Norman's hand sending waves of pain up his arm and through his body. Its bite punctured the skin around his fingers hard and he let out an anguished cry, feeling the jaw lock down tight. The agony almost caused him to pass out, before he felt his hand released, the cold air stabbing at it from all angles.

Looking down, he could see the bloodied smeared mess of what was his hand. The fingers were still intact, but the wounds were deep and pooling with blood. The sight made him dizzy, and blood dripped freely onto the snow below. In the distance through the falling snow, he could see the figure of the little dog running off down the slope. He shovelled the ice around him onto the injured hand, the coldness of it stung, and he dared not move the fingers for fear that there was any lasting damage.

Sitting there cursing his luck, Norman waited while a pool of icy blood slowly bled away from the spot where his hand was planted.

THIRTY-EIGHT

"Well would you look at that," Noreen Adams said to her husband.

They both looked at the two sleeping men slumped in their seats.

"Well, I'll be," Frank replied; his face almost allowing a smile to surface. "They just arrived, didn't they?"

"Yes. Let them sleep. They look so comfortable there. Besides it's late. Might be a good idea if we catch some ourselves."

She smiled at her husband who reached for her hand. He rubbed it, feeling the smoothness of her palms against the coarse grain of his own. It felt like soap and he raised her fingers to his lips, kissed them before looking her in the eye.

"Who knows what tomorrow will bring?"

***

I'm waiting for the bus to arrive. I'm already running ten minutes late for work. I curse the timetable and begin to run to the next bus stop. I begin to wish that I could see above the traffic and I'm amazed to find that one of my footfalls is stuck in the air! For a second it confuses me. I stop suddenly and repeat my wish to see above the traffic. I feel a breeze lift me and I find it difficult at first to check my balance. I'm swimming in the air! With some gentle paddles I ascend until I am high above and can see far across the city with the lines of cars clogging the highways.

Delirious with excitement I descend slowly to the gasps of a gathering crowd below. They all ask how I managed to levitate, and whether I can teach them. My mind swirls with the

opportunities presented. I could cash in on this. Write a book. Become a millionaire. 'The Secrets to Flight' by Victor James. Heck, I could even fly to the moon! The crowd parts and a young boy approaches and presents me with a small figurine pirate.
"Can you sign this Mister?"

The sudden realization brings a flooding rush of emotions to the surface, mainly exhilaration. The city landscape disappears and I find myself standing in an empty white, walled room. A small figurine is standing in front toppled over on one side. I close my eyes and practice the breathing exercises taught by Breagal. After what feels like a few minutes, I can hear a voice in the distance.
"Lock onto my voice."
It's difficult to find what direction it comes from. The room itself seems small without openings. The voice rebounds around in my head feeling at times distant, and at others like the speaker is standing right beside me. Opening my eyes momentarily I am surprised to see the room has changed dimension. Blotches of colours can be seen smearing the sides, if it can be said to have sides, for its shape is difficult to understand. The colours swarm and change as I look at them, somehow moving and growing in scope. Again the voice sounds in my head, this time to my left. I close my eyes to pin it down in my mind's eye.
"That's right. Lock on. Keep the pirate in your mind. That's right."
I walk in the direction of the voice and it grows in volume, or at least it appears to in my mind.
"Keep walking. Easy breaths. Keep the pirate at the centre of your thoughts."
I continue to walk, breathing deeply, trying to relax, hands in front and careful not to bump the walls of the room but feeling nothing. The intake of breath through my nose smells different, bringing back old memories from my past, the earthy smells of countryside air and cut grass. The smell seems to influence my feet, as now I find them walking

across what feels like a mud track, shoes making a *shlock* sound as I pull them out.

"Almost there," the voice says again in a reassuring tone that further settles my growing nerves of walking in the dark.

Other sensations enter into my consciousness now. A cold breeze flapping at my shirt making my shoulders shudder involuntarily under the chill. Something gently tapping me on the head, but when I reached a hand up to see what it was, it had gone. After it taps me on the nose, I feel the drip of a snowflake melt onto my lip.

"You're here. Open your eyes."

***

Breagal faced Victor and the men stood staring at each other for a moment as the flakes of snow passed between them in the darkness. A faint moon glow helped to give shape to their surroundings, revealing they were alone. They turned together to view the landscape.

They were standing on a flat hilltop that afforded them a view of several kilometres in all directions. Behind them were a series of craggy mountain ranges that seemed to scale gradually before climbing suddenly high into the darkness beyond. The light was dim, but the laying snow helped to shed some visibility on the nearby land. On either side they could see an expanse of terrain with a scattering of trees and with no discernible sign of civilization. In front of them, on the horizon, a number of structures poked through the blanket snow. Even from their elevated viewpoint it was difficult to ascertain what they were, but given the line that snaked between the buildings and around, it looked like it could be a village or some form of civilization.

That fact was confirmed suddenly by Victor, who was the first to spot it, squinting his eyes in the dim light and pointing to a spot at the southern trail of the track.

"Is that a fire?"

THIRTY-NINE

They began running down the hill, Breagal leading and with much greater athleticism than Victor had thought possible for a middle aged librarian. Footing was treacherous but the decline from the hill was relatively smooth and the snow was freshly laid, helping their footfalls find the grip of the terrain below.

The only sound they could hear was the stomping of the snow under their badly equipped shoes. Victor glanced down and then over to Breagal.

"Hey, what gives with the clothes?"

"What?"

"Don't you think we should have come better prepared for a stroll through the winter wonderland? If I'd have known, I'd have worn a coat to the hospital."

Breagal looked back briefly before continuing to charge on. His pace slowed after a little while, the earlier burst of enthusiasm clearly using up his fitness supplies. They walked along now, the older man panting, heavily taxed by the exertion. After a few minutes he managed to find his breath again.

"I wasn't 100% certain which point in the narrative we would insert ourselves."

"But now we do, so can't we just visualise better clothes?" Victor asked.

"Do you remember at the start of your training how you were in control of your lucid dreaming environment and could dictate and change things, even people or your surroundings?"

"Of course. Which is why it makes this so damn weird."

"Well..." Breagal said, "we are in Norman's dream now, so your influence over this environment is purely academic."

"Meaning?"

Breagal shook his head, seemingly annoyed at his student's lack of comprehension.

"We need to get to those buildings," he insisted.

They found a comfortable jogging pace again which suited them both and managed to maintain it for several minutes. Victor found that despite the cold, and the drift of ice snowflakes which melted on his face, he was beginning to warm again with the physical effort. There no longer seemed to be the urgency in the librarians pace and when they slowed to a walk, Victor picked up the conversation again.

"What do you mean that my influence is academic?"

"What I mean is that you need to remember this is Norman's dream," Breagal explained. "You're still you. You can't magic Moira Hart into this landscape, no more than you can fly across the land. It's his world which makes us extremely vulnerable now, even more than the world that we know back at the hospital because at least we can deal with most of the challenges up there."

Breagal swept aside the snow from his shoulder pad and rubbed his hands together, which Victor noticed were gloved.

"Nice gloves."

"Don't worry," Breagal said and noticed the sardonic smile on the younger man's face. "We'll be better prepared next time for the conditions."

Looking upward at the drops of ice drifting down they could see that the stars above were now fading away on the outer edges. The light around them seemed to grow slightly as visibility increased, and Breagal turned, quickening his pace again. They could see the shapes of the buildings ahead, which appeared to be fairly rudimentary and simple in design, mostly one or two storeys separated by a thin trail. Victor looked down at his shoes, which now resembled two shovels gathering up snow with each step. He leaned against a rock wall nearby, kicking the ice blocks that were his feet against it, shedding several layers.

"If I would have known I'd be running I would have brought my trainers," he mumbled. "Any other surprises in store for me, Breagal?"

Victor's shout had reached the ears of Breagal whose back was turned. He smiled and continued walking.

FORTY

The heat from the dog's breath seemed to breathe life on his face. Yenjin felt the rough textured tongue on his face like sandpaper. Opening his eyes and focusing, he saw an excitable Skye and allowed the dog to jump on his chest, forgetting for a moment the pain it caused his foot as his bodyweight shifted on the rocky ground.

"Surprised to see me girl? I'm surprised to see you too."

Yenjin looked around for some sign of Norman. The sun was a copper coin slotted into a cloud above, making a slow arc back to the mountain. The dog now stood on its hindquarters panting before putting her nose to the ground and sniffing a perimeter around his prostrate body.

The air was crisp with his breath forming in the cold. His body heat, combined with the day rays of the sun had managed to melt the snow on his lower body, dripping down through the clothes. The legs splayed on the rough floor were wet and chilled like ice blocks, the offending foot, sharp and pointed at an unnatural angle, which he dared not touch.

With concerted effort and great difficulty, he heaved himself off the rock, teeth gritted under the duress and used the boulder for support. Standing, Yenjin hopped around it to the gradual incline where he had fallen and broken his ankle the night before. He looked back to Skye who was staring at him in anticipation.

"You coming or not?"

***

The swelling had reduced but he could still feel the pain as it pulsed from beneath the ice that was wet with the melted snow and blood. The puddle of crimson had spread out from beneath him, and when he unearthed the hand to assess its condition, he was surprised to see that the damage wasn't as bad as first feared. Tensing it, Norman wiggled each bloody digit and breathed a sigh of relief. Although, the flow of blood had stemmed, it continued to trickle from the bite wounds, unable to congeal on a cold blue hand that he didn't recognise as his own.

The chill was not as fierce as earlier and, managing to rip off half of a shirt sleeve with his good hand, Norman wrapped it around the open bloody palm several times, using his teeth to fasten a knot tightly against the raw flesh. The fresh pain made him lightheaded, and he sat to collect himself. When he had recovered he stood again, and used passing trees for support to catapult him forward until he reached the summit of the incline.

Once there he shielded his eyes from the bright sun and looked ahead. The view was at once breath-taking and heart breaking. As far as he could see, there was a thick rooftop of forest in all directions stretched out far beyond. Their glistening white tops all reflecting a bright sunshine sky that had peeped out from under a sky of clouds as dense as the forest now facing him. Its heat now was of little comfort to Norman, who could see the thick impenetrable rough undergrowth ahead. Far to the left on the horizon there was a grey mountain range. He scanned the vista, searching for a tucked away manmade structure, trail of smoke, movement among the trees – anything that suggested civilisation.

"No. I don't see anything either," he said, and looked at the ground at his feet where he imagined Skye might have been. "Come on. Let's get to higher ground."

***

Norman cursed again, tangling in a vine that hung from the trees like trip wires slowing his progress. He chopped at it with a branch he had found several hours earlier, doubling as a walking stick and machete for the thicker groves he had stumbled through. His passage was made more difficult with ankle sores that chafed on every step. Taking a few moments out from the trek he had parked down on fallen logs to free the caked mud which still managed to wedge itself between skin and shoe.

While in those moments of respite, he batted away flies and other winged insects in the undergrowth, risking their lives for a swallow of the sweat that spilled from his face. They soon tipped off others in the forest until they clouded his vision, offering no choice but for Norman to stand again and stagger onwards. The forest covering had provided a natural roof, which broke in small pockets; the sunlight arrowed down from the tunnel in places shining on holy patches of ground.

Approaching the base of a steep incline, Norman spied a small alcove built into one of the faces of the mountain. Water had streamed into a rock basin and he shuffled over to it and cupped handfuls of it into his mouth before splashing some contents onto his face. Despite the pain, he managed to remove the shoes to access crusted socks which he peeled off before attending to his sores. Carefully, Norman applied water on the cuts and gently bathed them; the searing pain made him bite his lip. Folding up his trouser legs, he exposed his shiny red shins and swollen ankles to the cool air breeze while he washed the socks, dirtying the little pool of water.

Rejuvenated, he looked up at the incline, which appeared steeper the further his eyes climbed. The mountain broke through the roof of the trees and the sky beyond it was grey and clouded. The weak light stretched his own shadow long and Norman stared back at it.

"Just a little bit further."

Lowering his damaged hand into the basin, he let the water soak over his wounds, making him wince, before rinsing the blood from the improvised bandage onto the ground below. He hastily wrapped it, whipped on the wet socks and shoes, and began the ascent.

As Norman broke from under the shelter of the trees, snow drifted onto his face. He made a visor with his palm and shielded his face from the clumps which seemed to hang in the air. Steps which had been firm and sure moments earlier were now planted on a crumbling rock surface; boots meeting slick wet stone.

A swirling wind buffeted him when he cleared the tunnel of trees, slowly picking up pace and clouding his vision as the climb continued. There was a distinct temperature change and he could feel his hand throb against the cold, as if recalling the bite in a stored memory. Looking above, the greys had now darkened, menacing storm clouds botched tightly around the apex of the mountain. Turning back, he could see the blanketed canopy of trees in white; the little hill he had scaled hours earlier further beyond.

He continued ascending, the wind growing in intensity and flapped his clothes against his chest. Darkness seemed to creep up from nowhere and he paused for a beat and looked up the mountain face.

"What am I doing?" he said and, as if in response, the sharp little point of the figurine pressed against the top of his thigh and he patted it and continued.

The higher he climbed, the stronger the storm raged, wind angling snow sideways into his face.

Crawling low along the snowy bed, he pulled on bigger stones for support, wind whistling above. His eyes became slits against the gale and the snow made visibility no greater than a few strides forward.

"Gotta be there soon," he said and continued the half crawl, until he hit a wall of wind.

He dropped to one side, body tucked against the ground and turned away to recover the breath that was stolen from him. Waiting a few moments to gauge the severity of the storm, he decided to return to lower ground. Crouching and supporting himself with hands from underneath, Norman's legs reached out ahead to widen his base and begin the descent. The wind was at his back again, forcing him to take quicker steps which slid off stony faces. From nowhere he felt a push and was lifted forward onto two legs, shooting down the slope.

Suddenly his foot broke through a small fissure in the rock surface, sending Norman tumbling onto the hard rock on a bent knee. A swell of snow struck him from above, wiping the wince from his face. He managed to haul himself up on one leg, and tried to pull the other through the crack but found the boot wedged between the sides of rock opening.

The intense arctic shrill of the air squealed in his ears and sitting down, to get better leverage, tried to free his leg calmly but it refused to budge, each successive pull scraping the sore and swollen skin of his ankle against the craggy rock surface.

He bent over and began fingering the opening where his foot had broken through. The sharp edges were rough and using the other foot, he began hitting the opening to try and widen the gap, but the boot heel was too weak for the purpose.

In desperation, he looked around and was struck in the face with another burst of wind, which swayed his body forward. Norman tried to use the momentum to pull the foot through but the ankle pulled flush against the jagged opening.

The scream of pain was quickly swallowed up by the storm, as he thrashed about on the rock bed, slamming his fists into the ground. He looked to one side and then the other, seeing only a blanket of snow hailing around him. Frantic, Norman tore his leg upward with all his might, but the rock resisted, not giving an inch. In desperation he started hitting the surface with his balled up fist but the floor was firm.

It was at this point that Norman lay back exhausted and looked up at the dark clouds around him.

"Sorry," he said, before repeating it, shouting louder against the fury of the storm.

The relentless wind never allowed the tears to fall, tearing them from his face. He lay shivering in the cold, listening to the whistling air, picking out the nuances of its sound and capturing what he thought were individual voices. It sounded all at once familiar and dreadful as it engulfed him completely and, closing his eyes in exhaustion, he prayed that the end would be over quickly.

FORTY-ONE

They stood watching the final flickering dying embers being slowly extinguished and could still detect a slight heat emanate from the burnt structure. Finding a half scorched long stick nearby, Victor fished through the debris nearby, discovering nothing but ash. He threw the stick back into one of the pockets that was still burning. It caught the fresh wood and they watched the fire climb it.

"What do you think happened here?"

Breagal looked up at him then down at his shoes, clicking them together to remove the snow.

"I don't need to hypothesize. I know what happened here," Breagal answered before turning away and walking around the perimeter of ash to one of the still burning areas.

He crouched and held his hands out for warmth. The other man followed him and knelt alongside, looking at his companion as if to suggest he continue, which he did.

"I suppose I owe you an explanation, Victor. You've come this far, so it is only fitting."

"Well considering I just shot up in a hospital… I think it's only fair."

"Very well," Breagal responded. "This may be hard to believe."

"Being here, in this place is hard to believe. Like you said, I've come this far."

Breagal described Saul's dream diary, the series of passages that when pieced together gave an entire narrative. He also explained that Norman's dream sequence had followed an identical path, the initial stages captured by their friend before entering the coma. Several tell-tale signs convinced Breagal that Norman was fixed on that same arc. There were of course the dreams, an exact match. The rare occurrence that they would start where an older one had finished. Then there were the physical symptoms.

"What do you mean?"

"The nose bleed? Not trapped, residual blood as the doctor described, but rather a fresh injury arising from a successful attic escape."

"Escape? From what?"

"Hard to say," Breagal said.

The older man stood when he was sufficiently pleased that his hands were warmed and put them inside his pockets.

"A nose bleed? That's all you got? Again, a bit of a leap Breagal considering he did just have a car crash and was within an inch of death."

"The fever," he said.

"Which was?"

"Look around you? Extremes of heat. Fire and ice. Norman got too close to fire," Breagal said, and pawed at a footprint he made in the snow.

"And the hand injury?"

"From a dog. Flesh wound. This was a turning point for Saul. The first time he found himself alone, and as you can imagine," Breagal said, pirouetting on the spot with outstretched hands, "this is not the kind of place you want to find yourself alone for any stretch of time."

Victor stared at Breagal in silence before nodding his head. He turned back to the little battling fire that was shrinking all the time and plunged his finger into a little ash pile. Raising it to his face, he rubbed the soot between his fingers and watched the molecules catch the finest of winds and fly away. He stood and patted his knees, which had soaked through with the wet ground.

"So if this story has already been written, then we should know where Norman is, right?" Victor said. "We just follow the next dream, or whatever, that your brother wrote."

Breagal smiled at him. They both walked away from the fire and along the dirt road that divided the lines of standing houses.

"I wish it were that easy. You have to remember, my brother had the luxury of passing between both worlds – he could wake up from this one and return to normality, if you could call it that. In Norman's mind this is his world. His descent could be even greater than my brother's because he's here during every waking moment."

"So what are you saying?"

"I'm saying that I can only see so far ahead before we will be going in blind, hence why we need to trace his steps carefully."

"So where do we start? Breagal?"

Victor noticed that his colleague had stopped and was looking directly ahead. On the distant plain they could see a small shape gathering pace and headed toward them, almost indistinguishable with its white coat framed against the snow-capped hill, but a bark that rang out in the chilled air left no doubt.

"We start there."

FORTY-TWO

The small dog looked anything but vicious yet they still approached it with caution. It seemed intent to lead and they followed it for the best part of an hour up the hillside to a small house. Drawing closer, they noticed the door hung off the hinges, and an arcing dotted red trail in the snow led to its opening. The two men stopped and watched as the dog ran inside the building, barking.

"Some sort of animal?" Victor asked, stopping to look closer at the blood trail.

"I... don't know," Breagal answered.

"I thought you knew what was going to happen next?"

"For goodness sake. I already told you. I'm not psychic."

"Well, what happened next for your brother?"

"Doesn't make a fiddler's difference," Breagal scolded. "In my brother's entries, there was never any visit from the outside, and certainly not from a librarian and an accountant. We are making new territory here so be alert."

Victor swallowed hard. Looking closely at the door opening he could see wood panels stripped from the structure and jagged holes pierced in the sides.

"Something was in a rush to get out."

"Or get in. On your guard."

The sight of the small dog popping its head out the opening eased some of their distress and with it they moved toward the entrance. The door half blocked their entry and they put it slowly back on its hinges and pushed it inwardly. Peering in, the place was strewn with unopened cans of food, shelves ripped from the walls on each side. In the centre was a wooden counter, badly damaged but still standing like a solitary survivor of some war that had raged in the room. The place had been ransacked, and the floor was covered in mud from outside.

"I wonder what they were looking-"

A sudden groan from within the shop stopped the words in Victor's chest. The two men leapt backwards at the same time, Victor finding himself reflexively grabbing one of the cans as a weapon. They waited in silence, staring around for some indication of the source. Again the groan sounded, but this time they held their position, muscles tensed, ready to spring into action. The little dog wandered around from behind them and moved to the counter, where she barked once at them and then looked at something beyond their vision. With careful deliberation, the two men slowly edged their way toward the back wall and saw from behind the counter a sloped shape, both legs sprawled out, one of which was horribly twisted. The unnatural angle of the break almost made Victor gag and he had to hold his palm to his mouth to prevent it.

When they both had the confidence to step closer, they observed the seated man who, despite his strong muscular build, looked weak and broken. The sweat streamed down his pink face onto a thick neck where the shirt below was soaked. The large sinewy arms that hung limp by his side were upturned and flat on the ground, palms roughly textured under a mass of skin folds which shone red around the fingers. His eyes looked upward but in a delirium swimming in the back of his skull, giving no indication whether he noticed the two stunned onlookers.

"Christ! This man needs help!" Victor said, leaning down and staring into his eyes. "We're going to get you out of here."

There was a can beside the injured man just out of arm's reach, the food label torn from it which Victor used to dab the sweat off the man's brow. Victor looked down at the can noticing there was no ring pull or easy way to open it. He got up and began searching the room within, tossing over pieces of broken wood, sifting through the bed of heavy cans which rattled against the hard floor.

"Christ," he said. "There's got to be one of them open."

Breagal hadn't moved. His eyes scrutinised the man before looking to Victor who was upturning broken wooden frames and searching beneath the wreckage. He turned around and noticed the librarian staring.

"Aren't you going to help?"

Breagal shrugged his shoulders and looked back at the lying man.

"You're some piece of work!" Victor said, before picking up a can, and running outside the shop.

"You won't find any tools out there," Breagal said.

Victor placed it on the ground and stomped on it, but it had little effect. He checked the back of the door for a lock or something sharp to pierce it but found nothing. Walking with the can around the perimeter of the shop, his attention was drawn to a small door at the back, barely visible against the backdrop of the shop wall. Opening it slowly, it creaked on its hinges. Darkness inside was illuminated by his passage and he could see a tiny annex to the shop, a separate room just big enough to contain a bare mattress. There was an open can beside it, half full with beans. In front of the door and above the mattress was a screen with a panel, a knob attached in its centre. Victor stepped onto the makeshift bed, which offered very little spring as he looked at it closely. He observed that it was actually a sliding panel. It slid easily as he moved it silently to one side.

Through an opening about six inches in diameter, Victor could clearly see the main room of the shop where he had been a few moments earlier. Strung out, looking drugged, lay the body of the prostrate man facing him, eyes flitted between consciousness. In the centre of the room was Breagal, who was taking slow measured steps around the room, surveying the damage. Cradled in his hands was the small dog, belly being tickled by Breagal, tail wagging with a satisfied expression on its face.

Suddenly, Breagal shifted the weight of the bundle in his hands and jerked its head backwards. The snap was decisive and fatal. The dog instantly became limp in his arms.

Victor pulled his face back and closed the shutter quickly. He replaced his full can with the open bean one, left the annex, slowly re-entering the shop, hollering as he approached. Breagal was now leaning on the counter, the dog nowhere to be seen.

"I managed to find an open one," Victor said, face flushed.

Breagal was passive, moving to one side to let him tend to the man. Victor lifted some of the beans into his mouth which moved in reflex, managing to ingest some of the food.

"You know it's quite pointless, right?" Breagal asked.

Victor didn't respond although he was listening attentively.

"This is a dream character you are feeding. Nothing but a figment of the imagination."

The man's tongue was a fat worm, finding sustenance and groping for more of the food. His eyes were half closed, slipping in and out of consciousness.

"He has served his purpose. This is where his path ends. To feed it is folly. This isn't a real person Victor. Its name is Yenjin. He was in my brother's dream. A real hero. The battles he went through to get to this point, saving my brother and our friend's life were nothing short of miraculous, but his course has run."

"Yenjin," Victor repeated.

They had gotten to the bottom of the can and Victor tossed it. The delirious man was completely exhausted from the effort, his chin wet and red from the sauce.

"Dream character or not, I can't stand back and watch. It's not my nature."

Breagal smiled, shaking his head.

"That attitude could get you killed here."

"Where's the dog?" Victor asked.

"Must have run off. Come on, time to go."

They left the sleeping man against the counter, and walked out of the shop into the clearing again. There was a brisk wind in the air, which made them pat their damp clothes down. Victor closed the shop door, enclosing what little heat the shop contained for the fallen giant.

"Which way?" Victor asked.

"Back to the houses. We need a base from which to start our search."

Within the shop, Yenjin suddenly stirred with the sound of voices outside. The taste on his lips of something saucy brought other senses back. Sliding his back off the counter, he lay out flat on the shop floor, breathing deeply, feeling the cold but no longer willing to fight it. His vision was blurred and misty. Blinking slowly, he waited for the shapes around to come into focus. A weak beam of light entered from the side of what looked like a broken door. His eyes adjusted until the image cleared and, eyes wide, he stared upwardly at the object dangling from the door. Skye was hanging limp from a hook, pinned there with its limbs sagging helplessly. The eyes in her head looked at a point on the floor, but were lifeless in expression.

Yenjin shut his eyes tight but the tears still came and they didn't stop for a long time.

FORTY-THREE

There was no shortage of options when it came to finding somewhere to rest. Each house resembled the other; devoid of usable furniture or bedding, ransacked, gutted from the inside.

They finally settled on the first one that seemed cheerier than the rest, namely that this one had no blood on the walls. They were in a room, the ceiling of which had been torn asunder, Victor sitting in the corner, on the hard floor with his arms curled around his legs. Breagal entered and threw a few more broken sticks on the small fire pile in the centre of the room.

"You've been unnervingly quiet, Victor. Everything alright?"

"Just tired."

Breagal's face tensed as he held a wooden beam about a metre long and bent it until finally it snapped. He used one of the ends to prod and poke the growing flames, encouraging them to fan out.

"I was hoping you hadn't seen that."

Victor continued to look into the fire, although the illumination betrayed the poker face he was trying to assume.

"Truth is," Breagal said, throwing his wooden poker into the pile in frustration. "It was a kindness and a necessity. The poor dog and its owner needed to be put out of their misery."

"I thought you said they were dream characters and not real?"

"That I did and I stand by that. Although, they can influence things here just like we can. They were only going to make things difficult for us. Let me explain."

Breagal left the side of the wood heap to sit beside him, leaning his back against the smooth wall surface.

"The fire that you saw earlier? It was caused by the dog, knocking over a candle. Set the place alight. Almost killed my brother were it not for Yenjin. They managed to escape, but were foiled in their attempts to find cover, namely because the dog's barking brought unwanted attention."

Breagal watched the expression of the man's face, trying to decipher if any of his words had had a desired effect before continuing.

"On top of that, the dog was unpredictable. You saw the wound on Norman's hand. My brother had the exact same injury, same marks. He wrote about it. I saw it myself. Could you imagine having a variable such as it roaming around unattended? It would have been unthinkable. Unpredictable. And that, sir, is something we can't have in a place like this."

They both sat in silence and stared at the fire which was modest, and didn't seem to take to the wire framework of wood that housed it. Some of the twigs cracked, pulling their eyes back to the fire.

"Christ Breagal. Couldn't you just have locked it up in a kennel?"

"Well given the way you were reacting about my indifference to our injured casualty Yenjin, I figured the less you know, the better we would be for it. So I made a decision."

Victor frowned and shook his head. Breagal slapped his kneecap and rose with some difficulty. He took the second wooden poker that was propped on the wall beside him and returned to the fire.

"Listen Victor," he said over his shoulder. "I promise that I will keep you more informed from this point forth, however much you might disagree with my own sentiment. We need to be in this together after all. Fair?"

"OK."

"Excellent. Well this fire won't last too long. I'm going to go out to canvass the other houses for wood. There's bound to be something in this God-forsaken place that we can use."

"Shouldn't we be looking for Norman?"

Breagal nodded and looked up at the sky, following the trail of smoke as it drifted off, curling against the gentle breeze. The other man watched his gaze and noticed for the first time a night sky filled with stars more brilliant than he had ever seen before.

"The next entry on my brother's list shows a time delay until..."

"Until what?" Victor prompted.

"Let's just say, we'll be safe and sound here tonight, OK?"

"OK."

"There's little else we can do tonight in any case. When I return we can spend the remainder of this sleeping phase working on some breathing exercises to further anchor you to this plane. If you want, we can also mop up any other questions you might have."

"Need any help with the firewood?"

"No. I have it covered," Breagal replied and gave a wide smile. "Just make sure to keep it lit."

He turned and left the glow of the fire behind as it danced against the walls of the little room where Victor stretched out his legs and lay down.

Breagal left the main entrance of the house and turned right to walk up the street toward a cluster of houses on either side. After a few strides, he suddenly cut left and hid behind the corner of a house. Peeping out from the wall, he looked back at the building he had just left watching the opening for a few seconds until he was satisfied.

Under the cover of lined structures his sudden enthusiasm spilled from him until he could no longer hold it, and he burst into a sprint in the direction of the merchant's again. His heart raced, sweat ran down his face, obscuring his eyesight, as he angled his sprint away from the building and toward the outer fringe of the forest.

***

The soothing heat blanketed Victor as he rested. The fire now had ceded and was low in rising, the last remnants of it illuminating the open room bathing him in an orange glow. Tiredness had come quickly, unexpectedly, but not unwelcome as he had felt the change in climate hard to adjust to. There was a new noise above the crackling fire which, despite his relaxation, prompted him to observe it; first with detachment until all of a sudden it grew in volume, a crunching on snow that raised his attention levels back to the present.

Startled, Victor sat up suddenly and peered through the open door beyond. Seeing the figure, his body unclenched like a soft fist. Breagal had returned, and in his hands were a mountain of sticks, which he dropped to the ground before feeding individually to the flames.

"Christ, Breagal. You scared the wits out of me. How long were you gone?"

"A few hours I figure."

"Pop out to the cinema did you?"

"I trust everything was OK when I was gone?"

Victor cupped a yawn and nodded. Stoking the coals of the fire with the poker, Breagal began planting fresh twigs on top and they crackled under the intensity of the flame.

"Yes, sorry if the heating dropped. A lot of the wood in other houses had become damp and rotten. Not usable in this fire. It would have given off too much smoke. I'm here now anyway."

"Is it snowing again?" Victor asked.

Perplexed, Breagal followed his colleague's stare as it fell on his shoulders. He brushed the thin layer of snow off and chuckled outwardly.

"No. It must have fallen off some trees on the way," he said, beginning to snap some of the larger sticks down into manageable chunks for the fire to eat.

"Breagal, you're bleeding!"

The man looked down at his hand and noticed the blood that was dripping now onto the broken twigs.

"Nothing to worry about," he said and wiped the palm of his hand on the back of his trousers before inserting it in his trouser pocket. "Silly really. Cut it on a branch collecting this bundle. No harm done. Nothing quite like a good fire to warm the spirits."

Breagal sat down and crossed his legs close to the fire, the light dancing in his eyes. He wasn't able to maintain the position for long, his legs twitching of their own accord before he decided to kneel, holding them down with his bodyweight.

"Everything alright?"

"Yes. I do love campfires. Something about the great outdoors that really strikes a chord with me. Don't you agree?"

"Oh yeah, love it," Victor replied. "Especially camping in ransacked abandoned houses with blood on the walls. What the hell happened here?"

"A war."

Victor continued staring, waiting for more but the librarian remained silent.

"Between?"

"Not important," Breagal said, adding more fuel in the way of a thick tree branch onto the fire. "However, what is important is our plan."

"Go on."

"By my watch, with the medication in our blood stream thinning out we have only a couple more hours in this sleep cycle before we awake and are at the hospital again. There it should be just after dawn, perfectly synched to our own sleeping cycle."

"What happens if we don't wake up?"

Breagal's sudden chuckle made Victor uneasy, and waiting for the librarian to continue he stared into the fire feeling suddenly impotent.

"My dear boy! That is not something that I would allow to happen. Whilst we are here of our own free will, we will always find safe passage back home."

"Glad to hear it."

"Think of it like this. Imagine you are a balloon whose string is fixed to a small weight keeping it grounded. All that is you, that very consciousness that makes up who you are is contained in the balloon."

Victor felt a bug itch at his neck and scratched. He suddenly became aware that they would be exposed to the elements until they woke again. Breagal had turned his body to him and had resumed his Buddha position.

"As long as we have that connection, we can float into the dream state while still being grounded in reality. With Saul, his balloon string was snipped which made him drift aimlessly taken by the currents with no control."

"And Norman too?"

"What?"

"Norman too?"

"Yes and no."

"What do you mean?"

"You've seen how the physical reflection manifests from events in Norman's dreams."

Victor nodded and Breagal's face turned serious now, as the fire began casting shadows on his narrow features.

"If we can't get there before the next event then we're not talking about simply chasing down a balloon and clutching at thin air."

"What are you saying? We lose the balloon?"

Breagal clapped his hands together and the sound echoed around the chamber.

"Pop. No more balloon."

FORTY-FOUR

There was brightness behind the lids of his eyes that suggested morning. Without opening them, he breathed in deeply and replayed the last images in his mind. It came slowly as if emerging from the fog. The climb. Battered by snowy winds sending pellets of ice crushing against his brow and his eyes, making the journey unbearable.

A face came to his mind. Gentle and round, sandy thin hair with a gummy grin. The head was fixed to a giant's body, bulky shoulders sloping down into thick arms. He was holding a white dog barely older than a puppy. It licked the man's face, tickling him under duress.

"Yenjin!"

The thought snapped and his eyes opened. On his chest was the upstanding little pirate figurine that he had pocketed days earlier. It remained upright, looking at him; its orange shirt hiding a tiny golden pendant below, trousers blue and riding up to reveal stout legs, little shiny boots on either end. In its arm it held a cutlass and in the other a bottle of rum. The blue and yellow parrot perched on his shoulder completed the ensemble. Norman looked at the bearded face with one eye covered by a black patch and the little carved smiled.

"Shiver me timbers! Looks like I found me a freshie!"

Norman's shock at the strange voice was instant and he tried to mouth a response but out came gibberish from his hyperventilating body.

Suddenly he heard giggling nearby and a door opened to his side. In walked a woman, who he had no recollection of ever meeting. She was in her forties, a plaited black braid swung behind her as she moved. The woman didn't look in his direction but addressed someone just out of sight below him.

"Cleo! Come out of there this instant or I'll tell your dad that you've been messing again!"

Norman rolled over in time to see a small girl crawling out from beneath the bed. She began pleading with the woman who remained unmoved by her amateur dramatics.

"Well let's see how much fun you'll be having if I ground you. No more climbing. Come, help me with the dishes. Scoot."

The girl vanished through the door and Norman sat up, looking around stiffly. He noticed that there were thin sheets covering his body. The clothes he wore weren't his own. The room was neatly decorated and clean. Picture frames hung on the smooth walls, catching the light from a narrow window high above. Furniture was arranged around him with careful order. Eventually his eyes moved to the woman who was standing looking down at him, hands fixed at her hips and patiently waiting for him to acknowledge her.

"You're one very lucky young man, you know that?" she said, shaking her head in exasperation.

"Where am I?" Norman stuttered.

"Safe. For now, at least."

"I'm sorry, but I don't know…"

"Of course you don't!" she snapped. "Should have been damned with you. Kane told me what you did. You and that brute."

Norman's brain was still too frazzled to connect any of it together, but what was clear was the earlier peril had passed and he owed his life to this woman.

"I… thank you."

"You can shove your thanks!" she hissed. "Thanks won't protect my family from them. We used to be safe out here in the woods. But oh no. Not now."

Emotion came over her face and her mask slipped, but she managed to recover it.

"I don't understand…"

"Oh he'll make you understand when he gets home," she sneered. "What were you thinking? We've lost our livelihood, our future, everything because of you."

Norman looked down at the little figurine in confusion, as if hoping for a clue, which wasn't forthcoming.

"I'll do whatever I can to repay you."

"You'll do one thing."

"Anything."

"You leave tonight."

The woman made to leave but thinking twice, paused at the doorway before looking back.

"You know I wish we would have left you on the mountain slope. Storm had you beaten. Heck it had us all beaten. Were it not for that little sprite underneath your bed just now; had she not seen you and begged us to find you, we would've turned our tails and looked the other way. It's her you should be thanking."

The woman turned on her heel and slammed the door behind. Norman looked over at a chair in the corner and saw his pile of clothes, or rather a clean and pressed version that hanged neatly over the back. Easing his body back onto the comfortable mattress, he breathed a huge sigh of relief. In his peripheral vision he could see the door swing slowly open again and braced himself for another rebuke but was instead surprised to see the little girl creep into the bedroom.

She moved over to him with a shyness, unsure how to approach the stranger in their home who had suddenly awoken. She looked no older than six or seven years old, and her hair was tied back into a thick ponytail. Her freckled face was searching and curious, with a flat stubby nose which she picked at as she approached. A slug of liquid crept down from there, curious to see the stranger too before she snorted it back into its hiding place.

"Mama always get angry wid people she dunno. But s'OK. She alright."

Norman smiled at her, and the little girl returned one of her own devilish grins.

"And you must be Cleo?"

"Ahah."

"Your mama says that you saved my life?"

Cleo looked bashful but her beam widened. Her little snort released the green slug again and she used an already luminous shirtsleeve to mop it up.

"Thank you," Norman said.

He held out his hand, which the little girl stared at before shaking and collapsing into a fits of giggles on the floor.

"How did you find me?"

"Easy peasy. I saw you in de twees. You was widda dog. Say Mister, I don't find no dog wit you. Is it still out der?"

"No," he said. "I think she went back to her daddy. At least I hope so."

"What is her daddy's name?"

"Yenjin," Norman replied and smiled.

The girl started laughing and repeated the name over and over. Norman recalled the torrid time he had climbing the steep hill one handed, struggling with Skye. Then he remembered the bite and its memory made him look down at his hand. It was freshly bandaged and, flexing the fingers, felt much better.

"That was you up in those trees looking at us?"

The little girl pursed her lips and raising a finger bade him shush, and then said in a whisper, "Papa don like me goin' up so high, but I likes it. When I told 'em what I saws, they thought they would follow you to see where you was goin'."

Next door they could hear her mother shouting her name. Norman noticed that she had been paying careful attention to the little figurine toppled over on his chest.

"Do you like him?" he asked.

"Oh yes!" Her eyes opened wide and she jumped up and down by his bedside.

"OK OK! Steady!" Norman laughed and he picked it up in his hand and presented it to her. "I want you to look after this for me. Can you do that Cleo?"

"Yes. Yes. Yes! Defin-ite-ly!"

She approached it carefully as if it was a trap. She looked up at him and then down at the object, before snapping it from his palm.

"What's his name?" she said, as she turned it around in her small hands.

"You can call it whatever you like."

She paused and twitched the corner of her mouth upward, looking for inspiration before the thought flashed on her face. Delighted she raced around the room holding it aloft in the air, guiding the pirate in flight, before opening the door.

"Mammy, look what I got!" she shouted.

Norman listened as the little girl ran away, the footsteps receding deeper into the house, all the while chanting the two syllables of her new toy's name. Yenjin.

FORTY-FIVE

Norman changed out of the pyjamas, neatly folding and placing them on the chair in the corner, before slipping on his familiar garb and returning to the bed. He lay down and stared up at the ceiling. Carefully unwinding the wrap around his hand, Norman observed his wound for the first time. Each distinctive dent in the skin had crusted over in a scab, something that would have required a couple of days. The hand was still swollen but nothing like before. Cleaned and rested, it felt much stronger as he tensed it into a ball. The last vestiges of pain more a memory than physical.

It was a knock on the door that had roused him just as he was dozing. The room was a little darker than he remembered and he turned to see the door open slightly but the person on the other side didn't enter.

"Dinner is on the table."

He recognized it as the voice of the woman, before the footsteps carried away again.

Norman edged off the bed and followed the voice outside the room, entering a corridor dimly lit by two candles fixed to opposite walls. He passed two closed doors on either side, along the length of the hall, before it veered off to the left out into another room. He stood uncertain outside the opening, observing the scene in front and feeling ill at ease.

Sitting at the kitchen table were two frowning faces staring up at him. Between the man and woman, the little girl was standing on her chair, a huge grin plastered on her face, evidently pleased to see him. Four plates were placed on the small table and a solitary candle brightened the small room. Norman stepped inside with a lowered head and moved to the empty chair and sat down. He continued to stare down at his plate, aware of the intense glare of the man seated opposite who hadn't yet touched his food.

The others had already started eating as soon as the uninvited guest had taken his seat. Ravenous as he was, Norman found himself unable to eat under the scrutiny of the man and he hazarded a look up from his plate. Stocky build, bulging eyes that glared out from two puffy dark sockets, the man met his stare. The jet-black hair on his head was thinning and parted in the centre. The thinly drawn mouth seemed to be chewing as if in deliberation. Behind, affixed to the wall, was a shotgun resting on a custom made rack. It was well within reach of the man and Norman hoped that there would be no reason to use it anytime soon.

The man watched Norman's gaze hover over his shoulder, and his lips twitched into a crooked smile. When he spoke it split the awkward silence.

"You remember Big Bertha, don't you boy?" he said, mouth contorted in a sneer. "Of course you do. Should have taken you out, the mutt and that big brute when I had the chance."

"Kane!"

It was the woman who interrupted and the merchant looked at her. As if remembering his place, he took his attention away from the newcomer and to the plate of food in front, which he started to poke through. Norman also looked down and observed the dish for the first time, now that eating seemed like an option. A slab of grey meat occupied most of the plate, with a lump of green mashed peas on one side. Beside that was a small nest of lettuce leaves, finely chopped with a tomato perched on top. The helping was generous and Norman's stomach stretched in anticipation of the hearty meal.

They ate in silence for several minutes, including the little girl who hadn't taken her eyes off Norman for the duration. She smiled, trying to provoke a response, to which her mother scolded her to focus on her greens. The little pirate was tucked inside her breast pocket.

"I hope Una has told you that you're not staying here?" the merchant asked.

The woman dropped her utensils to the table, they clattered against the plate, and looked at her husband in frustration.

"I thought I said that we could discuss this later? We're all tired and hungry and the dinner table is no such place for discussion."

"Yes, I know that sweetheart," he insisted. "But, be that as it may, I can't just sit here and have dinner with someone who brought hell to our door!"

The dinner party were surprised to hear Norman suddenly speak in defence for the first time.

"Mam, sir. I want to thank you for saving me and taking care of me, changing my bandage, cleaning my clothes."

The man looked at his wife expressing shock. He opened his mouth to speak, but Norman continued.

"I also know that it was risky for you to do it. I want you to know that I'm grateful more than you'll ever know in words, and that I'll be on my way in no time if it be your wish."

"It be all of our wishes boy!" the man retorted, before stabbing the fork into the gristle of meat and wolfing it down his pie hole in one swift action.

Silence fell upon the group again, and all that could be heard was the scraping of utensils against the ceramic plates, as dinner was drawing to a close.

"Where d'you come from, Mister?"

It was the little girl this time and Norman looked at her then around at the other diners, to see if he was allowed to answer.

They stared back nonplussed and Norman told them about his experience, starting from his time with Yenjin which was still as far back as he could remember.

They sat in a respectful silence when he had finished his narrative, uncertain what to say, except for the merchant. He stood suddenly and began clearing the plates to a small basin nearby.

"Well," Kane said. "We each got our own sob stories, but it doesn't change anything. You're on your own boy. We have to protect ourselves."

"Kane!" his wife scolded.

"No Una! We've done enough for him as is. You've certainly done enough for him. We saved his life, but you heard him, wherever he goes he brings trouble. We can't be a part of this. We've managed fine out here on our own. Besides, those things seem to be moving further and further out from the hole that they came from. Who knows when they could be knocking on our door next?"

"Mama, are da monsters comin' here?" asked the little girl.

"No honey," she replied. "Your daddy is just being dramatic."

"Dramatic," he sneered. "The only God-damn one speaking sense around here is what I am."

The stubby man sat back at the table and looked at Norman who was watching the interaction.

"Listen. We can't have you here. I know you've lost a lot and… I wish I could say I'm sorry for your loss, but I can't. We've all lost. As head of this household, I ain't having you here, so I hoped you enjoyed your meal. I suggest you go back to your friend and the mutt and find some other charity case to take you in."

This time there was no intervention from the woman. No counter argument. Norman stood up and thanked the group each in turn, before turning and walking toward a bolted door on the side.

"Please Mama, can't he stay one more night?" the little girl pleaded.

Her weak voice began to break into gentle sobbing. Norman slowed his pace, waiting to hear the response. Even with his back turned he could sense the non-verbal conversation going on back at the table between the parents, until suddenly the mother spoke.

"Wait!" she said, as Norman reached the door. He turned to meet her eyes now and he sensed something had thawed there. They seemed softer than earlier.

"It's almost dark outside. You can leave first thing in the morning."

Norman smiled and almost hugged the woman before she delivered a final volley at him.

"Don't think we're going soft and don't get too comfortable. Make no mistake. We still want you gone."

FORTY-SIX

The two men woke within seconds of one another, rubbing their eyes and looking around. Gone was the heat from the fire, and they now felt the gentle whirring of the air conditioning around them. Breagal looked at his watch and stretched out, rubbing his tired face. The curtain around the bed had been drawn back in one corner and they both looked out through the gap to see a row of occupied beds along the floor.

Victor yawned, holding the back of his palm up to his mouth. His feet still felt chilled, memory of the snow fresh in his mind. They both stood up and walked over to the body of Norman who slept, gently unaware of their efforts the previous night.

Breagal moved to the far side of the bed, and removed the patient's hand from under the blanket and studied it.

"Well?"

"This is a good sign," Breagal said. "It's healing well. He's found the merchant's house."

"So he's safe?"

"He's not out of the woods yet," Breagal said, suddenly noticing the unintentional double meaning and smiled inwardly.

"What's our next step?"

"Well," Breagal started as he moved back to the seats, collecting his briefcase that was stored there, "I'm going back to work, and I suggest you do the same."

His companion looked at him perplexed. Breagal saw the confusion in his face and moved to ease his friend's concerns.

"Norman is safe for now, and will be for the next few hours. There is absolutely nothing we can do until tomorrow when we'll return and continue our exploration."

Victor shook hands with the librarian who winced. They both looked down at his hand, noticing the lacerated slash across his palm. It was the hand that had bled over the sticks at the campfire.

"If you needed reminding of the danger in the other world Victor, let this be it," Breagal said and patted him on the shoulder.

With that he turned and left through the curtain opening and out into the hospital ward. He was alone now with Norman for the first time and observed the breathing apparatus beside him.

"We're coming for you, buddy," he whispered and bent down to kiss the forehead of his friend.

***

That afternoon in a small room some two hundred miles away, a forlorn figure stood, staring out onto the courtyard. To the uninformed it looked like he was surveying the grounds from this high vantage point, but instead he saw it all yet saw nothing.

If he had had any spatial awareness he would have noticed a blue sedan pull through the high-rise gates of the walled complex a few minutes earlier. The driver of the car had entered, scaled the steep staircase and knocked before entering the room. Had the patient of Elm Hurst Psychiatric Ward been consciously aware, he would have noticed that beside him now stood the tall lean figure of Stephen Breagal, smiling sweetly.

The librarian embraced him in a hug and then drew back suddenly, searching into the glassy eyes of his brother, seeing what he thought was some glimmer of consciousness still hidden from view. Holding his hand in both of his own, he leaned forward and whispered into his ear.

"We're coming for you, brother."

FORTY-SEVEN

Norman woke fully refreshed finding the first light of the dawn morning entering the room. Quickly dressing, he left the bedroom and walked the corridor to the kitchen. At the table, he was surprised to see the woman sitting there, cradling a mug of hot liquid between her hands. She was blowing into it now, shifting the steam vapour that rose from it like a smoke signal.

She nodded her head by way of greeting and Norman returned it, before walking around her to the door which he cranked open. He was about to exit before he heard her speak.

"Wait!"

Norman stood in the doorway with his back still turned to the room. He heard her rise and approach. Turning, Norman could see that she carried a small brown bag, which she handed to him.

"What's this?"

"We might be tough and cold in this part of the world, but we aren't animals. At least not yet. Some food. Not much."

Norman thanked her and she looked away, unable to meet his eyes. Again, he turned to leave but the woman held his shoulder.

"If you find that it's too tough out there or if you can't find your friend... come back. I don't want to be responsible for what happens to you out there."

Norman nodded, thanked her again and an awkward silence passed between them. She took her hand from his shoulder and turned around, not wanting to show but,

Norman saw her brush something from her face with her open palm. Coughing suddenly, she regained some composure and stood firm again looking at him. He could see her eyes were brimming with water and Norman felt the pang in his breast.

"Where will you go?" she asked.

"I'm not sure. Is there anything around? Are there other people?"

"No. You were the first person I'd seen in weeks. Everyone we know fled and is in hiding somewhere. You'd need to be a damn sight lucky to find anyone else out here."

Norman felt the weight of the bag in his hand. His fingers tensed around it, keen to demonstrate that they had recovered.

"In that case, I have a friend to get back to. He'll be wondering where I am."

"Well if you're headed back the way of Kane's shop you should head with the sun on your back. Find high ground to get your bearings. You'll see the outer edge of the forest from there. Good luck," she said with finality, and the ice was on her eyes again.

The door closed gently behind him and Norman could see the day with blue clear skies above. The snow had melted from the trees now, but still lay in spots on the ground. Feeling the warmth on his back he walked away and into the tunnel of trees on his side.

Suddenly curious, he looked back to see the house where he had been resident for the past few days. It took a few moments before he recognized the grey door he had just left. It was camouflaged against the cliff side with moss covering the edges. He couldn't see a rooftop and it dawned on him that he hadn't been living in a house, it had actually been a small cave dwelling hidden against the mountainside. Recognizing the small sink pool of water to one side where he had quenched his thirst days before, he shook his head in wonder.

Realizing that he was at least a morning and half an afternoon from the place where he left Yenjin, his pace quickened and he skilfully navigated through the undergrowth that continued their efforts to pull him back. The walk was much easier but his enthusiasm was almost to his detriment, as his fast pace almost caused him to lose footing again and slide on the snow. Berating himself for his lack of patience, he slowed the pace and after several hours made it to the top of a hill where he had first spied the mountain bursting through the canopy of trees; the same mountain where the storm had almost taken his life. There was nothing but gentle descent now until he reached the boulder where they had slept.

It was slippery under foot with the steep gradient, loose stones and rock inviting a tumble. Norman stepped slowly in spite of his excitement. Carefully using the overhanging branches and shrubs nearby, he finally reached the bottom of the clearing where it levelled out. Abandoning all concern for safety now, he found his legs move into a sprint, calling out Yenjin's name.

When he reached the boulder, it was clear to see that there was no one there. Neither man nor dog. Looking around he shouted in all directions but received nothing in response. Carefully tracing the ground on which they had lain, he saw the rock that Yenjin had used to prop himself upwards. There was still a stain of what looked like blood there. Its weak trail led not in the direction from where Norman had come, but back up the gentle rise of the opposite hill, back toward the little village. There was a wide burrow in the snow bed almost in a straight line. It was quite shallow but the blood trail seemed to follow it. It looked like something had been dragged or pulled through it. Looking closer, he could see the footprints of a small animal alongside. Four little pock marks barely visible in the snow.

"My God," Norman said. "You're still alive."

Bounding up the incline, he dodged the trees as they raced past, scrambling alongside the trail that his friend had made.

The trail continued in a straight line until Norman could see the ending of the forest canopy further ahead. A radiant blue sky, warm and inviting, propelled him forward looking around for any sign of Yenjin and calling out lest he be within earshot.

Instead of going up and through the clearing, the blood trail took a sharp angle left, catching Norman off guard as he slowed to trace the new direction. The snow was thinner here and he couldn't detect the clarity of the prints anymore, however the blood still remained and Norman found the path getting tighter as the trees around struggled for space. Jostling for position among the trees, they dumped some of their snow load on his small shoulders as he sidled past, causing him to jump from fright. Like a dog with a scent, he managed to pick up pace, visualizing a path ahead, expecting at any point to find his friend bloodied, delirious but most importantly alive.

His grip had been sure and firm on the level clearing but as soon as his stride hit a spot on the turf he felt something snap underfoot. There was a sudden tightening around his ankle and Norman found his leg pulled from beneath him. He didn't have time to react as the momentum carried his second leg away and he fell flat on his back, hitting the back of his head hard on the floor. The blow knocked him unconscious, arms flung out to the side dropping the bag from his hand. Arms trailed through the floor of the forest as his body was dragged forward. Suddenly it lifted off the ground, hoisting the man six feet in the air suspended under a thick tree branch.

Leaves fluttered down from trees above with the weight of the swinging object until it finally settled and all was calm again.

There wasn't another movement until a few hours later, when Norman stirred and looked around, but he was finding it hard to connect his thoughts with the noise in the distance. The sound of a siren beating its drum.

FORTY-EIGHT

Keep walking…. Almost there…

Victor's emergence into Norman's dream was more straightforward this time, and when he arrived, opening his eyes, he found that they were atop the same hillside as before except for one difference. There was now the echo of a siren, which he couldn't understand. It was shrill in the air and seemed to come from the mountain, like a heartbeat, far in the distance to their right. Feeling himself grounded, he looked toward his companion in uncertainty but Breagal's attention now was fixed away from the source and toward the little town they had spent the night before.

When he looked back at Victor his face was panicked. "Follow me. Fast!"

Victor trailed the librarian as they ran down the gentle slope, the snow almost melted now and the tough terrain below still firm. Breagal was running in a crouch position as if afraid of being spotted and Victor assumed the same form, trying to match the early blistering pace of the older man. When they hit the level terrain, his back straightened turning into a full on sprint and the younger man found it difficult to keep up.

They were nearing the town now, and all was quiet around them except for the blast of the siren. When they reached the trail that parted the houses, Victor felt the terrain shift. He felt more give and his shoes slapped against the muck. Trying to keep up with the front-runner, he looked down, noticing the path had been recently churned up, the mark of heavy soles all around them.

"What the..."

On their right hand side, they barely had time to notice the burning building from before. Their fiery beacon from the hilltop had been extinguished, grey ash drifting up from it, carried by the gentle breeze.

"In here," Breagal suddenly announced, turning off the street to the left and entering a stone building.

The inside was similar to every other building that they had seen so far, except a broken staircase had half collapsed on itself leading to a second floor. Carefully ascending, Breagal reached the top before offering a hand to Victor to do the same, which he managed to do with no great ease. The librarian walked along the small landing of the house and entered an empty room, lying down below a tiny window ledge. Victor walked over to join him and, as he approached the window opening, Breagal pulled the man down hard, causing his companion to fall to the ground.

"You mind explaining to me what the hell is happening?"

Breagal's breath took a few moments to settle and he rolled over onto his back and waited. When his lungs had recovered he sat up on one elbow and looked at the concerned face of Victor.

"My apologies friend, but we had to act fast. There is something you need to know."

"Go on."

"That siren?"

Pointing upwards they both listened to the constant drum still bellowing from beyond.

"That seems to compel them to action. My brother wrote about it. His dreams were haunted by this sound. You need to find shelter when hearing this sound, lest they found you in the open and then..."

He didn't finish the sentence but Victor saw the danger etched on his face.

"Who's them?"

"Men, but different. You'll see soon enough."

"So the siren sends them out?"

Breagal nodded in response, now lying on his chest, propped up on two elbows looking out the window. From their vantage point they could see a portion of the street below.

"So when do they come back?"

Breagal took his attention away from the street and looked at his companion before considering and then looking at his watch.

"They come back when the siren stops. However, my dear brother did note that each time the siren sounded, especially in the latter stages, it became longer. This allowed them to explore further and deeper each time, searching every nook and cranny far and wide. Obviously with that, they took longer to return."

"What are they are looking for?"

"Why, Norman of course. Any semblance of life – of consciousness. It's his dream after all. It's giving life to these monsters. The longer he stays here, the longer these animals live."

Suddenly, as if on cue, the siren stopped wailing and the two men held their breath. Their ears strained but could only hear the sound of a few birds chirruping down below.

"Now what do we do?"

"Now we watch and wait."

***

Breagal sensed by the hour that passed that this particular expedition by the troops had been a long one. Checking his watch again, he looked over to Victor who had become bored with staring out the small window and was now lying on his back resting with eyes closed.

Victor opened his eyes, looking to his side, catching Breagal's stare. The librarian felt a little embarrassed to be caught staring at the resting man and almost apologized before the younger man spoke.

"Listen!"

Breagal's breaths were slow and steady, at odds with his racing heart. Propping back on his elbows his gaze narrowed on the section of road visible to them from this viewpoint. Keeping head down, his ear was cocked to one side, trying to tune into the sounds around them. There was a distinctive sound far in the distance, a rumble of sorts, steadily growing from their left hand side. Both men heard it clearly now and huddled around the window, careful to maintain their hidden positions.

"Is that boots?"

Breagal shushed Victor. The heavy footfall on the path below marched in beat, rising in volume until they saw the first figure pass by only ten metres from their window. Both men stifled cries, seeing the dark mud splattered figure of a man in khaki military uniform, dragging in his hand a severed head from the scalp of hair, bobbing it along the stony pebbles below. Their wide eyes followed the man but a few seconds later the stone window ledge barred their view. Following shortly behind were a procession of men in the same garb, some carrying trinkets, or what appeared to be body parts, in their hands. The death march was in silence and the two observers from the window were careful to follow it.

Victor counted thirty of the men marching past in single file, before moving out of sight. He looked at Breagal whose hand was now raised to his mouth, not trusting it to keep silent as they lay witness to the shocking assembly of human body parts. Their footsteps now were growing quieter, but Victor thought he could detect a fresh set.

Returning his gaze to the street, he was surprised to see a small group at the back. A quartet of four men carrying two thick beams on which stood a large upright wooden box fastened in place by straps. Victor squinted his eyes to see if he could see the contents inside, but it was too dark. Suddenly from within, two hands reached out of the box and gripped the bars. The sunlight caught the panicked face of the inmate, desperately looking around. The tears were flowing from his face, distressed cries calling out. They pierced the silence and were calling the name Yenjin. Victor stumbled back from the window, breathing hard. He knew the voice and face instantly.

Breagal's hand reached up to his face, the quiet words escaping from a mouth opened in shock.

"It worked."

FORTY-NINE

Minutes passed by, both too stunned to react, and it was Victor recoiling from the window in shock who finally spoke.

"We have to...we have to save him."

He quickly scrambled to his feet, and with a forceful tug Breagal's hand reached up, pulling him back down again where he fell in a heap. There was a dazed expression on Victor's face when he sat back up and his eyes flitted around in his head, unable to focus.

"Listen friend," Breagal began, holding the hyperventilating man's face between his hands. He talked calmly now, trying to soothe his companion. "All is not lost. You can trust me on that but we have but one play left."

Victor's breathing remained fast but his eyes had locked onto the librarian's, listening intently.

"The road ahead is unknown to me but what I do know is that we need to follow those animals back to whatever hole they came from and await our opportunity to liberate him."

His face was imploring, seeking approval in the younger man's eyes. The steady slow sound of marching boots had ended and the men suddenly found a silence upon them again. Victor nodded his head, trying to grasp what the librarian was saying.

"Just tell me what I have to do," he said, breath now returning to normal and his focus intent on the blue eyes of the man opposite.

The librarian stood and motioned for him to join as they walked to the stairwell again, before hopping down to the ground floor. Edging his head out the doorway, Breagal looked both ways before stepping out into the open clearing.

"What did you mean upstairs?"

The librarian turned, surprised to see that Victor hadn't followed. He was still standing under the doorway and Breagal gave a confused look which prompted him to repeat the question.

"I'm not sure what you mean."

"I heard you say 'it worked'. What worked?"

"I…" Breagal stuttered, searching the ground with his eyes for an answer.

"Where were you the last night we were here?" Victor asked and stepped out from the doorway, closer to the librarian. "The night you were collecting firewood. You were gone an awful long time."

Breagal traced his own steps back a little, noticing the other man seemed a little hostile, and held out his hands in defence.

"I can explain Victor."

"I'm listening," he said and pulled up a couple of paces short of the other man.

"I think we're both agreed that Norman doesn't have the luxury of time on the conscious plane," Breagal said and received a nod to continue. "My brother's entries followed a long tangent, weeks in reality which we couldn't afford."

The frown on Victor's face as he scrutinised the librarian didn't offer comfort to Breagal who felt he wasn't explaining things very well.

"You recall the shop we were in? Saul met with the owner, deep in the woods. After an initial dispute, where he was exiled, he returned and they managed to resolve things, living with the family for quite a while. Again," Breagal stressed, "time which we didn't have."

"What did you do Breagal?"

The librarian held up his hands to try and offer reassurances, shaping his argument as best he could.

"I accelerated things a little."

"What does that mean?"

"I brought Norman closer to us, much sooner."

"You got him caught!"

Victor stepped forward suddenly and Breagal backed away from the younger man, imploring him to hear his logic. Victor looked around the landscape, shaking his head and moved back to the doorway and began kicking the wall with the point of his shoe.

"I only did it for his best interests Victor!"

"How do you figure that one out?" the man said and turned to Breagal, livid with fists pumped by his sides.

"Calm down. Come on now. We can't afford for you to get too excited or you'll break the state."

The remark made Victor laugh in spite of his anger and he churned a short path up and down the dirt track until he had regained composure again.

"If we would have followed the normal course of events, we wouldn't have had the time to reach Norman. I had to do something drastic. Trust me on this."

Victor looked into the man's face. Breagal's hands were closed together in prayer, propping up his nodding head.

"You couldn't have just sent him a message? Suggested a meeting point?"

"It would make no difference," Breagal said. "This is his constructed world. His mind will try to convince him of its reality. You remember in your own dreams, your mind tried to justify certain bizarre scenarios to continue the dream state. It's the same with Norman. Any reference to the outside world will fail to convince him – no letter would offer that. He's unlikely to even recognise us."

Victor took a moment to consider the new information, shaking his head, trying to reconcile it with the training he had received and finding it hard to swallow.

"Sometimes I wonder whose side you're on."

"I'm on your side!" Breagal said and moved over to him, risked putting out an arm which patted his shoulder. "Now we know where he is. The alternative was searching for days and weeks in the forest. The merchant's dwelling was very well hidden, by all accounts. Trust me. I read it."

Victor took a deep breath, looked at the face of Breagal and accepted the encouraging look he gave before walking out, turning right up the dirt track. About a kilometre in the distance, in a dotted line, they could make out the body shapes of the men blazing a trail west. They seemed to be following an imaginary line directly ahead, leading to a huge mountain in the distance. When Breagal felt that enough time had passed for his logic to seep in, he restarted the conversation again.

"We need to follow suit. We can't let them out of our sights at this point. Are you still with me?"

Breagal needn't have asked, for as soon as the words had left his mouth, Victor had already picked up his pace, striding with intent. The librarian watched the purposeful stride and smiled.

***

The danger was absolutely clear. They had been following the troop for several hours in plain sight. They passed neither structure nor dwelling that could double as cover. They kept the solid pace of the pack a kilometre behind, barely enough visibility to distinguish the rectangular object lofted from the back of the procession. Under Breagal's suggestion they loaded their pockets with fist sized stones from a rock wall in the town. Every hundred metres they dropped a stone on the ground to mark their path. Soon realizing that they were walking in a straight line, they unloaded the remainder into a small pile off the side of the track.

They walked in silence, Victor spending the time ruminating on where his friend was being taken and the imminent danger far and beyond what he had expected to encounter. As he kept pace, he continued to look down, watching his steps, planting them into the already staccato pattern laid down on the mud below.

Breagal meanwhile was lost in his own reverie, recalling the final mangled diary entries of Saul.

"Any idea where they're headed?"

"My brother wrote about it. It's a place called Namastre. Some sort of holding pen hidden within the mountain."

Ahead of them the troops continued at the steady marching pace. The faint blue outline of a giant mountain, its shadow now cloaking the upper portion in grey, loomed large on the horizon as they approached.

"It's approaching evening," Breagal said, looking at his watch and making a quick calculation in his mind. "We probably have another thirty minutes left."

"That's not enough time!" Victor implored. "How are we going to catch them? We'll lose them!"

"There isn't much we can do together," the librarian replied. "The dosage only lasts so long before you need to come out of the dream cycle."

"Well, can't you just give a bigger dose?"

"I wish I could. My supply is finite."

"Isn't there something else we can do?"

Breagal considered for a moment walking alongside, their strides synching.

"There is, as far as I can see it, only one other option."

"Tell me."

Breagal weighed his words up carefully.

"If I pull myself out of the dream, I can administer you with shots of Profanol. You would be taking my dosage. It means that your dream sequence won't be interrupted, and you can continue to follow the pack."

"But where will you be during all of this?"

"I will be carefully observing you and Norman of course, for any signs of distress. Should there be cause for concern, I can pull you back out at no risk to yourself."

Victor's eyes focused on each of his own steps tracing the harder terrain now, processing this new information as he probed further.

"I don't like the idea of being cut loose in this place on my own. I don't know how to get out of here."

"Here's how it would work," Breagal responded, sensing Victor's commitment was close.

The librarian explained that he would give Victor another dose as soon as they returned; it would be two days' residence in the mind of Norman Adams, instead of one. At the end of the second day, he would be pulled from the dream as normal, whereby they would discuss what he had found. To re-enter the dream state, Breagal would take a smaller quantity, just enough to assist Victor's dream hop.

When he had finished talking, Breagal looked to his right and could see Victor weighing things again in his mind. Had he not been looking to the floor and instead at the older man's face, Victor would have noticed the nervous tension there as the librarian made the pitch.

"OK. I'll do it," Victor said.

A wave of relief came over Breagal, expressing itself in a huge smile he struggled to contain. He looked away from his companion momentarily before returning a face now composed and serious.

"Good lad. Besides, you wouldn't want this old man slowing you down in any case," he added with a sudden cheer in his voice.

"You seemed spritely enough when that siren set off!"

"And I'll pay for it later," Breagal said, stretching his back as if revealing a pain there.

Taking a deep breath of the evening air, they both looked ahead again. The shadow was stretching further down the mountain and darkness was approaching. Breagal put his thin arm around the shoulder of the shorter man now, walking alongside.

"It's a heavy burden to carry, but I'll be watching from the wings. I'll also make sure that no harm comes to Norman up above."

"Thanks Breagal."

They walked like this for several minutes before Victor spoke again.

"How long do we have left?"

"Not long. Maybe a few minutes. I'll try and get out sooner than you and administer that shot. I've got more experience than you in this state so it should be manageable."

"Is there anything I need to know? Anything you read that I should know about before I keep following?" Victor asked.

"No. You're fully up to speed my boy."

Suddenly Breagal's watch began beeping and, turning to Victor, he asked him to lie on the ground.

"Deep breaths now, Victor. You'll feel a wave try and take you back to consciousness. Fight it. Anchor yourself in this plane. Feel the hardness of the path on your back and the cool breeze as it whistles around you. Dig your nails deep into the soil and feel the damp earth between your fingers. This is real. Sense its richness all around you."

Victor could feel himself being taken slowly, like he was drifting on the breeze. His eyes closed and he began to fight against the current, hearing the soft sounds around. He scratched the surface of the soil below, which was oddly soothing. It felt rich and textured between his fingertips. His attention moved to his head, which had been resting on a small bed of pebbles; it was discomforting but he dared not move. It had gently reminded him that he was lying out in the open. Opening his eyes now, he looked for the source of the words that had spoken a few minutes earlier. He felt the wave that had pulled, draw back suddenly and at once felt centred again on the dream plane. Breagal was nowhere to be seen.

He was on his own.

FIFTY

The librarian didn't take long to act after he awoke. Almost in reflex, on opening his eyes he pulled the briefcase from under his seat and snapped it open on his lap. A quick glance around the room told him that it was safe, the only movements in the dawning light the consistent breathing of the prostrate patient opposite. Everyone else was still deep in slumber around him. Fishing out the syringe he plunged it into a vial and slugged a large measure, tapping the air bubble inside. Victor was sitting beside and Breagal quickly located the vein on his arm and pressed the contents into his bloodstream.

Observing the sleeper for a few moments he allowed himself to smile. Closing the case, he gently rose and placed it back on his chair then left the room. Several minutes later he had returned with a wheelchair. With some difficulty he managed to lurch the dead weight of Victor James onto it, securing the briefcase on his lap before slowly rolling it out of the ward. He looked behind to make sure that he hadn't been seen, but the coast looked clear. Wheeling the drugged man through the big double doors of the hospital, they were now crossing the gravel of the car park. Breagal spotted his sedan there, and he found the humour to whistle as he approached.

***

He began to feel the edge of tiredness creep into his mind. It hadn't been difficult to follow the pack ahead in the darkness with the silvery glint of the moon above casting a fine sheen across his path. He still kept the same distance however, and the initial tentative steps which had turned into a bold stride had now resembled a shuffle in the last few kilometres.

Suddenly, he noticed the course of the men alter direction slightly. They had reached the base of the large mountain and instead of scaling what would have been a near vertical face, they instead steered left around a rock face hidden from view. Panicking at their sudden disappearance, Victor sprinted to where they had entered, finding an opening that banked hard downward into a valley. Scrawled on the grey rock face in white chalk was the word "Namastre" with an arrow pointing to the opening.

He entered and immediately heard the footsteps echoing off the walls from below, but with the dim light conceded it would be difficult to traverse. Instead of taking the route deeper into the canyon, he made the decision to find a place nearby to scope out and watch. Spotting an overhanging rock ledge near the entrance he hauled himself up and hid his body from view. When he was confident in his position, Victor craned his head over the ridge, surveying the land below. Too dark to see, he employed his other senses. Boots thudded against the rock and there was the occasional sound of tumbling rocks hurtling deeper below, before finally, silence settled.

The walk had been long and cold and he sat back against a rock face, careful not to disturb any stones nearby. Yawning he rubbed at his eyes and felt them dry and weary. Gently closing them he detected the gradual temperature increase with the rising sun not yet in sight. He stretched out his legs, the spent muscle still tightly coiled and sore.

Suddenly in his peripheral vision he saw a movement to his right, and swivelled around too late. A strong hand wrapped around his throat, hoisting him high into the air, pinning his head hard against the rock. He could feel the muscular grip tighten around his windpipe, feeling the air there cut off and he began gasping in desperation. Frantically he pulled at the arm of the beast to release him but it was too strong. His vision became spotty now and he felt the blood rush to his head. His hand searched the wall behind wildly for a loose stone or rock, but found nothing.

Energy was seeping from his body and he could feel the blackness coming upon him. The grip eased all of a sudden and he felt uncertain feet touch the ground again; in his immediate field of vision a head appeared. Victor was still trying to swallow air deeply through the small opening and he felt like his consciousness was about to slip from him. Just before he fainted, the hand that held him dropped from his throat before a voice, full of emotion, cried out in pain.

"Why did you kill my dog?"

FIFTY-ONE

When Victor awoke, his hands instinctively moved to his throat. The attack had come from nowhere and he breathed deep, feeling the muscles of his throat tense, pained with each hungry breath he swallowed. He felt the air cold on his raw throat and it caused him to break into a coughing fit that emptied his lungs. Doubling up on his side, he winced and waited for it to pass. After some minutes, his breathing had returned to normal and suddenly remembered the imminent danger. He snapped his eyes open in panic and looked around.

Slumped against the rock face, sliding off to one side, sat the hulking frame of the man he had met in the merchant shop. His eyes were staring at Victor though he detected there was no longer a threat in them. The man's large face was smeared with mud with clearer trails below his sorrowful eyes as if he had been crying. Propping himself on his elbow Victor studied the man closer now and could see that his large arms were a mass of blood, seeping out from beneath the thick mud that had crusted there. One leg was buckled beneath him and on this he sat. The other one was in front and the foot dangled there freely from the socket.

Approaching carefully, Victor bent down to the man whose own breath was low and shallow. The attacker could barely keep his eyes open, but managed to look up. Slowly his lips moved to speak, and it required a huge effort to do so.

"I'm sorry for choking you Mister. But my Skye..."

He broke off, and a huge tear formed in the corner of his eye, before dropping onto a cut cheek, bouncing off onto the dusty floor. Victor suddenly remembered the name of the man. Norman had shouted it from the cage.

He studied the figure, reasoning that he must have weighed close to 300 lbs., most of that solid muscle mass, completely redundant now given the state of his foot. He completely dwarfed Victor and he sensed that if the man had wanted to kill him, it wouldn't have been at all difficult to snap his neck. His earlier fear left now, and sitting down beside the man he felt tiny in comparison.

"That's OK," Victor replied. I want you to know that I would never hurt your dog. I was trying to help and feed you back at the store. You remember?"

The big man reflected on this before answering.

"So if it wasn't you…"

"I'm sorry, but it was the man who was with me. He shouldn't have done it. It was wrong. I'm so sorry."

Yenjin shook his head, closing his eyes tight as if remembering again the limp shape of his dog dangling from the hook with its snapped neck. Several moments passed before Victor tried again.

"Yenjin? Your name is Yenjin right?"

The man rolled his large head up on its axis, expressing surprise.

"How did you know?" he asked with a weakened voice, barely audible.

"I'm friends with Norman."

"He… mentioned me?"

"He told me how brave you had been. How you saved him lots of times and were it not for you he would have burned in the house fire."

Yenjin smiled, closing his eyes, recalling their successful escape then his head dropped back to his shoulder, mumbling something.

"Yenjin, Norman's in trouble."

With considerable effort he looked up again at Victor, eyes trying to focus but not altogether there.

"What?" he slurred, barely enough energy to keep his head raised as it bobbed on his thick neck.

"I mean... those things... they took Norman!" Victor explained to him but it didn't seem to register with Yenjin, whose dazed expression remained.

His head fell onto his chest now and the entire weight of the man slid from the rock flat where his back had been propped, falling flat onto the ground. His head struck it first, skidding against the sharp stones there, opening up a fresh slice of his forehead where blood began forming.

"Christ," Victor said. He succeeded in rolling the man onto his back, stretching out the battered legs in front.

The small reserve of strength in Yenjin seemed to be disappearing rapidly. He was barely conscious, the breaths becoming broken and unsteady. Looking around, there was barely enough room on the ledge for them both now and from above Victor could see sun now visible, peeping out from a ridge in the cliff face. Its glow illuminated the cavern below them, and he could now make out distinct shapes in the distance.

Studying his surroundings under the new light for the first time, he was surprised to find that the cavern was deeper than he had imagined, hemmed in all around by the natural stone wall of the mountain. A winding path looped around the outer edge, circling a hole in the centre. It wound around and down further below them.

Craning his neck, Victor leaned over the side and followed it as far as he could. He could see many revolutions underneath, a collection of black bodies that looked like ants from this position. Watching them with morbid fascination the pack split, some busying themselves around a box which lay nearby. A small band of them raised it in the air and placed it on what appeared to be a pulley system. Victor could see the shadow below the box suggesting it was in suspension. Two of the figures were turning a wheel against the wall. He watched in horror as the cage inched along the lateral rope away from the ground beneath, disappearing from view.

Frantic, Victor jumped down from the ledge and bounded down the looping path. The view below was still obscured and it took two complete revolutions before he pulled himself to the ground and looked back down. He could detect a faint cry below and saw the box dangling from a rope, rocking from side to side. There was a second box alongside on the same rope, with what appeared to be another figure contained within. There was no movement from this one however, and Victor could see that the figures were suspended high above a huge open hole below. The faint smell travelled up through to him now and he caught the stink of faeces and fought against gagging.

"I'm too late."

FIFTY-TWO

He was impatient, waiting for the sleeper to stir and looking at his watch again he began to get agitated. Victor roused gently from his sleep and Breagal smiled and let out a long breath.

"Take your time. Easy now."

The lights had been dimmed in the room, helping to preserve the sleep of his guest. The smell of jasmine flavoured the air in the study and Victor opened his eyes and looked directly up at the ceiling above.

"In your own time now lad," Breagal reminded him, and Victor turned, shaking his head as if waking from a terrible dream.

"My God. It's worse than I imagined."

Bringing his chair closer Breagal's expression grew worried. He looked down at Victor and asked him to reveal everything from the point at which they had parted.

Victor was about to start before jerking around and noticing his surroundings for the first time. He sat up confused, and faced the seated man.

"Why am I in your house?" he asked, bemused.

"I had to take certain steps, you see. I had to make sure that your sleep cycle wasn't interrupted."

"Hold on a minute," Victor asked, suddenly becoming angry. "You moved me from the hospital?"

"Calm down, please," Breagal implored. "It was in everyone's best interests you see."

"No I don't see, Breagal," he snapped back, standing up. "I don't see how it is in my best interests that while I'm asleep you can take advantage of me."

Breagal smiled and reddened at the cheeks.

"Come on now, my boy. What do you take me for? No one took advantage of you," he laughed. "How do you think Norman's parents would have reacted next morning or indeed all of this afternoon if you had still been under the cloak of sleep? They probably would have thought you had gone comatose too!"

"Don't be flippant Breagal. You know what I mean."

"I'm afraid I don't, dear boy. A minor detail. Pray, please take a seat and tell me what happened."

"You don't get it. While I'm asleep you take it upon yourself to move me, without me knowing about it? A little heads up would be appreciated."

He held his hands up in apology.

"Mea culpa. I'm sorry. I did what I thought was right. I should have consulted you first of course. Please accept my apologies. Your interests were always top of my priorities."

"Clearly not," he snapped back before sitting back down on the thin yoga mat.

Victor relayed his uneventful trek in the night until near dawn when he had slipped inside the rock wall at the place called Namastre. Recalling the layout of the dome structure, he described how the men had looped the cage onto a suspension rope and pulled Norman out over the dark abyss below. It hovered there alongside a second cage, and he could hear the distant cries of his friend from below.

From his viewpoint, he continued to observe over several hours, enduring the foul fetor that wafted up from the pit below. When he had finished his account, he looked at Breagal whose seat had been turned away. He had been silent throughout and Victor saw his hands were clenched tightly together, the bony whites of his knuckles tensing.

"The other cage," Breagal asked, voice wavering. "Did you see what was in it?"

"Yes, I saw. It looked like there was another person inside."

Breagal drew a deep breath, shooting it out quickly, as if expressing sudden relief.

"What was the person doing?"

"Umm. Nothing."

"What do you mean, 'Nothing'," Breagal snapped. "He had to be doing something!"

"I guess whoever or whatever it was, was just sitting there. The cage was still and I didn't see any movement in it. All that moved were Norman and those...beasts."

Breagal leaned forward on the chair, resting his hand on his chin. He looked lost in thought. Victor stood and, finding his personal effects on the coffee table nearby, shovelled them into his pocket. He looked at his watch which showed that it was just after 6 p.m. He had just completed two, eight-hour dream shifts back to back.

"What are those marks on your neck?" Breagal asked from behind, looking up now and eyeing Victor's neck.

"Oh this?" he said, touching his throat gently. "I caught it on a tree vine as I was chasing the pack. No harm done."

"Should get it looked at. It looks sore," Breagal responded, before looking back down at a spot in front and returning to deep contemplation.

"Yeah, I will."

Victor picked up his phone and noticed a missed call from Norman's landline.

"Back in a minute."

Breagal wasn't listening; he was considering the narrative and piecing it together with what he already knew from the diary entries he had studied earlier. He barely noticed the door of his study open again a few moments later. His wife walked through and startled him from his thoughts.

"Not up to much, heh?" she said and pointed her head toward the little circle of crystals on the floor.

Breagal stood and tried to explain but she waved off his entreaty.

"Stephen, this is some dark stuff you're getting into. Look what it did for your brother. I don't want anything to happen to you."

Her voice was a mix of anger and emotion, and he moved close and held out his hands to hold her hips. She looked up into his eyes, him smiling and touching his forehead to hers.

"It's OK," he said. "I'm just helping out a friend. Nothing major. I promise, dear."

Margaret Breagal nodded slowly, and he lifted her head under the chin and kissed her softly on the lips.

"You sure everything's OK?" she asked.

Their hands found each other and he gave her an encouraging squeeze and seeing his smile, she unhooked herself from him.

"Your dinner's ready," she said and took a breath. "I've made enough for your friend if he wants to join."

He watched her leave, looking at the lock which he had failed to bolt when Victor had left. Breagal moved to the other side of the room to latch it but the other man passed through and glanced at the librarian. He couldn't hold the look and walked slowly over to him, staring down at the floor.

"They're turning off the life support in the morning. We've run out of time."

When he looked back up, Breagal saw that Victor was weeping and the librarian closed the space between them and held him in an embrace. Breagal soothed the man with quiet words, rubbing his back, but the librarian's face was hard and showed a determined look. It looked like he might have to get his hands dirty after all.

FIFTY-THREE

Breagal took his eyes of the road and looked to the passenger, who was still drying the tears from his face. The briefcase was on his lap and Victor was fidgeting with the handle, slapping it back and forth, distracting the librarian who felt it unwise to reproach the younger man given his sensitive state. Instead, Breagal patted his forearm, hoping to bring some comfort, but his touch felt forced.

Finding themselves stalled in traffic, they sat in silence waiting for the turn off ramp for the hospital to open up on the right.

"I know you're hurting Victor," he said in a soothing tone. "But it can't be a total surprise that the machine is to be turned off. It just means we can't afford any slip-ups in the time that we have."

Breagal said the words slowly, hoping that his directness wouldn't provoke the wrong response in his companion. Victor pulled down the flip mirror, looking at the red bloodshot eyes that stared back. Clearing his throat, he sat up straighter in the seat. The traffic edged forward and, seeing the sign for the hospital, Breagal indicated right, nose of the sedan poking out from the traffic line.

"We still have time," he reminded the passenger, who returned his stare and nodded in agreement.

"How do we get near him? How do we get him out of there? It's just..."

"I know it looks bleak now, but you'll find a way," Breagal said and as if thinking out loud continued, "There must be something about the siren. It's power there."

His words trailed off, suddenly distracted. A small opening appeared between them and the car in front. Pulling sharply right, the car exited the line and entered the next lane, oncoming traffic beeped loudly at the sedan as he cut straight across the traffic. The car bounded over the pavement illegally, bouncing the driver and passenger off their seats momentarily against the car roof before finally skidding to rest between two cars in the gravel car park of the hospital.

"Either we find a way, or make one," Breagal said.

***

The ominous news had spread and Victor could see a small group of people at the end of the hallway hovering at Norman's bed. The curtains had now been fully drawn back and he watched, hugs being exchanged, and sombre condolences being offered to Norman's grief-stricken parents. As they strode along the corridor he was surprised to note that the faces were mainly those of his colleagues. Emotion ebbed at his throat before he swallowed it back down.

They joined the group and Victor shook hands with each of his colleagues and introduced Breagal. Closet book worms already recognized him from the library.

"Stay you away from those wires now Clance," Victor said and smiled weakly. "Wouldn't want you breaking anything."

The other man stepped back from the bed and held out his hands to show that he had no intention of getting any closer. His smile, like those around failed to light the rest of the face, a quick flick of the lips that felt strange to hold with any conviction in the circumstances.

"Been a while mate," Clancy said. "You must be out of sick days at this point?"

"You think Richmond would allow me sick days off? Not a hope. I've taken most of my holidays these past couple weeks."

Finding Norman's parents, he excused himself from the casual banter and approached, warmly embracing them both.

"It's the humane thing to do, Victor. I hope you understand," Noreen implored.

"I understand," he replied. "It's your choice of course. Both of you. Still nothing from the doctor?"

"Nothing barring a miracle. He hasn't responded in any of their tests. It's like he's in a world of his own right now."

Victor moved to his sleeping friend. His face was pale and hollow, the oxygen tubes still affixed to his mouth. Chest still moved mechanically and to one side, the machine's heart monitor display still pulsed seventy-three beats per minute. Breagal was behind Victor, sympathizing with the parents and after a few moments the librarian was by his side again, close enough that only he could hear the whisper.

"It's time."

FIFTY-FOUR

They were sitting in Breagal's car waiting for the Profanol to take effect. It was late and they could see the lights in the hospital building being switched off one by one. On the second floor, where he figured Norman to be, he could make out two silhouettes behind the curtain. The other guests had all filed out one by one, and there was no doubt who remained.

He had just taken a double dose shot to his vein in agreement that a longer time in the dream plane might be the best option lest he return prematurely.

For his part, Breagal had taken a small dosage, enough to bring him into the dream state, after which he would sit out and observe Victor. They both had their seats tilted back and lay in the darkness, the heat from inside the car gently soothing. They sat in silence, impatient until finally sleep entered.

***

Come closer. Carefully. Breathe deeply.

Feeling the terrain under his feet change from the matted car floor to stiff ground beneath, Victor found himself at the same spot as before. Sharing his view on the hilltop was Breagal and they found that they were both staring at the same place, beyond at the huge mountain in the darkness.

"I don't have much time," Breagal said, finding the words difficult to come. "You need to find a way to get close to those cages and release them."

Victor reflected for a moment, before brushing away a concern.

"You take care of things down here, and I'll take care of things up there. You have my word," Breagal said and held out his hand.

They shook before joining together in an embrace that caught Victor off-guard. He took a deep breath and they both nodded to each other, before suddenly he watched as the image of Breagal began to thin out before disappearing from the hilltop.

Alone again, Victor shivered against the cold before breaking into a jog down the hill. He saw the familiar base of the mountain, refusing to let his pace waver, a grim look of determination on his face. Starlight from above revealed the line of stones they had laid out two days earlier, helping to correct his course. His focus narrowed straight ahead, and if he had reason to look behind he would have been surprised to find Stephen Breagal, appearing again on the hilltop, quickly ducking to the ground, hidden from view.

From the lying position the librarian raised his head and watched the distance slowly growing between the runner and himself. Glancing at his watch he estimated that he had an eight-hour shift ahead. He waited a few beats, before getting up, took a deep breath and started to jog.

***

By the time he had reached the mountain base again, it was early morning. The sun shone on the rock wall and Victor allowed himself to ease back into a slow walk, letting his breath settle. He wiped the sweat that had collected on his brow and seeing the crudely drawn sign of Namastre on the wall, Victor slid his body within the narrow gap and once again found himself inside the domed canyon.

It was completely still within and his first instinct was to climb the small rock footholds on the side, leading to the ledge above. With ease he pulled himself up and over and to his surprise saw the big heap still lying there. There was barely a breath in the man but his face, or at least the parts not matted with blood or dirt, showed a deathly pallor. His chest no longer sucked breaths and Victor struggled to even see the ribcage rise.

"Yenjin. Yenjin!" he whispered into the man's ear without receiving a response.

Pinching a fold of skin on the thick bloodied forearm didn't work either and Victor's head dropped, realizing that his trump card was useless.

Carefully navigating off the ledge and back on terra firma, he began moving along the circular path spiralling below. After reaching the third revolution he counted another ten until the bottom. Directly below he spied the figures in the cages again. Their shadowy outline wasn't quite sharp enough for Victor to make out, but he fancied the more active figure to be Norman, and with his movements the cage dangled on the rope line. He couldn't see where it was attached and decided to slowly descend two more revolutions.

His breath caught in his chest as the scene from below suddenly became clearer. He could see the band of about thirty soldiers all huddled together on a landing below where the path finished. All covered in black armoury, their heads were shorn with bloody smears and dirt scratched across their skin. They appeared perfectly human except for the orange luminous eyes boring out of their skulls.

There was a small murmur of noise from the pack, unintelligible to Victor, and he watched in morbid fascination as it appeared they were communicating with each other. Their mouths stretched open unnaturally and they seemed to be walking in a trance, the occasional jerky movement as they bumped together making his skin crawl.

Assessing the stony path ahead that looped down, Victor decided to take in one more revolution, pressing his back tight against the stone wall to remain out of sight of the group. When it was completed, he crawled slowly toward the edge again, unwittingly taking a huge slug of the putrid smell into his lungs. The odour smelt like decaying flesh and human waste and it almost made him gag, raising a hand to his nose. Breathing through his mouth he could almost taste it curdling at the back of his throat. He pulled himself from the edge out of view and swallowed a deep, cleaner breath, which cleared the smell.

Finding himself better prepared, he peeped out again, pinching his nostrils. His spot gave a full view of the scene beneath. Some fifty yards below he could see the pack again roaming around, bodies tight together on the small landing. Between a gap he could see that the suspended rope that had held the cages aloft was tied to a wooden wheel, with great big handles on its outer edge. To Victor's mind it looked like a steering wheel of a vessel of some sort joined to a pulley system, used to pull the cages out into the centre.

As he leaned over to get a closer look, a stone that had been embedded in the path broke off under his weight and suddenly fell from the path. Victor winced as he watched it tumble down, crashing off the paths below, the sound echoing off the walls amplifying the effect. All at once, the eyes of the pack looked up to where he had been crouching, and from deep within the canyon a siren began booming, shaking the ground around him.

Victor leapt to his feet and began running as fast as he could back up the winding path. The noise of the siren hurt his ears, but he ignored the pain, taking giant strides up and away from the gathering commotion below. With each loop, he could see the group advancing from below, their eyes menacing and focused on the runner. In the gaps of the siren call he could hear their heavy boots and grunting from the deep, striding with heavy purpose now, the pack all closing in on him.

Above, he could see the final revolution and felt his body coursing with adrenaline; he had nearly reached the top. The sounds seemed tantalizingly close now and he could feel their stinking breath on his back. On the last loop, the wall gap reared into plain view, but more worryingly was the absence of the chasing troop below. They too were on the final revolution, he realized in terror, and at that moment he felt the icy grip of a hand grab and pull his shoulder back, swirling him off balance. He hit the deck hard and saw one of the beasts, wide-eyed, leap on top of him. Its heavy weight lay stretched across his chest, the stench was palpable and Victor tried to heave the man off without success. The guttural noises were all around him now, teeth gnashing in anticipation as slowly all the figures had caught up, crowding around, blocking out the sun high above.

    Underneath the pile a desperate Victor James fought desperately, kicking and punching. He heard the siren stop, and considered that it might as well have been his heart, realizing that his aborted rescue attempt had just turned into a suicide mission.

FIFTY-FIVE

Breagal was wheezing, unable to keep pace with the relentless younger man. It was still dark around but light was nibbling at the sky to the east. He found a grassy spot off the muddy track and lay there watching Victor advance. Breathing deeply and allowing it to find its natural rhythm again, he allowed his eyes to close. The image there quickened his settling breath again as he saw Saul captured in a cage and dangling over the open gaping hole below. He shook it from his mind and practiced the relaxation techniques, taking a deep breath before holding and releasing gently. He began focusing his attention on various parts of his body, feeling himself present there. Relaxing the breaths now, he felt the tension in his body slowly fade.

When his eyes had opened, the early morning light was brightening the darkness around. Looking up he failed to spot Victor on the horizon. Breagal got up, re-joining the beaten trail and began marching toward the mountain at a steady pace. After an hour the blue mountain loomed up at him, and he could see the trail follow a path left. He moved that way but stopped in mid stride as the piercing shrill of the siren exploded from deep within the bowels of the mountain. Breagal's body crumpled to the floor, hands covering his ears from the deafening pitch. Panicking he turned back on his heels, running as fast as he could, all the while looking over his shoulder and expecting the beasts to burst into view around the walled enclosure.

The sound ended almost as soon as it had started and finally Breagal stopped to look back at the mountain, a confused expression on his face. He waited several minutes for another siren call, but it was only followed by silence. Returning, he found himself turning left on the trail and staring at the grey rock wall, reading the sign.

"So, this is where it ends, big brother. I'm finally here."

He followed its arrow through a narrow hole in the wall face. The view at once staggered him and he approached with sudden trepidation. He could see that the path now looped down and around along the outer edges of the cavern, boring its way deeper into the earth. He took several steps inside and traced the path with his eyes not seeing clearly where it finished. Breagal then took a few steps further down the gentle decline before carefully approaching the edge and crouching. His eyes squinted, still unable to see beyond.

He was about to turn around and stand but suddenly a figure leapt from above, its full weight hitting him hard and taking his breath. The momentum carried him tumbling over the edge and he found his back hit a rock below, shooting an indescribable pain up his body. He was wrestling with the other body on top of him, feeling blood in his mouth now and his limbs were digging all around, trying to grab a hold of something solid as they continued rolling. Finally, he felt the brutal assault stop and found his body flung out on a flat plain. Feeling a crippling pain in his back, he opened his eyes and cried out. There was moisture underneath the rag that was his shirt and, reaching around, felt the sharp edge of a stone that was lodged there. His head swam with the pain and he rolled onto his knees in discomfort.

By his side he saw the attacker, a huge man, and blood flowed freely now from his mouth. He looked down at the bulk and couldn't believe what he was seeing. The big man spat a wad of blood in his direction and, looking up at him, mouthed one word.

"Murderer."

Breagal couldn't begin to rationalize it, but managed to divert his attention away from the bloodied man and looked up, seeing the walled entrance above. He had fallen some twenty metres and with fortune had landed on the next path.

Suddenly, the siren started, terrifying him back to his senses. He looked below and could see the beasts staring up, orange eyes glistening as they broke into a sprint. To their right, Breagal saw the wooden cages teetering on a rope. The line was connected to opposite walls several revolutions far below looking as thin as dental floss against a dark pit. He struggled to his feet and stepped toward the edge, looked down to measure the distance of the fall, before stepping back and shaking his head. Breagal shouted desperately in the direction of the cages, but his voice was swallowed up by the growing noise in the canyon as the troop boots slapped off the hard surface, sending echoes around. Breagal's face broke and seeing their advance, staggered up the path, unable to fully straighten his back.

He reached the entrance ahead of the pack and looked back desperately for a brief second, hearing them close but not yet within sight. Looking at his watch he cried in despair, turned and ran out onto the open plain, back humped as the stabbing stone wriggled deeper inside his muscle. Moments later he heard the sound of their footfalls change, no longer echoing off rock, instead hearing it hit the hard earth.

"Wake up," he screamed.

His sight blurred as tears filled his eyes. He repeated the cry, stumbling ahead with no real purpose, the vast plain stretched out far and wide around him. He screamed the name of his brother, but it was drowned out the second it left his mouth as he felt the pack jump on him, sending his body into a nosedive as he crashed into the mud.

FIFTY-SIX

Standing up made the cage rock gently on the rope, its movement making him woozy. The smell that reeked up from below had become more familiar, almost tolerable but it still stung the man's eyes as he rubbed at them. He found it difficult to piece together his broken thoughts, the memories beginning to melt under the intense heat that came from below. Looking down at the pit between the bars of the prison, he could see the putrid brown lumpy filth that was bubbling there like the open mouth of a mud volcano.

Thick plumes of white gas popped from the great bubbles that wafted it high, the curdling sour smell directly penetrated their wooden cages. Norman continued to look down, staring at the sides of the pit for a reference to consider how long it would take to hit the surface if he slipped through the bars.

On one side he could see another cage that had been there when he arrived. The person inside was older, huddled in the corner of the cell, arms clutched around the bars. He seemed a couple of decades older and had dull, lifeless eyes and blotchy, red skin, peeling on a sun burnt forehead. The man's clothes were ragged, hanging from his thin frame in ribbons. Norman tried to speak with him but there was no indication that the man had heard. He remained still, staring beyond to an imaginary point in the distance. The cages were close enough together that Norman could reach out through the bars of his own and he began to rattle the other cage, serving only to terrify the prisoner who now covered his eyes with a dirty sleeve.

Norman's attention diverted to the other side where a group of black figures were bunched on a landing that jutted out from the mountain. He could faintly recall from somewhere a wall of darkness creep up on him, the feeling of dread, swinging upside down in the air. The memory was fragmented, broken, as he tried to tease it out but found it swallowed up by the thick odour, a dense fog in his mind. He felt it scramble his thoughts, a headache pulsing in his brain, veins in his temple vibrating.

The sun was above them and he felt its sudden warmth but sat back down shielding his eyes from the growing light. Licking his dry lips, he looked around for a source of water. His box was suspended high in the air with his neighbour, metres from the nearest rock wall. Tendrils of the dirty white plume from below continued to finger their way up through his cage. He tried to waft it away but he was fighting ghosts, that continued their assault on his senses. It coated his tongue and the back of his throat, making him dizzy until he lay down flat, feeling the wooden beam slats hard on his back.

A deafening noise from within the mountain blasted out, frightening the two caged figures. Norman clamped his hands to his ears for fear that his eardrums would burst. The pain was excruciating and under the narrow slits of his eyes he could see the group of figures suddenly take flight and speed away. He followed their pursuit and could see a man running away at the top of one of the turns high above. He watched in detached fascination as the figures caught up with the runaway, wrestling him to the ground. After several moments Norman was relieved to hear the siren stop and he took his hands from his ears, the sound still ringing in them.

The group carried the bundle from up high and made their way slowly back down to the ledge where they had been huddled earlier. One of the group moved into an arched doorway against the side of the mountain and came back carrying a cage. The man appeared to be unconscious and was tossed into it and the entry was closed, fastened tight with some cord. Norman watched, morbidly fascinated at the scene unfolding. The cage was hoisted onto a rope which was threaded through the spokes of a large wheel.

Two of the black figures pulled on the wheel and slowly the cage was sent off the edge of the path, the lifeless feet of the prisoner dragging on the path below before they took off and hovered mid-air. Several more turns winched it closer to Norman, rattling the string of cages as they stood suspended high above the pit.

Norman shifted around confirming that there was only one other box apart from his own. His thinking was becoming cloudy, finding it difficult to concentrate. The movement of his own cage added to the strangeness he felt, displacing logic and reason before they began to branch out. When the new cage had pulled close, he looked at the face of the unconscious captive. There was a certain oddness about his features that made him stand out from the man in the other cage behind. Norman reached a hand out and began shaking the cage violently.

This time it brought a reaction from the prisoner, and Norman watched with interest as he stirred from his sleep. He rolled from his back and onto his side, drawing his legs up from the holes to allow him to manoeuvre and carefully rose to his feet, planting them on the wooden beams underneath. The man was tall and the cage prevented him from standing erect. Hunching over he finally turned around and Norman had a clear view of his face for the first time. The man's eyes were clear and full of emotion as they searched Norman's face; seeing something there, mouth dropped in awe.

"Buddy, is that really you?"

The siren suddenly burst out from close by, bouncing off the rock walls around them, vibrating the line of cages. Norman pulled his eyes away from the new prisoner, hands clapped to his ears. In an arched doorway carved against the mountainside, a gentle hue of red light flared in tandem with the screeching noise.

It illuminated the grey walls within. The black figures scurried off, and Norman hauled himself to the front of the cage, peeping his head through the bars and looking upward for a movement there. Craning, he spied the top half of a man's body high above on the upper rings. His body was bent over and looking down at them. It was too far away to see his face, but he thought he could see the man's mouth open, perhaps shouting something. The shrill of the siren was too loud and swallowed the noise, and the man ran back up the short remainder of the loop. Norman could see the dark figures were halfway up now and continued their relentless pursuit. Two of them stopped where the man had been standing as if investigating something there, but the force of the pack continued chasing the man high above as he completed the top revolution and moved out of sight.

Suddenly the two black figures who had stopped halfway up the mountain fell from the path. Norman watched them tumbling downwards at a ferocious pace, hitting the rocky slopes hard and unable to prevent their onward descent. The bodies were mangled and broken by the time they had reached the prisoners level and the fascinated observer watched as they rolled all the way down and tipped silently into the pit beneath them. The boiling slime slowly crawled over the bodies of their jailors until they were submerged below.

The newcomer in the cage next to Norman had also watched the scene and the two neighbours found themselves breathless, looking up at the ledge where the beasts had fallen to their death. A shape stirred there, poking a bloody head out and looked down at them.

"What the..." Norman said shocked, and was even more surprised to hear recognition in the voice of the man next to him as he shouted.

"Yenjin!"

FIFTY-SEVEN

Victor looked around for some way to get out of the cages but he could see they were suspended high above a pit, the aroma of which had now collected in his nostrils making him swoon a little before finding his balance again. It's revolting, he thought and he tried breathing through his mouth as best he could. The siren was still bleating now and he found it hard to think. The figures had left them unattended in pursuit of the man high above and Victor's mind searched for a way to get out of the cage.

"We have to get out!" he said to Norman beside who looked at him like he was crazy. "Do you understand what I'm saying?"

The man was on one knee, a pained expression on his face, eyes closed and a hand rubbing his hair.

"It's the air Norman. Try not to breathe it."

Victor was looking all around and along the rope without finding any means to help himself. He moved to the front of the cage and shouted against the siren up to Yenjin, who either hadn't heard or wasn't following his orders. Either way they still sat there helpless, feeling their best chance of escape slipping through their fingers.

The siren stopped suddenly. Seizing the moment Victor shouted up to Yenjin who was still laying against the ledge, peering down at them.

"We need your help Yenjin! I'm trapped with Norman. Those things are coming back!"

Pressing with urgency he hoped the big man could find a final reserve from somewhere. The two prisoners watched the large stooped figure raise himself off the ledge as he began to drag his body down the path, half hopping and crawling. They watched in desperation as he looped around them high above, all the time with Victor casting a nervous glance at the entrance opening, expecting a flood of soldiers to arrive there at any moment. Progress was slow and the man lurched forward violently, falling down stretches of the path and hitting the rock wall face. Victor's heart leapt in his chest at each stumble and, after what seemed an eternity, he was on the ground level with them and seeing him close now, they could see the almost maniacal determination in the giant's face. His teeth were broken, grimacing against the pain, and his head was a swollen pulp, with bulging eye whites reddened with blood. The trail that he had made was bloody against the stony path surface, but he had reached the clearing where the troops had assembled before.

"The wheel! You need to turn it!"

Looking to where the man pointed, Yenjin cried out in pain as he managed to balance his frame onto his good foot and pull close to the rock wall. There he fumbled for the wheel, vision impaired, blood flowing over his eyes. He wrapped his giant hands around the handles and pulled desperately. Victor looked to the entrance above which was still empty, before looking back at the wheel. A forlorn, breathless Yenjin stood beside the wheel, looking at him in resignation. He had been unable to budge it.

"No!" Victor cried out in anguish. "This can't be it!"

As he crumpled to the floor of his prison, he watched as the huge weight of Yenjin slowly slid off the wall and fell lifeless onto the ground below. The big hands on the wheel dropped with it, leaving thick, red bloody prints.

"Yenjin?"

It was a voice behind Victor and looking around could see Norman's face pressed against the frame of the cage. He looked at the collapsed man now, detecting something move in the man's eyes.

"I remember now," he said. "But it's hazy."

Yenjin and Victor looked at Norman now in anticipation.

"You saved my life," he said, eyes closing, trying to remember. "Yes, that's right! In the attic! You saved me from the fire in the house."

"Don't forget about the forest either," the big man croaked, suddenly finding the energy to speak, smiling in spite of his bloodied and broken face.

"That's right," Norman said. "I came back for you but you were gone. I wanted to save you."

"You did, son. You did save me."

With an almighty effort, the heap staggered to his feet again, swaying on an unsteady leg. In his peripheral vision Victor could see a black line seep into the mountain from on high. Looking there he could see the troops had returned and were sprinting down the canyon, completing loops around them. The siren burst out all around them again, deafening in its pitch, Victor screamed out but was unable to even hear the voice as it exited his mouth.

"Now Yenjin!"

Yenjin leaned on the wheel and began turning the wheel with every ounce of his being. They felt the cages budge a little and looked at the man whose back was turned to them. He was trembling all over with the effort, and Victor suddenly felt himself being winched back along the rope line. As soon as the cage had reached the ledge, he began jumping on the beams below his feet in panic. After hearing one of them snap, he wedged his foot against it and it broke off. The hole created there was just big enough for him to slip his body out and, running to the wheel, he accompanied the giant who had expended tremendous effort. The eyes were swimming in his head now, but still the grip remained fast. Victor assisted and pulled the handles, momentum soon carrying Norman's cage safely onto the ledge.

Yenjin fell to the ground exhausted and looked at the scene in front. Audio had gone for him now and he could dimly see his friend liberated from his cage by the efforts of the other man who had displayed considerable strength of his own in breaking open the prison structure. One loop above them, just beyond the solitary cage that still swung on the rope with the little man cowering, Yenjin saw the line of black figures, mouths contorted into a silent scream. His eyes were too heavy to continue watching and everything was fading to black. He could feel the pain ebb out and away from his body, which came as a relief. The breaths rattled in his throat and he found them stressful and let them stop. He let the last breath hang before finally closing his eyes.

***

Norman's parents were standing beside their son at the hospital bed holding each other tight. Tears fell freely from their faces and they both held his hand in their own. Clearing her throat, Noreen Adams looked at the man who was standing by the machine. Nodding, the doctor flicked the switch and the machine extinguished its last breath into the patient's chest.

***

Victor hauled his friend Norman Adams from the cage. He was aware of the ranks of soldiers closing in on them from above. There was no way back up there and the only option open to them now was the little doorway against the cave where the red light pulsed with each beat of the wailing siren. Holding hands, they ran to it now over the prostrate body of Yenjin. Disappearing from view inside the cave, the walls narrowed into a tunnel and they raced inside, bathed by the red glow from within. Between the beats Victor could hear the excited screams just outside, accompanied by the thrashing and sloppy tearing of a feast as they accelerated deeper into the heart of the mountain.

The deep red hues were beginning to soften but the intensity of the drum grew louder than ever. Victor barely had time to recognize, but noticed the inner walls were becoming damp around them. The red had now changed to blue and then a gentler green calming glow coming in waves, as they moved closer to the source of the sound. Behind them, above the din of the hungry feast, was the sound of hard boots hitting the inside of the tunnel. In pursuit and closing now, the first few bodies had been distracted by Yenjin but the group continued on.

Suddenly Victor felt his friend's grip weaken and watched in horror as Norman crashed to the floor, clutching his chest. His back coiled, shifting his pelvis up in the air. The slight body spasmed and thrashed against the floor then, after a violent jerk, it lay motionless. The green light bounced off the slick walls around them and lit up the face of the Norman as Victor saw the dead eyes look up and away from him.

FIFTY-EIGHT

Panic gripped Victor as he looked down at the lifeless body of his friend, the snarling noise of the troops drawing closer. He knelt down and started to give CPR, banging on Norman's chest. He continued pressing air into his lungs and could see long shadows dancing on the ceiling beyond, just around the corner. Desperate, he crashed a double fist into the sternum of Norman and to his surprise a weak breath slipped from his friend's mouth.

Looking into his eyes, there was a flicker of movement there and watching him blink, Victor felt reassured, scooping him over his shoulder. He now saw the troops in plain sight and, with considerable effort, ran away from them, turning around the corner.

Their tunnel suddenly opened up into a small rectangular room, which was completely illuminated in a soothing green colour. The sight almost staggered Victor and he noticed on the left side the source of the glow, a large crystal almost his own height deeply embedded into the rock wall. They ran into the centre of the room and Victor could hear the weak rasping breath of Norman in his ear. Scanning for a doorway, or exit they appeared trapped. Putting his friend down and against the surface of the magnificent green crystal, Victor's eyes searched for an opening on the walls using his hands to feel along the wet rock surface. The voices were coming at them again and, desperate, he turned to Norman whose eyes were beginning to close.

He was slumped, barely in a seated position; arms had fallen onto his lap and a finger opened out and pointed into the corner weakly. Victor looked there and could see on the rock wall surface the green sheen of light across its face. He searched frantically around it but couldn't find the object of Norman's attention. Hanging his head, the emotion welled up in him and he let the tears come, closing his eyes and hearing the rush of the troops down the small tunnel.

When he opened them he saw a shimmer on the floor, which seemed to play tricks with his eyes. Clearing the tears, he was startled to see that the mirage was still there. Crouching he saw the floor in the corner was different on the surface; it was a pool of liquid, the green sheen camouflaging it against the rest of the terrain. It had not been immediately obvious from his standing viewpoint but from a squat position he could detect the shiny surface. Running over to it he looked down and his breath caught. He could see through it like a window and saw as if suspended from the ceiling, the body of his friend at the hospital. Standing to one side was a white-cloaked man with a navy turban and thick black beard. If the man wasn't immediately familiar, the two people across from him were – Norman's parents.

Victor turned around, seeing that the troops had now entered the opening of the small room. The green light flashed on their faces and they ran to Norman who was between them, stretched out against the wall. Victor sprinted to where his friend lay and managed to haul him to his feet, out of the stretching hand of the first beast. A second groped for them and Victor ducked, feeling the hand swipe at the air around his face. Spinning, he pulled the deadweight of his friend across the floor toward the portal, and cried out in pain feeling teeth seize his ankle.

Norman dropped from his arms suddenly, sent crashing to the ground just short of the pool of water. Pain shooting up his body, Victor reeled around and struck the face flush with his fist, the bite around his ankle letting go. Ignoring the pain, he scrambled back to his feet and in one movement pulled Norman off the ground, but standing on his injured foot, buckled with the effort and found himself falling again.

The fall had turned his body and he watched as soldiers bathed in green and with orange glaring eyes all piled forward, desperate hands outstretched like claws clamouring for them. Victor could feel them falling away just out of their reach as they dropped below the water.

FIFTY-NINE

Awakening, Victor reached out his hands in front, batting away the imaginary demons in his mind. Senses slowly came back to him and looking around he could see that he was inside the car of Stephen Breagal. The librarian was still asleep in the driver seat, and Victor tried to stir him but couldn't manage it. He looked ahead seeing the grand structure of the hospital, the early morning sun dazzling the windows with stretches of bright yellow light.

He flung open the car door and stepping out almost fell, suddenly feeling the searing pain in his foot. Looking down he saw the blood there soaking through his white soak, but continued against it. Hobbling through the car park, he felt each step squish under the pool of liquid that had accumulated in his shoe.

Ignoring the pain, he hobbled the entire way up the stairwell, not waiting for an elevator to the second floor. The blood from his shoe printed against the ceramic tile as he staggered past the reception desk. The receptionist rose from her seat, calling him back. Bursting through the double doors of the ward, Victor limped his way down the corridor, drawing bemused glances from staff and patients.

At the end of the corridor he could see the two figures of Norman's parents standing beside a doctor and he quickened his step against the pain climbing there. It almost made him black out, but drawing closer he could see the expression on their faces which unnerved him. They were in floods of tears and moved closer to the bedside of their son. Victor reached them and followed their stare.

The chest rose slowly but was steady and Victor watched the eyes open and stare up at him. The breathing mask had been removed and a small smile crept onto Norman's face as he recognized his friend. Victor moved to his side and the doctor was about to intervene, but Mrs Adams prevented him. He bent to kiss the forehead of his friend and they both began crying, the tears coming at once.

"You wouldn't believe the dream I just had," Norman said, smiling weakly up at him.

Victor laughed and nodded his head in agreement. "Try me."

EPILOGUE

The two young men were seated at a table casually observing the people in the room. The TV in the corner was blaring too loud, steadily increasing in volume since they had arrived fifteen minutes earlier. They looked at the culprit again, an older man perching on one of the chairs, aged in his sixties. He was wearing striped black and white pyjamas and used a broomstick to punch the volume button on the TV, which was high up in a bracket above in the corner of the room. His seat was one of two occupied at the outer edge of a line in front of the machine. The other occupant faced away from the set and the elderly lady with blue rinse hair seated there had been knitting for the duration of their stay.

"At least someone seems to be enjoying themselves."

His friend laughed as they watched the old woman cackle at her own imaginary set in front, speaking to the empty chair at her side.

"This place is getting under my skin. How about a pint after?"

"I can't," Norman replied. "I'm meeting Nancy tonight."

"Nancy? You don't mean Nurse Nancy from the hospital, surely?" Victor asked and received a nod in the affirmative. "You old devil. Fair play bro. She's gorgeous."

"Thanks, it's only dinner."

"And the rest!" Victor added with a wink.

He raised his closed hand in a fist pump and, a little embarrassed, Norman did the same, tapping it in mid-air before they both began laughing.

"How are things going with you and Moira these days?"

"Yeah man. Good so far," Victor said, fidgeting with his collar and unable to contain the smile that lit his face. "Early days you know, and we're taking things slow but we get on well. I really like her."

Suddenly a second old lady, who must have been nudging eighty, appeared from the hallway in a gentle jog. She was wearing a blue singlet and shorts over her pink nightgown. On her head were large audio phones, hard-core dance music booming from within. The little device was grasped firmly in her pale, veined hand, bouncing with the rhythm. Bemused, they watched her stride slowly past, drawing excited cheers of encouragement from the woman who was knitting, who she acknowledged with a wave.

As she approached the far end of the room, their gaze fell on an older gentleman with long shaggy grey hair. He was dressed in blue slacks wearing a white buttoned up dress shirt to the collar and sat on the carpeted floor beside a knee high bookshelf. The man began pulling each book out one by one, opening it and using a thick crayon to mark the inside cover, before replacing it neatly on the shelf. He suddenly felt the gaze of the two men on him and turned to wave. Victor and Norman returned it awkwardly and the man, evidently pleased with himself, turned back and spilled another row of books onto his lap.

"I see you've met Jesus Christ?"

They looked around to see a heavyset black woman in white overalls grinning from ear to ear.

"The Jesus Christ? Wow, what an honour!" Victor said.

"Haha. Yeah, he's one in about seven billion a'right. A real hoot. Jesus for the 21st century. He'll sign autographs and ev'rying. I guess there are worse people and worse places you could be," she said.

The two men laughed at the comment.

"You can say that again," Victor replied.

"Everything OK?" Norman asked.

"Oh yes!" she said. "No problem at all. Sheila will bring

'em both to you shortly. I'll remind you again though, I ain't sure how much information you'll get out of 'em."

"Thank you, Miss."

"Sure thing, honey."

They both looked at Victor who had turned to study a young man of Arabic ethnicity near the window. Since they arrived, he had been sitting there the whole time reading a book. Casually dressed in blue jeans and a white cotton fleece, for all intents and purposes looking out of place there, he appeared more normal than the residents around him.

"What's his gig?"

"Hmmm. A strange one alright. Claims he's Lazarus. You know him from the Bible? Well he thinks that Jesus' touch gave him eternal life. Some sort of double-edged sword or whateva ya call it. The price he had to pay to come back to life almost 2000 years ago. Yeah, like I said, we get all sorts here."

"Interesting."

"Look whose here!" the woman said in mock delight, and moved to the two men that entered.

Sandwiched between them was a thin attendant, struggling to hold them both steady by the crook of the elbow as they shuffled toward the table slowly.

The two seated men were aghast when they saw the former librarian. His hair had grown long and unkempt, grey streaks hung from the temple. The lustre and brightness had disappeared from his eyes.

"Now boys, you have two visitors today. This is Norman and his friend Victor. Aren't you the lucky ones?"

There was no reaction on their faces and the carer guided the men gently into their seats directly opposite the younger men, before standing off to one side looking on with the other attendant.

Norman looked up at them and asked if it was possible to have a few minutes alone with the brothers. They confirmed that it wouldn't be a problem and walked off together gossiping into the corridor behind.

The two younger men looked at the patient opposite.

Norman stared into the sunken eyes of Saul, recalling the pain almost a year earlier of narrowly missing the man on the road and the subsequent car crash. He had since discovered that the journal he had been studying actually belonged to this man. So many questions formed in his mind, but crystallized into one single thought which he now gave voice to.

"Why did you leave me on that roadside?"

The physical scars had healed but the emotional pain was still raw. The man looked directly ahead and almost through him. There wasn't so much as a flicker in his eyes, and Norman recalled the scared look on the face of the man in the cage in his dream.

Meanwhile, Victor had been staring into the face of Breagal, searching for something there. Now that the man was in front of him, he couldn't feel anything other than pity. The man's eyes sloped off and down to his side, giving a sombre expression unlike his brother's confusion. Victor had a lot of questions which would no doubt remain unanswered, given the man's vegetative state.

After a few minutes passed, the two younger men looked at each other deciding that there was nothing that could be done. Rising, they said their rushed goodbyes and walked away, alerting the two attendants waiting in the corridor that their business was finished.

Breagal's gaze straightened suddenly seeing the two men walk away. A tear formed in his eye and rolled down his thin unshaven cheek. In his mind, he was shouting at them now, but the two words wouldn't carry to his mouth. He saw them shake the hands of the attendants before looking back in their direction. They hovered for a moment as if considering, before turning and the door gently closed behind.

The librarian's whisper was low, barely audible above the TV set had anyone been close enough to hear. Had his brother been conscious he would have heard the pained words clearly.

"Help. Me."

FUTURE RELEASES BY THE AUTHOR

SIGIL

The quaint village of Ballygorm is shocked one bright summer morning by the tragic news that one of their own, a successful young builder and devoted family man has been found dead, hanging in an apparent suicide.

But Parish Priest, Father Tom Regan is sceptical. Inspired by his TV detective hero, Fr Regan uses his twin role as confessional confidante and the village's religious figurehead to investigate the mysterious death and he suspects foul play.

Piecing the clues together, he finds that his outwardly pious and tight-knit community has been harbouring a murderer in a village where everyone is a suspect.

Release – June 2016

-

RAISING LAZARUS

Student Molly Walker visits Lockworth Prison to interview some of the inmates as part of her final year University thesis.

She meets a young man, incarcerated on a prostitution charge and forms an unlikely bond with the serial offender despite their contrasting backgrounds.

The man believes he has been cursed with eternal life, the consequences of a gift his family begged a wandering prophet and teacher for some 2000 years earlier.

Sceptical, Molly digs deeper, exposing the dark underbelly of the city to better understand the mysterious stranger as the man's life long crusade unfolds, a mission which could drastically change both their lives and send shockwaves around the world

Release – End 2016

For more information, you can visit www.aidanjreid.com

Made in the USA
Middletown, DE
24 January 2020